No Kissing Under
the Boardwalk

Read more Kate Angell

Sweet Spot (Richmond Rogues)

No Tan Lines (Barefoot William)

Unwrapped (Anthology)

He's the One (Anthology)

No Strings Attached (Barefoot William)

No Sunshine When She's Gone (Barefoot William)

The Sugar Cookie Sweethearts Swap (Anthology)

No One Like You (Barefoot William)

No Breaking My Heart (Barefoot William)

No Time to Explain (Barefoot William)

No Kissing Under the Boardwalk

KATE ANGELL

KENSINGTON PUBLISHING CORP.

www.kensingtonbooks.com

KENSINGTON BOOKS are published by

Kensington Publishing Corp.
119 West 40th Street
New York, NY 10018

All Kensington titles, imprints, and distributed lines are available at special quantity discounts for bulk purchases for sales promotions, premiums, fund-raising, educational, or institutional use.

Special book excerpts or customized printings can also be created to fit specific needs. For details, write or phone the office of the Kensington sales manager: Kensington Publishing Corp., 119 West 40th Street, New York, NY 10018, attn: Sales Department; phone 1-800-221-2647.

KENSINGTON and the K logo are Reg. U.S. Pat. & TM Off.

ISBN-13: 978-1-4967-1823-5
ISBN-10: 1-4967-1823-2

First Kensington trade paperback printing: October 2018

10 9 8 7 6 5 4 3 2 1

Printed in the United States of America

First electronic edition: October 2018

ISBN-13: 978-1-4967-1824-2
ISBN-10: 1-4967-1824-0

Alicia Condon, Editorial Director,
you are patient, dedicated, encouraging,
and I thank you.

Debbie Roome, my very best friend.
We've been friends "forever."
I've always appreciated your support.
Your husband, Ted, is a true hero.

One

"**O**swald! *That bikini top better have come from the lost and found at the lifeguard station.*"

Zane Cates's words reached Tori Rollins across a wide expanse of sugar sand. His tone was stern, concerned, and directed toward a dalmatian pup. She cringed. Scrunched her nose. She followed astrology. Mercury was in retrograde. She blamed life's screw-ups, impacts, and aftershocks on the planet. Mercury could be a prankster. She'd been puppy-pranked.

A playful Oswald had tugged and stolen her polka-dot swimsuit top. She presently lay facedown on a beach towel on the smooth expanse of white sand. It was October, and the snowbirds had yet to flock south. She'd located a secluded spot and untied her top, not wanting tan lines. She hadn't planned on falling asleep, but she had. Attending high school, then working the night shift at Zinotti's Pizza, ate up her time, exhausting her. Saturday afternoon, and the warmth of the sun soothed. Had lulled her. One unexpected pull on her top from Ozzie, and it slid beneath her breasts before she could grab it. Gone.

Escaping puppy paws kicked sand on her Hawaiian Tropic–oiled arm. The roly-poly dalmatian scampered off with her top in tow. Tripping over the white on black polka-dot cups. Tumbling forward, nose in the sand, quickly recovering, then picking up speed.

Oswald. Zane's sneaky pup. Spotted chaos. Notorious for his antics. Cute and conniving, Oz stole whatever he could wrap his little mouth around. Zane had yet to break him of the habit. Beachgoers' lost Frisbees, flip-flops, paperback books, water bottles, whistles, and sunglasses to the scamp. Items Zane then apologetically returned to the owners. The dalmatian had now gotten the best of Tori. Great, just great.

She desperately needed to cover herself. She hadn't worn a T-shirt over her bikini top. So she grabbed a pair of cutoff shorts, white-seamed and fringed. She pressed them to her chest. Rolling onto her hip, she sat up. Wishing she'd come to the beach better prepared, she called after the pup, "Not funny, Ozzie. *Stop!*"

There was no stopping Oswald. The dalmatian's tail wagged as he scooted around the corner of the boardwalk. Disappearing. She sucked air. Set her jaw. Waited for Zane to appear. He did within seconds.

Zane Cates was a presence unto himself.

His reputation preceded him. A good-looking guy, clean-cut, smart, athletic, friendly, and outgoing. Whereas she was aloof. Always kept to herself. It was a protective measure, taken to hide the fact that she was an outsider. Always had been. Her parents had difficulty holding jobs, which forced the family to relocate each year. She'd abandoned friendships with every move. There'd be no future attachments in the resort town. She did alone just fine.

He walked toward her now. He was careful where he stepped. Rambunctious Oz ran circles around his feet, nipping at his ankles. She took him in. A solid six-foot, broad-shouldered, bared-chest, wearing black board shorts. He was mature for eighteen. Confident. He recognized his place in life. The Cates name was well known. His ancestry, deep rooted. His great-great-great grandfather had founded Barefoot William. Zane had three brothers and one sister. All equally popular.

He soon reached her. His toes touched the frayed, faded edges of her beach towel. He had big feet. He towered over her. Casting shade. He twirled one strap of her bikini top around his finger. "This belong to you?" he asked, knowing the answer.

"See anyone else topless?" Her tone was dry.

He glanced over her shoulder. "Only you. Dogs aren't allowed on the boardwalk and beach. We were coming from the dog park when Ollie got rowdy and slipped his collar. He ran to you, scored your top." His sincerity was soon lost to his smile, which was broad and teasing. "Sorry, Tori."

He knew her name. Surprising. They hadn't been introduced. She eyed her bikini top. Held out her hand. "Mine. Give."

"Yours in a sec." He gazed at her, his dark eyes probing. "You're new in town."

Small talk? He had to be kidding. She responded, if only to get her top back. "I've been here six weeks." Since the start of the school year.

He nodded. "Yeah, I've seen you around. You're in my Honors English and World History classes."

He'd noticed her. Unexpected. She'd given him the discreet side-eye. Not something she'd admit. Girls in the senior class were hot for him. He got a lot of attention. Her appreciation would mean little.

She wiggled her fingers. "My top."

He held back still. For whatever reason, he was prolonging her unease, taking advantage of her situation. "So who's Tori Rollins?"

She was far from special. She heaved a sigh. "What you see is what you get."

He lowered his gaze to her chest. Gave her a hot look. "You're more than a nip slip," he teased.

A nip slip. She startled. Pale, hard-tipped, her right nipple peeked at him through the denim fringe. She didn't embarrass easily. She hated the heat in her cheeks now. She quickly adjusted her cutoffs. Then eyed his board shorts. Stared at his groin. A substantial bulge. She was a virgin, but big was big. Her nipple turned him on.

"I like what I saw." No shame whatsoever from Zane. Full smile and single dimple. He shook out his legs. Shifted his stance. Actually laughed at himself, deep and masculine. "Some things are harder to hide than others."

Her throat had gone dry. Her palms were now sweaty. "My top," she said insistently. More a demand than a request.

He released it.

She caught it.

"Need help putting it on?" he asked, straight-faced.

She rolled her eyes. Other girls might accept his offer, but not her. "Turn around. Take off," she muttered.

He pivoted on his heel. Shuffled his feet in the sand. Yet didn't walk away. She eyed his backside. Some guys developed early. He'd already grown into his skin, more man than boy.

Tori scanned for passersby. Not a soul. The nearest person was a speck on the southern shoreline. She awkwardly worked the polka-dot top beneath the cutoffs clutched to her chest. She went on to adjust the shoulder straps and secure her breasts in the cups. Then set the shorts aside. She tied the back strings. Tightly. Breathed easier. Despite the fit. Her swimsuit was three years old. She'd filled out last year, going from an A to a C cup. The sides pinched. Pushed up her boobs, revealing curves and cleavage.

Oswald dropped down beside her on the beach towel. He rolled over, wanting his tummy rubbed. He whined for her attention. She gave in, scratched his belly. Then circled and connected the black dots on his white fur with her finger. He was cute. Despite being a thief.

"Decent?" Zane glanced back before she could respond. His gaze lingered on her breasts. Fortunately there was no visible nipple. He hunkered down. "Mind if I sit?"

"It's your beach."

"True, but I share."

Oz refused to move from the center of the towel, so Zane settled on the end nearest her. The terry cloth was six years old. Sand sifted through the threadbare fabric. Their bodies bumped. Shoulders brushed. Thighs grazing. He sat too close. Too still. All warm skin and muscle. His scent was lime and sunshine.

Silence held between them. Lengthened. Awareness touched her. An unexplained skip in her heartbeat. An unimaginable flutter in her stomach. She had no idea *why* he sat beside her. Unless he was killing time. She let the clock tick. Waited him out. The late afternoon shadows from the boardwalk crept across the sand. Reached for her feet. She wished she'd painted her toenails. But polish was a luxury. Her life was nickel and dimed.

The dalmatian soon crawled onto her lap. His head drooped on her knee. He closed his eyes, and his body went soft. He slept. She stretched out her legs, stuck her toes in the sand. Gritty.

Zane cupped his hand, scooped a palm full of sand, let the fine particles filter through his fingers as he initiated, "Where're you from?"

Portland, Reno, Chicago, Boston, Fargo, Little Rock. Name a city or town, and her family had likely driven through or lived there. But her personal life was private. "Around." Broad and untraceable. Evasive.

He raised an eyebrow. "Care to narrow it down?"

Not really. But she'd appear rude if she didn't. She

wasn't out to offend him. Still she took her sweet time. "Georgia."

He pinpointed, "Atlanta?"

Good guess. She slowly nodded.

"I was there recently," he told her. "My dad, younger brother Rylan, and I caught a Braves–Richmond Rogues game."

"You like baseball?" seemed appropriate to ask.

"Not as much as Ry. Baseball is his life. Major League is his future." He sounded proud, positive, as if it were a foregone conclusion.

"You seem so sure."

"My father taught us to go after what we want, until we got it."

A supportive dad. "What's in your future?" slipped out.

"The Air Force Academy."

"Ambitious."

His expression was serious, thoughtful. "I began the admissions cycle in March of my junior year. I've gone over the process at least a hundred times. I'm eighteen, a United States citizen, and unmarried, no dependents. I've completed the pre-candidate questionnaire. Once it's reviewed, I hope to be granted candidate status. It's a lengthy procedure."

"How so?" she asked, showing interest.

He drew a breath, explained, "Prerequisites: a congressional nomination, strong academic performance, extracurricular activities, character evaluation, personal interview, fitness assessment." He ran his hand down his face. "Sorry, I sounded like a recruiter. More than you needed to know. I got carried away. Didn't mean to bore you."

"Impressive." She was far from bored. His enthusiasm touched her. A tangible connection. "When would you get the entrance notification?" she asked him.

"Next year. Between February first and mid-July."

"I hope you're accepted." She meant it.

"Yeah, me too." He visibly hesitated. His voice deepened, became confidential. "I want to enter the Total Force Integration. TFI allows active duty pilots to fly in Reserve and Air National Guard units. The Air Force requires a ten-year service commitment after an officer graduates from pilot training. I'm fascinated by storms and"—he seemed unsure she'd understand—"someday want to be a hurricane hunter."

"Oh . . ." was all she had. Slowly, she added, "From fighter pilot to hurricane hunter. Daring."

"I've been called mental by my sister. Insane Zane by my brothers. Reckless, daredevil, crazy-ass by my friends."

She disagreed. "I think you're very brave."

"You do?" Surprise tinged his voice.

She half-smiled. "Scary brave, flying into the eye of a hurricane."

He justified, "The information obtained goes out to emergency managers to issue timely evacuations."

"Evacuations . . ." Her thoughts retracted sharply. Memories, seen through an eight-year-old's eyes, seized the moment. Still vivid. Fear constricted her throat. Her mouth was dry as she softly said, "My family lived outside Charleston, South Carolina, when Hurricane Hugo hit in 1989. We were late leaving the area and barely escaped the brunt of the storm."

The past painted a bleak picture. Schools and stores closed. Her parents' rust-bucket truck. A cooler of sodas and sandwiches. Three sleeping bags. Traffic stalled on the highway. A dark sky. A darker panic. A powerful wind shook the truck. Rain slapped the windows. Lightning flashed and thunder boomed. Tornados circled. Tori's stomach churned all the way to Tennessee. She felt queasy even now.

Zane sensed her distraction. Her introspection. Her sudden vulnerability. He leaned toward her. Their shoulders pressed as he gently tucked a strand of her hair behind her ear. Wild auburn hair that frizzed in the humidity. He touched his finger to her chin, turned her to face him. "You're pale."

"Hurricane Hugo struck a decade ago, but it feels like yesterday." She'd never shared the experience with anyone. She had kept it deep inside her. Yet now she lowered her guard with Zane. He planned to be a hurricane hunter. He could identify with her.

He lightly brushed his thumb along her jawline. "Your family survived."

"We outran Hugo." Barely. Only to drag into Nashville, gas tank on empty, front passenger tire losing air. Once again, her parents had difficulty finding work. They finally exchanged her dad's handyman skills and her mother's maid service for a room at a motel. It was rundown and musty smelling but provided a roof over their heads. Food came from vending machines. Her folks slept on the bed. She'd zipped into a sleeping bag. After a month of paychecks, the family moved on. North to Bloomfield, a small town in Kentucky where a bed-and-breakfast provided her parents employment. A small apartment over the garage became their home. For a year. Before they were on the road again.

Tori tossed her hair, cleared her head. She wondered how much longer Zane would occupy her towel. A bit longer, it seemed, as he continued with, "How 'bout you? College?" He'd taken more interest in her in ten minutes than anyone had in ten years.

Her dream was tucked in her heart. Never shared. Not even with her parents. Could she trust him with her most intimate wish? Silence stretched on as she struggled with her decision. Releasing her dream would give it substance. Zane sat beside her, as real as any moment she'd known.

He nudged her with his elbow. "I'll keep your secret. Promise."

"Interior design," she said softly.

His brow furrowed attentively. "I have friends going into engineering, medicine, education, law enforcement, and business administration. Interior design?" He shrugged. "Not a clue. You must have a good eye for decorating."

He would be right. "Textures, patterns, display, my mind's a kaleidoscope of color." Not bragging. A fact.

"Kaleidoscope, huh?" Thoughtful seconds passed. "I'm a basic color kind of guy. Black, white, gray."

"Achromatic shades are good."

He frowned. "Pretty boring compared to you."

"Color gives me life." The words were quietly spoken.

"How so?"

It was too difficult to explain. She couldn't put her emotions into words. Life had been hard. Color and design distracted her. Imaginative decorating had helped her survive. Made her strong. She didn't want to throw herself a pity party. Not in front of Zane.

Her recall was sharp. At age six, she'd spun her mental color wheel, making it an intangible, yet creative game. She brought brightness into her bleak world. A cardboard dollhouse became a palace, complete with throne, canopy bed, and magic mirror. She decorated with her own color palette. Princess pink and silver dreams. A fairy-tale brilliance.

At age nine, bedtime hovered darkly. Sleep evaded her in her tiny bedroom. The walls closed in, and she pushed them back, picturing her narrow air mattress as an actual twin bed. A bed made with raindrop aqua sheets and a butterfly-yellow-patterned comforter. A fluffy-marshmallow-white pillow. There'd be a glitter star night light to break the darkness. She covered the barefoot-cold cement with a round, heart-patterned rug. Each night she'd close her eyes and redecorate the room. The youthful images stayed with her. Grew with her into her teenage years.

By sixteen, she appraised each room she entered, taking inventory, inventively picking flooring and wall colors, and imagining furniture to complement it all. Texture made her fingers itch. Leather, chenille, brocade, cotton, linen, microfoam. Interior design was in her soul. Her future goal. She was starved for the success her parents had yet to achieve.

Zane waved his hand before her eyes. "You still with me, girl? So color's your life?"

She blinked, nodded. Retreating into herself was safe. Being with Zane made her feel unprotected. Exposed. She made light of her feelings. "Design, color, is in every breath I take. I inhale blue and exhale purple."

He grinned. "I like your outlook on life."

His words were a first. Kindly spoken. She relaxed, went on to say, "Design is a highly competitive field. It's difficult getting noticed. You need credibility . . ." Sigh. "College and a portfolio."

"The best colleges for interior design?" His question showed genuine interest.

She'd done her research. Had spoken extensively with her guidance counselor. "The best schools are in Europe. Florence Design Academy and the Interior Design School of London. Not affordable. For my undergraduate program, I'm looking at the Pratt Institute, Brooklyn campus. A living lab of craft and creativity. They offer scholarships and financial aid."

"How're your grades?" It was a frank question. "ACT, SAT?" he asked, mentioning standardized exams.

"Solid." Despite her transitory lifestyle and attending three high school districts in as many years. She used all her free time to study. Read. She would graduate from Barefoot William High School at the top of her class.

She looked to the Gulf, and not at him. The water shone with a mirror's gloss. A cool pool blue crested with gold dust. High tide, and the waves struggled to shore, then surrendered. A cloudless sky, bleached white by the sun. The air was still, as if holding its breath. She released her own. What to do? What to say?

Oswald's puppy snores made her sleepy. She covered her mouth, yawned. She'd love a nap before work. Not enough time.

"Oz likes you," Zane mused.

"Puppies like those who pet them."

"Ozzie's more than a back rub. He rips off everyone but is particular and doesn't snuggle with just anyone. You've become someone to him."

She'd never been someone to anyone. Not a person. Not a pet. Her family was dysfunctional. They shared few hugs, no words of affection. She'd pretty much raised herself.

"I like him," she admitted. When he wasn't stealing her bikini top.

"Like my dog, like me?"

His question surprised her. "You're okay, I guess."

"Just *okay*?"

More than okay, actually. Hot and handsome. A respected townie. Admired by his classmates. Out of her league. "I don't know you well enough to think differently."

"Get to know me then."

Not a good idea. "I have a job and little free time."

"Where do you work?"

"Zinotti's Pizza. Weekends are super busy." She'd be making pizzas and subs until her hands hurt.

"Can you trade shifts with someone? Take the night off."

"Can't afford it. I need the paycheck." She wasn't a Cates. She had no fat allowance or family money.

She worked five nights a week, willingly picked up extra hours when someone didn't show. She glanced at the watch clipped to her beach bag. Four o'clock. She needed to clean up, change into her uniform, and get to Zinotti's by five. Time to fly.

She eased Oswald off her lap, began gathering her things: water bottle, sunscreen, radio. Once everything was collected, she pushed to her feet. Then slipped on her cutoffs. Zane's gaze slid up her legs along with the denim. She raised the zipper. The missing brass button caused the opening to split over her navel. An open V.

He rose too. Asked, "You working tomorrow?"

Sunday. "A double shift. Why?"

"I thought we could hang out. I could show you around."

"Give me the Barefoot William experience?"

"I'm part of that experience."

"I don't know . . ."

"Don't know what?"

He confused her. She curled her shoulders protectively. "Why me?"

"Why not you?"

She'd seen the girls he attracted. The pretty ones he sat with in the lunchroom. The popular ones he walked beside down the hall. Sat with at assemblies. The laughing ones he gave a ride home after school. Zane drove a 1967 black Impala. A muscle car. It rumbled. Tori didn't fall into the thin, blond, have-it-all category. She protected her heart. "I'll pass."

He bent, scooped up his puppy along with her towel. He shook out the terry cloth. Handed it to her. A towel for the ragbag. Oswald licked his chin. "Should you change your mind," he persisted, "I'm good for carnival rides and amusement arcades. I'd hire a pedicab. Buy all the junk food you can eat. Steal a kiss under the boardwalk."

A kiss. Her heart gave a silly little squeeze. She pointed toward a sign near the wooden steps that connected the wide storefront walkway and beach: NO KISSING UNDER THE BOARDWALK.

"Sign applies to tourists not townies."

Hard to believe. He would show her a good time, of that she was certain. But at what cost? She avoided casual friendships. Him as her boyfriend? Unlikely. Laughable, actually. No chance whatsoever. She didn't want to be his senior year diversion.

"Thanks, but no thanks." She turned toward the board-walk. "Got to go. See you around."

"Yeah . . . around."

Around landed Zane at Zinotti's five nights in a row. Thursday afternoon came and went. He skipped out of football practice early, grabbed a quick shower, and once again sought out Tori. His pup had stolen her bikini top, and he'd spoken to her for only an hour. Yet there were people he felt something toward without reason, people who got under his skin. Warmed his heart. Surprisingly, she was one of them. He'd never felt anything like his response to her in his life. It was more than a physical charge. He liked her. A lot.

She stayed on his mind. He kept her to himself. She was too hard to explain. No one would understand. Not his family. Not his friends. His feelings were strong and unsettling. Confusing. She made him crazy.

She hadn't given him the time of day since the beach. She avoided him at school, dashing out of the classroom and disappearing in the crowded hallway when the bell rang. She always got on her bus before he reached the parking lot. Disappointing, as he would've given her a ride home.

But she couldn't dodge him at the pizza parlor. He was a paying customer.

He again took over a red leather booth. A deuce near the counter and ordering window. With a stretch of the shoulder, he could partially look into the kitchen. He watched Tori toss the dough, then roll her shoulders over what he assumed was a prep table to prepare an order. The heat from the pizza oven had reddened her face. She delivered orders when the waitress and cashier were busy.

And here she was, bringing his pizza, extra cheese and pepperoni. She wore a red Zinotti's T-shirt and white jeans. Her hair was pulled up in a tight, high ponytail. Her blue gaze, uneasy. Her expression, tired.

He initiated, "You work too much."

She shrugged. "I work to get ahead. We're short on help in the kitchen, so I came in for a couple hours."

"What's a couple?"

"What's it matter?"

He patted his stomach. "Eddie gets pissed when customers sit for a long time." Eddie Zinotti was the owner of the place. He wanted turnover in his booths. "I'm hungry right now, but I'm not sure I can sit and eat until midnight, if that's when you get off."

She looked at him questioningly. Dubiously. "You'd wait for me? I'm scheduled till ten."

Zane nodded. A short date was better than no date. "No school tomorrow," he reminded her. "Teachers' planning day. So how about it?" he asked with his first bite of pizza. Her decision shouldn't be difficult. He didn't want her overthinking his offer. Still she made him wait. And wait.

He'd nearly finished an entire slice before she gave in, saying, "Eat slowly."

"I can do slow." He grinned, momentarily appeased.

A corner of her mouth tipped up as she turned to leave. He watched her walk away. Purposeful steps. All cute and curvy. He was a physical guy, and Tori had a great body. Firm breasts. A pretty pale pink nipple. She made his palms itch. Sweat. Horny sat with him in the booth. He had a relentless boner. He untucked his Barefoot William Athletic Department T-shirt from his navy gym shorts. Covered up her effect on him.

She reached the kitchen door, swung it open. Paused, and glanced back at him. Her expression was now tentative, and somewhat sad, which he didn't understand. Had she changed her mind? He wanted to spend time with her. Wanted to get to know her better. Yet she refused him an hour or two. She disappeared a second later, and he half-expected her to sneak out the back door. He hoped he was wrong.

He resumed eating. Unhurriedly. Counting his chews. Twenty per bite. While sipping his soda with deliberate slowness.

It was Family Night at Zinotti's, and parents with small children packed the place. Most ate and left quickly, before the little ones got restless. Eddie Zinotti circled the restaurant. A man of medium height, with dark hair and intimidating muscle. He smiled and spoke to customers, handed out early-bird discount coupons. He frowned at Zane and his empty plate. Zane flagged down the waitress and ordered a basket of cheesy bread sticks.

The front door opened, closed. He was soon joined by his second cousin and best buddy, Race Wallace. They'd bonded in the playpen, later becoming rivals in individual sports: tennis, golf, wrestling. Allies in group competition: football, basketball. They shared similar interests. Sports dominated their free time. Then mechanics. They worked on antique cars. When it came to girls, they had a bro-code. If they were interested in the same babe, they both backed off. Both were now seniors. Both had applied to the Air Force Academy.

"Dude, here you are," Race said, sliding into the booth across from Zane. He wore a T-shirt scripted with *Beach It Hard* and faded blue jeans. "You busted from practice. Not answering your cell phone. I've made the usual rounds. You were hard to track down."

Zinotti's wasn't Zane's usual chill and hangout. The beach and boardwalk were his backyard. He frequented Molly Malone's Diner for an after-school burger. Often skim-boarded the water's edge near the lifeguard stand. He regularly fed quarters into the pinball machine and air hockey table at the amusement arcade.

Zane nudged the plastic basket across the table. Two cheese sticks remained. "Yours," he said. He couldn't eat another bite. His gut hurt.

Race eyed him. "What's the deal? Pizza, bread sticks? You carb-loading?"

The waitress, whose name tag read BLU, crossed to them. A sexy twenty with spiky blond hair, light green eyes. Hand on her blue-jeaned hip, she raised an eyebrow and asked, "What can I get you?"

Race speculated, "Whatcha offering?" Sexual undertones colored his deep voice.

His flirting fell flat. "The menu's on the wall blackboard over the counter."

Race squinted. "Forgot my glasses. Read it to me, babe?"

Zane rolled his eyes. Race had perfect vision.

"Have your friend read it to you." She nodded at Zane. "When he's not watching Tori. I'll be back once you've decided."

Race watched her walk away. "Nice ass. I think she likes me."

"You think every girl likes you."

"They don't?"

Most did. "There's always an exception. Blu Burkhardt's no longer in high school. She graduated in my brother Dune's class, two years ahead of us."

"Older works for me."

"Maybe not for her."

"We'll see." Race raised an eyebrow, questioningly. Backtracked, "Who's Tori?"

Zane scrubbed his knuckles along his jawline. How best to answer? "New girl at school."

"New, huh?" He was obviously puzzled. Race couldn't immediately place her. "She works here?"

"Pizza maker."

His friend faced away from the kitchen. That didn't stop him from glancing over his shoulder and through the ordering window. Two people worked in the kitchen. Tori and a mature woman.

Race grinned. "Ah, ponytail with flour on her cheek. Unless you've gone cougar," he added, referencing an older woman dating a significantly younger man.

No cougar. Zane narrowed his gaze. He hadn't noticed the flour. No more than a fingerprint smudge. Race had an incredible eye for detail. He nodded. "We have classes together but hadn't met. Not until last Saturday. It all went down at the beach. She was sunbathing. Oswald stole her bikini top. I returned it."

"Peek-a-boobs?" Race conjectured.

Zane kept the nip slip to himself. "No, she covered up with cutoffs."

Race cut her a second look. "She's hot. Ozzie's a great wing-dog."

"I'd like to take her out after work." His tone was uncertain.

"Who's stopping you?"

"She is."

Blu side-scooted through the kitchen doors, carrying a tray of meatball subs. She delivered the food to a nearby table, then stopped back by their booth. "Ready yet?"

"I'm ready for you—are you ready for me?" Race asked.

Blu stared him down. Her expression said *not now, not ever.*

Race exhaled. He went on to ask Zane, "How much longer do you plan to sit here? I can drag out a large pizza for thirty or forty minutes or scarf down a calzone in ten."

"Go with the pizza," said Zane.

"Large with the works. Pepsi," his buddy decided. Then snuck in, "I'm Race, by the way, should you need a name for the order."

"No name required. You're Table One."

He wasn't deterred. "What kind of name is Blu?"

"My mother's an artist."

"She painted you into a corner with a name like that."

"Race? Odd."

"Life's a sprint. I'm fast." He grinned. No return smile. He cleared his throat, added, "Family name. Great-grandfather."

"Whatever." She shrugged, left them.

Race drummed his fingers on the table. "Girl's tough."

Zane contemplated. "Blu's smokin'. Zinotti's is always packed. Chances are good she gets hit on a lot."

Race side-eyed Blu. "Ignoring her might get her attention."

Zane snorted. "Ignoring isn't following her every move."

Race took his advice. Blu brought his pizza and soft drink soon after. He didn't look up. "Thanks," under his breath.

She unexpectedly lingered. Silence stretched between

the two until Zane asked, "What time does Tori get off work?"

"Table One was her last order. She cut out five minutes ago. Back door."

Gone. Zane's stomach sank. Tori hadn't officially committed to their date. Still she slammed him. No wave. No good-bye. No consideration. He stood so quickly he jarred the table. Race grabbed his drink to save it from spilling. "What kind of car does she drive?" he asked Blu. He hoped to catch her in the parking lot.

"Tori walks back and forth from work."

She couldn't have gotten far on foot. "Direction?"

Blu hesitated, no doubt protecting her friend's privacy. Seconds ticked.

Zane didn't understand her reluctance. She was wasting his time. "Where?" he pressed.

Blu pursed her lips, finally saying, "White Heron Apartments."

A low-income complex two miles east. Near an old, rundown outdoor movie theater. These days it wasn't much more than a big field with a tilted, torn, weathered screen, where kids parked and made out. Zane hoped she kept to the sidewalk on the main road. She'd be easier to spot. Blu handed him his bill, he glanced at the amount and passed her two twenties. Then headed out, dodging two families who were conversing near the door.

"Hey, wait," she called to him. "Your change."

"Keep it." He was in a hurry.

"Big tipper." Her voice was appreciative.

"I tip bigger." Race's words drifted after Zane, just as he cleared the door.

"Bragging isn't cash." Blu left him to check on her other customers.

Zane shook his head. Race's chances weren't good with

the waitress. But that wouldn't stop his friend from trying to date her. For Race, rejection heightened the excitement of the chase.

Zane jogged across the parking lot, searching for Tori. He came to a stop right before he reached his car. He lived and breathed the vintage model. He was a decent mechanic, having worked part-time at Gray's Garage on weekends. He'd learned everything he knew from Wilbur Gray, a master technician. Zane enjoyed keeping the body in mint condition and the engine running smoothly. The Impala gleamed beneath the parking lot pole light.

More impressive than his vehicle was the girl standing near the hood. Tori Rollins. Her head was lowered as she scuffed a tennis shoe on the ground. Sensing him, she looked up, her expression wary, as if doubting her decision.

He expelled a breath, his throat dry. Relief walked him to her. "Hey," he managed, keeping it light.

A small nod. Nothing more.

"Blu told me you'd left."

"I told her to tell you."

Blu had taken her sweet time. Why had she been so cautious? It didn't matter now. Tori waited for him. His heart swelled inside his chest. He inwardly smiled. He would prove to her tonight that he was worth her while. Whatever it took.

"So . . ." He slapped his palms against his thighs. "Can I introduce you to my town?"

She looked down on her work clothes. Pizza sauce splattered her T-shirt. Cheese smeared her jeans. "I'd like to change first."

He held the car door for her. "I'll drive you home."

She settled on the passenger seat. Secured her seat belt. She gave him the address of the complex. As they pulled up, he saw that it was constructed in the shape of a horseshoe with three-story apartments bordering a circular driveway. Minimal outside lighting, cracked cement sidewalks, and barren grounds made the place less than inviting.

In the visitor's parking lot, he killed the engine. He waited for her to invite him in. Instead she stared out the front windshield, nervously fingering the buckle on her seat belt. After a lengthy mental debate she said, "Come in if you like?"

"You sure?" He gave her an out. "I can always hang in the car. Listen to music."

"My parents work the night shift at Beachside Memorial Hospital. My dad transports patients from the Emergency Room to X-ray. My mother does food prep in the cafeteria. Nana Aubrey, my mother's mother, will be sitting in her rocking chair, a photo album on her lap. Her husband passed away last year. She's suffered a mild stroke and depression and is sad, still grieving. She's staying with us now, but she lives with her memories. Gram seldom talks. She can't always finish her sentences. I'll introduce you, but she won't remember that you've met."

Zane felt suddenly grateful. His grandfather had also lost his wife, but Frank remained young at heart, dedicated to his family. The beach resort crowded him, so he lived rural, alone in a stilt house. An orange grove dominated the acreage, along with peach, banana, and grapefruit trees. He picked his own fresh fruit. His life was peaceful and happy, with lots of visitors.

They exited the Impala. He walked beside her along a winding sidewalk to a corner first-floor apartment. She slipped a key from her jeans pocket, unlocked the door. She pushed inside. He followed. There was no entrance hall; they stood in the living room. Small, dark, and warm. The light from the television cast its blue glow on a white-haired woman seated in a cushioned wicker rocker.

Round, rimless glasses bridged her nose. She huddled low in a purple robe. Her motion was slow and rhythmic, and the chair grated at the joints like arthritic wood. She clutched a rectangular album, while a meteorologist on the weather channel recited temperatures across the country.

Tori crossed to her grandmother. She rested a hand on the older woman's shoulder. "Nana Aubrey, I'm home." No reaction from her grandma. "I have a friend with me, Zane Cates."

Zane came up beside the rocker. "Nice to meet you, ma'am."

Blank-faced and silent, Nana Aubrey continued to rock her chair. Zane looked to Tori, caught the sadness in her eyes before she glanced down on her clothes, sniffed. "I smell like pizza," she said. "I need to shower and change."

"Take your time. I'll visit with your grandmother."

Tori nodded, warned, "Your conversation might be one-sided."

"Doesn't matter."

She kissed her grandma on the cheek, then left them. Her shoulders were bent. A heaviness slowed her steps.

He stood next to a side table, topped with a withering bouquet of pink carnations. No glass vase. The water in the plastic jug had evaporated. The crumpled petals echoed the mood of the small room. Rather depressing. He felt the emptiness. Loneliness. A sense of loss. The apartment didn't feel like a home. No impression of family. No permanence. It seemed unsettled. Bare walls. No decorative pictures. No personal effects. Minimal furniture. A small sofa and the rocker. The Rollinses could walk out the door with the clothes on their backs and no memories of this place. No regrets. Gone.

He ran one hand down his face. He had no idea what to say to Nana Aubrey, what, if anything, she might understand. He carefully went with, "Tori and I are friends. We met at the beach." He left out Oswald's stealing her bikini top. "We go to the same high school."

No change in the older woman's expression.

"I've lived in Barefoot William all my life," he told her, his tone gentle. "I want to share my town with her." Pause. "I like your granddaughter," he confided, figuring the grandmother could keep a secret. Tori had indicated Nana Aubrey wouldn't remember him being there anyway.

Or would she? A slight shift of her head, a nod perhaps. Maybe not. He wasn't sure. The rocking creaked to a stop. A commercial came on, brightened the television screen, and the volume jumped. At the exact moment her lips moved, muttering, "Eighty degrees." Unexpected and surprising. Had she just given him the temperature? She was watching the weather station.

He drew a breath, agreed. "Pleasant night. We're going to take a walk on the boardwalk and pier. Enjoy the amusements."

"Ferris . . ." Incomplete.

He guessed, "We could ride the Ferris wheel."

"Like."

His throat tightened. "Thank you." He appreciated her insight. He would take Tori on the ride.

Nana Aubrey returned to watching TV. Tori entered the living room moments later. Looking damn hot. A total turn-on. No tight ponytail now. Her auburn hair brushed her shoulders, slightly damp from her shower, wavy and free. No makeup. All fresh-faced and natural. Pretty. The asymmetrical navy stripes of a loose-fitting shirt slanted over her hips. Cuffed distressed denim jeans showed ladder-tears on her left thigh. Burgundy and blue paisley tennis shoes. She looked good to go.

And he was a goner. He wasn't going anywhere. Not

with an erection that tented his gym shorts. Tori gave him a fleeting look and glanced away. He flexed his thighs, recirculated the tension at his crotch, and talked himself down. His dick wasn't a good listener.

Tori went to hug her grandmother. "I'll be home by midnight."

Zane doubted Nana Aubrey kept track of time. He wondered if she even knew what day it was. What month. He raised an eyebrow at Tori, concerned, needing assurance her grandma would be fine alone.

"My mother made Gram dinner before she went to work. She'll sit, rock, and watch television until I return home. Then I'll put her to bed."

Zane leaned down, lowered his voice near the grandmother's ear. "Nice talking with you." He swore her face softened for a fraction of a second. Yet her distant-eyed stare never left the TV.

He and Tori got back into the Impala. He drove to the beach and located a parking place in the Cateses' private lot near Center Street. The street divided the sister resorts of upscale Saunders Shores and honky-tonk Barefoot William. The Cateses' immediate and extended family owned every shop, arcade amusement, and carnival ride along the cement boardwalk and down the full length of the wooden pier.

The two slid from the vehicle and strolled the sidewalk to the beach. The night rolled out a crescent moon and a gentle breeze. All the shops fronted the Gulf. The stores had adjoining walls and colorful doors. All the doors were propped open, welcoming late-evening shoppers. Music echoed inside the shops and out, encouraging tourists and townies to snap their fingers, to clap their hands, and even to spontaneously dance. Smiles abounded. The air vibrated with laughter and good times. No worries, be happy.

Tori shouldered through the crowd, walking slightly ahead of him. She had to sidestep slow-moving pedicabs giving beach tours, jugglers, stilt walkers, unicyclists, and pogo stick jumpers. The novelty performances drew big tips. She pulled up short near a lemonade stand. The scent of freshly squeezed lemons was tart. She leaned against the bright blue pipe railing that separated the boardwalk from the beach. Tilting her face skyward, she drew a soul-cleansing breath. Then exhaled slowly through parted lips.

Her voice when she spoke was as soft as a sigh. "Thank you, Zane."

"For . . . ?" What, exactly?

"Being nice to my grandmother and bringing me to the beach."

He did so willingly. "I like older people." He enjoyed spending time with his grandfather. "And I wanted you to see Barefoot William through my eyes."

But instead of her seeing the town through his eyes, he saw it through hers. Her usual reserve had been released to the night. Her eyes sparkled with excitement as she took it all in. He casually reached for her hand, and she laced her fingers with his. Pole lights and neon storefront signs brightened the night. He spotted several close friends, nodded, but selfishly kept introductions and conversations to a minimum. This was his time with Tori. He made every minute count. No infringements.

They strolled the pier, investigating its banks of food carts. He bought her a basket of chili-cheese fries. She offered him a taste, but he shook his head. He was still full to bursting from his earlier pizza and cheese bread.

Her fries disappeared, and she became distracted by the Boomerang Hut. A fascinated crowd had gathered outside, comprised of as many adults as children. His second cousin Boomer was the boomerang wrangler. Boomer demonstrated how to throw the silver fluorescent night-time boomerang so it would circle back to the thrower. People purchased the boomerangs as quickly as he could hand them out. Under Boomer's guidance, each took a turn. The majority of the shiny wooden airfoils soared back to the pier, although a few lost momentum and landed in the Gulf. Alert and agile, Boomer leaped and caught the toys when customers ducked on their return. He was quick enough that no one got hurt.

Boomer caught Zane's eye, raised an eyebrow toward Tori. He waved a handful of boomerangs. "Give it a try?" he asked.

Zane nudged her with his elbow. "How 'bout it?"

"I've never thrown one."

"Most haven't," Boomer was quick to say.

"What if I fail and it falls in the water?"

Boomer grinned. "Won't be the first boomerang to drown."

"Okay," Tori agreed.

Boomer passed her a boomerang, then gave her private instruction. He got behind her, angling her shoulders and right arm for perfect projection. Zane cleared his throat, a territorial warning, when his cousin pressed too close. Boomer put more space between them.

Tori was far too serious. Too stiff. Three boomerangs soon met a watery grave, swallowed by the waves. Defeat swept her sigh. All fun vanished. Tonight was meant to entertain, not to frustrate and disappoint.

Zane shadowed her. He squeezed her shoulder. "Together," he suggested. His big body wrapped hers, and, hand over hand, they sent a boomerang out and over the Gulf. It flew long, arced, and swiftly returned to them. Tori pushed back against his chest, not wanting to get hit. Zane reached around her, caught it easily.

Wide-eyed, she parted her lips and exclaimed, "We did it."

We. He liked the sound of that. "Go again?" he asked. He liked her flush against him. Curvy. Warm.

She shook her head. "No more. I'm ending on a high." She turned to face him. They stood so close her hair teased his cheek, neck. "You go now."

Boomer passed him six boomerangs. If boomerang throwing were an Olympic sport, Zane would win gold. He wasn't usually a show-off, but he wouldn't pass up this opportunity to impress Tori. He separated himself from her, then took aim. A strong snap to his wrist, and, in rapid succession, he threw each one. The silver boomerangs sailed like shooting stars through the dark sky, flickering over the water before curving back to the pier. Quick reflexes had him nabbing five within arm's reach. He jumped for the sixth, which returned slightly over his head.

The crowd oohed, awed, whistled, and clapped.

"You've got ninja skills," Tori said with admiration.

He warmed to her praise, admitted, "I worked the Boomerang Hut two summers ago. My first attempts were far from perfect. The Gulf ate my profits. Daily demonstrations gave me a lot of practice, though, and I improved."

They walked on. This was his home. Zane never got tired of the carnival rides and amusements. He let his inner child out to play. The crowd thickened on the pier. Lines for the rides snaked along the wooden railing. Laughter brightened the night, punctuated with squeals and shrieks from those riding the bumper cars, scrambler, and children's roller coaster with its elevated railroad track designed with minimal turns and mild slopes. Exciting, but not scary. Wave Swingers drew the loudest screams. The swing ride was fitted with chairs suspended from the rotating top of a red-scooped carousel, which tilted for additional variety of motion, as it whipped out over the Gulf.

Tori and he passed on the rides for now. Instead, they honed in on Hooper's Hoops, a kiosk that sold hula hoops in a variety of colors, from hot pink and sand tan, to metallic silver.

They watched a teenage girl swirl four hoops about her hips. "My cousin Kristen," he told Tori. Tori's wistful expression had him asking, "Ever hula hooped?"

She shook her head. "Never tried."

"Time's now."

She waved him off. "I'm not sure . . ."

"You successfully threw a boomerang," he reminded her. "This is a night of firsts."

He sensed that she wanted to give it a try, but didn't want to make a fool of herself if she couldn't keep the hoop twirling. "You couldn't be any worse than Pint-Size in pink."

She studied the little girl giving it her all. "She's three or four. Even a child's hoop swamps her."

They listened as Kristen instructed the tiny blonde. "Hold the hoop at your waist with your hands apart at a comfortable distance." The mother helped her daughter get into position. "Place one foot in front of the other to gain balance," Kristen continued. "Rest the hoop against one hip, then spin it. Rotate your waist in small circles. Be patient, until you find the perfect rhythm."

Pint-Size tried and tried again. She put every effort into getting the hoop started. Wiggling, jiggling, but wasn't successful. The hoop dropped on her sandaled feet. An encouraging mother and lots of giggles later, and the girl succeeded with a single spin. Kristen whooped. The crowd applauded. The child took a bow.

"Well . . . ?" Zane challenged Tori. "You, then me?"

"No way. We go at the same time."

He knew his limitations. Hula hooping was one of them. No easy feat. It was more than a forward-backward sexual motion. The side-to-side part eluded him. Still, he was game. He didn't mind embarrassing himself if she had a good time.

Zane introduced Tori and Kristen. Kristen offered them an assortment of adult hula hoops. Tori chose a clear plastic hoop with metallic gold glitter in the tubing. Zane picked solid black. Kristen moved out of their way. "On your mark, get set, go!" She cheered them on.

They faced each other. His focus was fully on her. Tori bit down on her bottom lip, concentrated, and got her hoop going ahead of Zane. He was distracted by the sensual swing of her hips. He fumbled getting started, all thumbs. After several attempts, he finally managed an uneven circular motion. His hips weren't made for hooping.

Seconds later, his thoughts went south. The motion of their bodies simulated sex. With each spin of the hoops, she thrust her hips forward, and he pushed his back. Then he rotated his hips toward her, while she arched her butt away from him. They caught their rhythm; their speed increased. It was all incredibly suggestive. His dick jackknifed. Turned on. His gym shorts were no help at all. They didn't hold down his erection. If the hoop dropped from his waist, it would hook on his penis.

Tori's gaze held his. She tentatively smiled. Soft curving lips. Lips he suddenly wanted to kiss. Instead he locked his jaw. He wasn't one for public affection. Privacy suited him better. Under the boardwalk. Despite the NO KISSING sign.

Sidestepping, he stopped his hula hoop before it fell. He lowered it over his groin, let it drop at his ankles. No mishaps. With deep breaths, he managed to bring his boner under control.

Tori was perpetual motion. She danced a two-step. Amazingly talented. Kristen carefully passed her a second hoop, then a third. Tori managed to keep all three circling. For some time. Her hips and breasts swayed. Mes-merizing.

She finally threw back her head and laughed. A raspy release of happiness and pleasure. The hula hoops slowly swirled down her body. Overlapping and flip-flopping, stacking themselves on her tennis shoes.

"Nice going," Kristen said to Tori as she collected the fallen hoops. "Great body control."

Zane silently agreed. Her body was flexible, capable of amazing circular rhythm. His buddy Race would say, *She could hump a hoop.*

He next proposed something to drink. His treat. Soda, lemonade, ice cream float, snow cone. She declined and located a drinking fountain instead, satisfied with water. He then offered blue or pink cotton candy, fried Oreos, and funnel cake. She passed on all three.

Farther along the pier a concession called Shades caught her eye with a large display of sunglasses. A pole light il-luminated two mirrors that cornered the collection, so people could try on numerous pairs and admire their ap-pearance.

Zane immediately scored dark-lensed aviators. He already had a pair, but still considered a second. Tori hesitantly scanned the dime-store to designer styles. Eval-uating. Thoughtful. She fingered and flipped several price tags. Her breath caught. She worried her bottom lip.

Zane noted her indecision. He leaned close, kept his voice low, assured her, "Browsing doesn't mean buying."

"The vendor won't mind?" She was anxious.

Zane shook his head. "He's used to lookers. Take your time." His uncle Charlie ran Shades. Momentarily turned away from them, he busily rang up sales. He was a big man in his sixties, retired from public service and wanting to pad his pension. He complimented his customers on each purchase.

Tori located the rack priced two-for-one. It took her a long time to narrow down her selections. Her final pairs were far from traditional. More fun and unusual. Quirky. A red, heart-shaped frame with pink lenses and a black-and-white, zebra-striped frame with dark purple lenses. She alternately tried them on, looked in the mirror, dipped her head, and blushed, as if embarrassed for checking herself out.

"Hey, Zane, great choice in aviators," his uncle Charlie commented. He went on to compliment Tori. "Both pairs work for you, pretty lady."

Charlie's approval heightened her blush.

Zane introduced them, then added, "My uncle's an honest salesman. No bullshit for a sale. You make the sunglasses look good."

Still Tori went back and forth, switching off the frames. Indecisive. She eventually returned them to the sunglass stand. "Not a necessity," Zane heard her mutter.

Necessity? The word stunned him. She obviously lived a life of choices. Choices he'd never had to make. Life came easy for him. He had a decent allowance. He bought what he wanted, whenever he wanted. No second thoughts. He could always tap his parents for extra cash.

He worked his jaw. He didn't want to offend her, but neither did he want her to walk away from the sunglasses that interested her. How to best handle the situation? He'd never been one to dance around an issue, so he retrieved the crazy shades, handed them to Charlie, along with his aviators. "On account," he told his uncle.

Charlie placed the sunglasses in separate cases. Then put them in clear plastic bags and handed them to Zane. "All yours." He added, "Nice to meet you, Tori. Stop by anytime," then went on to assist other customers.

Zane eyed Tori. He'd expected a smile. Appreciation. Neither was forthcoming. Instead her eyes darkened, flick-ered a dangerous blue. Her mouth flattened, the corners pinched. The face of annoyance. Man, oh man. What the hell? He felt a confrontation coming on and preferred it to be more private than public.

He scanned the area. Immediately chose his destination. He pressed his palm to her spine and steered her toward the Ferris wheel. Her stiff back and dragging steps slowed their progress. They arrived as the ride was being loaded. Only one car remained. They slid onto the aluminum seat. It rocked slightly. Zane would've liked to sit close. To wrap his arm about her shoulders. Instead he gave her what little space there was and set the sunglasses between them.

The operator recognized him. "Evening, Zane."

"Hello, Rory," Zane returned. "We're going to ride a while. I'll signal when we want to get off."

"One round only," Tori muttered.

The operator secured the safety bar across their laps. Then set the ride in motion. The Ferris wheel jerked slightly, then swept upward. Smooth. High into the sky. The view belonged on a postcard . . . the entire board-walk and pier stretched out before them. Twinkling and magical. Colorful lights lit the spokes on the wheel. They sat in silence for six turns.

Until he asked, "You mad at me?"

A breeze blew in her face, tossing her hair. In a stilted tone, she accused, "You bought me sunglasses."

He rolled his tongue inside his cheek. "Who said they were for you?"

"Who are they for then?"

"Maybe me."

"A fighter pilot in red, heart-shaped frames? Question-able."

"I'd thought more zebra on my going solo." His first flight.

"Aviators suit you better."

"The zebra and hearts suit you."

"I've money in my pocket if I'd wanted them bad enough."

"I wanted them for you."

"But I don't want them," she stubbornly insisted. "Don't assume you know me. I was browsing. You have no idea what I want or need."

He pulled a face, asked, "What could you possibly want more than crazy sunglasses?"

"Seriously?" Her tone was grave. "I want to buy a hot lunch at school. To purchase a weekly bouquet of flowers for my grandmother. To get new shoelaces at the dollar store when mine break at work. To chip in for gas in the family car. To feel rich with five dollars in my pocket." Her naked truth.

He had no words. Her honesty put him in his place. Made him feel ashamed. He'd pushed too hard with his teasing, possibly embarrassed or hurt her. She had her priorities. Her *necessities*. What he took for granted, she sacrificed for. He felt like an ass.

"I'm sorry. This was none of my business."

"None at all," she stated. "Don't do it again."

He needed to make amends. He sucked air, made one last attempt. "Do you ever accept gifts?" He hoped so.

"Depends on how long I've known someone."

"We've known each other nearly a week."

Reluctance on her part. "What's the occasion?"

"Let's make the sunglasses an early Christmas present."

"Seventy-six days until Santa. I don't think so."

"Early birthday gift?"

"Next September. Nearly a year away."

"Celebrating our first date?"

"Memory of our first argument?"

He snapped his fingers. "Makeup sunglasses."

His words had the desired effect. She gave in, gave a minimal grin. "I can accept that."

He felt bone-deep relief. The pressure left his chest. Knots loosened in his stomach. Life felt right again.

Tori settled deeper on the aluminum seat. He eased his arm about her shoulders. She went soft against him. He liked the feel of her. No pretense. Natural.

"I think I like you, Tori Rollins," he whispered near her temple. Keeping it light. Testing her response. Not wanting to scare her.

"Take your time. Let me know when you decide."

He needed no time. He had decided the moment Oswald stole her bikini top. He was half in love with her already.

Two

Spring 2000

"Admit you love me, Tori," Zane teased. They stood barefoot in the sand at the beach. Facing each other. Half hidden by the NO KISSING UNDER THE BOARDWALK sign. He'd first kissed her behind the sign, on their sixth date. Then continued to kiss her often throughout their senior year. It was their favorite landmark.

He curved his hands over her shoulders now and drew her to him. He held her close, chest to breast. Their hipbones bumped. Their thighs meeting. His body hummed. She gave him more than butterflies—he felt the whole zoo.

Her sigh echoed through his body. "It's too soon."

Too soon? She had to be joking. Love had come hard and fast for Zane, knocking him on his ass. She was taking her sweet time admitting she loved him too. He *knew* she cared; his gut told him so. He wasn't insecure or needy. They were involved. An exclusive couple. Still he anticipated the words that would cement their relationship.

She was a different person now compared to the girl on their first date the previous fall, when she'd been seriously uptight . . . her heart closed. She had slowly warmed to him. Opened up over the months. Spending her free time with him. Sharing her life. He now wanted her commitment. Him. Her. Together.

Moonbeams, star shine, and the darkening night held them in silvery shadows. He rested his forehead against hers. Kissed the tip of her nose. Then each cheek. Lightly kissed her lips. He felt her smile against his mouth, and he smiled back. His heart was happy.

"I need to get home soon. I've got a test tomorrow and I have to study. Calculus doesn't come easy for me."

"I'm easy for you."

"Indefinite integrals, limits, derivatives are hard," she said on a sigh.

He was hard. The rise and fall of her breasts beneath a BAREFOOT PARADISE tee brushed his chest. Her nipples pebbled, poked him. His dick inside his jeans poked her back. He was a standing boner around her. Always. She was a virgin. She trusted him not to take advantage of her. He never pressured her for sex. They'd shared deep kisses. Intimate touching. Heavy breathing. Dry humping. Close encounters.

She cupped his butt, squeezed. "However much I like your body, close down, big guy."

He widened his stance. Relented. "I have homework too. I've got an economics paper due at the end of the week, assessing the economic performance of the United States."

"That should keep you busy."

"I'd rather we get busy."

"Not tonight."

He nipped her bottom lip. "You're no fun."

"I was fun last night."

Most definitely, he silently agreed. The backseat of his Impala would attest to that. Skin on leather.

Tori leaned back slightly. "I can't slide my last semester. I want to graduate with honors. We should be hearing from colleges soon."

"Anytime now." His chest tightened a little. "Race received his appointment letter to the Air Force Academy yesterday. He's already notified Admissions of his acceptance."

"So I heard," Tori told him. "He came into Zinotti's last night, letter in hand. Showed it to Blu. She congratulated him. Offered him a handshake when he went in for a kiss."

Leave it to Race to use his acceptance as an excuse for a make-out celebration. Blu saw straight through him. He wasn't one to cool his heels and wait for a girl to come around. He was a player. He regularly dated other girls, all the while pursuing her. She barely gave him the time of day. Despite the fact he ordered pizza several times a week and tipped the price of his meal. Sometimes more.

Race lived carefree, on the edge of crazy, but wasn't careless. He was too damn smart. Serious would come with his arrival at the Academy. There would be time restraints on first-year cadets, an intense orientation, the need to prove himself, and a ton of stress. He would be kept busy. Race was having fun now. Cutting loose at every opportunity.

"Your letter will arrive." Tori was confident. Positive.

He appreciated her optimism. The wait wasn't easy. She was on his side. Always encouraging. He drew a breath from deep in his gut. "Approximately twelve hundred out of nearly ten thousand applicants make the grade. I want this, Tori. More than anything I've ever wanted in my life." Pause. "Except you."

"You'll be accepted."

"It's there or nowhere. I didn't apply to any other colleges. I don't have a plan B like you do."

She grew thoughtful. "Pratt's my first choice. I also applied to University of Florida, Gainesville; and Florida State, Tallahassee. Colleges with strong Interior Design programs that offer full scholarships."

Tori had forethought. She'd covered her bases. He liked that about her. She was conscientious. She looked at life from all angles, evaluated the circumstances and every possible outcome. He so often jumped without looking first. Without looking for a safety net. It was who he was.

She tightened her arms about his waist and gently stroked his lower back. A circular motion that soothed him. "You're the best of the best, Zane. Not all letters from the Academy are sent at the same time, right?"

"Right. Still, I'd like to get my appointment sooner than later."

"Maybe tomorrow."

"Maybe tomorrow for you too."

He was aware that she met the mailman each afternoon, between the end of the school day and when she started her evening shift at Zinotti's. It was depressing to flip through the mail and not find that highly anticipated letter. They consoled each other. Many of their friends had received admittance notifications. Their futures were now mapped out.

Being in limbo sucked. "Hang out with me a while longer," he entreated. Her company calmed him. Thoughts of the American economy were the furthest thing from his mind. The paper could wait.

"How about a snow cone?" he asked. He knew her weakness.

She stepped back. Faked a glare. "You're procrastinating and taking me down with you."

"I'm restless." His nerves were jumpy.

She gave in. "Twenty minutes max. Snow cones and a final walk down the pier."

Twenty minutes were better than no minutes.

They located the snow cone cart. Tori ordered lemon, so tart her lips puckered. Zane went with blueberry. She laughed as the berry stained his lips. He kissed her, shared the blue, then swept his tongue inside her mouth, cold from the shaved ice. He savored her lemon. Smacked his lips. "You taste good."

They walked the length of the pier, silent while enjoying their snow cones. She didn't force conversation, happy with her own thoughts. He hoped her mind was on him. He never stopped thinking about her. He held her in his heart.

She finished off her snow cone. Too soon. "Home, Zane," she requested.

"I can't talk you into staying?" Last-ditch effort.

One corner of her mouth curved. Wistful. "You've talked me into a lot over the past few months," she reminded him. "But nothing you could say tonight will keep me from Calculus."

"We could take Oswald for a walk."

A second's hesitation. "Not fair. You know I love your dog." She'd never had a pet and gravitated toward the dalmatian.

"One block."

She sighed. "Against my better judgment."

"You'll still have plenty of time to study."

"I prefer to study before it gets too late. My mind is mush after midnight." She was a day person; he was night. "You're a bad influence on me, Zane Cates."

"I'm good for you, Tori Rollins."

"You're a distraction."

She distracted him too. He'd rather be with her anytime, anyplace, than with anyone else. They tossed their snow cone paper cups in a trash container. He then took her hand and led her back to the parking lot. "Ozzie awaits."

They arrived at his parents' house in Olde Barefoot William. A beachside neighborhood. Here lay the Cates inner circle. The immediate and extended family lived in old Florida-style homes and cottages that had been handed down for generations, and were as eclectic in architecture as they were harmonious. The houses were shingled and shuttered, with wide porches. They'd withstood hurricanes and time. A few had had minor face-lifts.

Zane pulled his car into the driveway. The house was quiet. Dark. His parents had gone to a movie. His younger sister Shaye was at a friend's house. Rylan was at the local batting cages. Baseball was in his blood. He practiced every free moment. His two older brothers, Dune and Aidan, were in college. Florida schools. They checked in on the occasional weekend.

They climbed out of the Impala. The front porch light illuminated the crushed pink shell walkway. Red hibiscus bushes lined the footpath. The scent of roses floated from his mom's flower garden at the side of the house. Zane noted the grass needed to be mowed. One of his chores. He'd take care of it tomorrow. The job took less than twenty minutes on the family's small riding mower.

Oswald heard them arrive. The dalmatian barked his welcome. Zane entered the house, leashed him. Oz greeted Tori with a lunge, paws to her chest, and a lick to her chin. Happy and exuberant to see her. She hugged him, then knuckle-rubbed his ears.

Zane was patient. He gave them their minute together. Ozzie had lots of human friends, but he favored Tori. In return, she'd wrapped her heart around his dog.

He rested his hip on the entry table and absorbed the pulse of his home. It was a house that gave hugs. Overstuffed furniture crowded the living room with seats for seven. Three televisions satisfied everyone's programming wishes. The walls held childhood secrets and happy memories. It was a room that had witnessed love and compassion, opinions and the occasional argument. His parents were indulgent, yet firm. His brothers and sister were tight. If one did something wrong, they all took the fall and punishment.

Tori gave Oz a last pat on his head, and Zane nudged the door open with his foot. "Walk, Ozzie." The dog shot out ahead of them.

The sixty-foot retractable leash allowed Oz plenty of freedom. He trotted down the sidewalk, then cut up several driveways. He knew everyone, and everyone knew him. He would bark, wanting attention, and whoever was home came out to pet him.

"A popular guy," Tori mused.

Zane grinned. "This has been his nightly routine since he was six weeks old. My relatives would acknowledge me with a nod, then make it all about Oz, offering him a dog biscuit or new toy. Oswald loves squeaky toys. His favorite was a yellow duck, which he quacked all the way home last week. Ten noisy, ducky blocks."

"Blocks . . ." Tori calculated. She poked Zane in the side. "I agreed to walk one block. We've gone six now."

Busted. Zane was hoping she hadn't noticed how far they'd gone. He'd held her hand. Brushed his hip against her. Stolen a few kisses. He'd selfishly stretched out their time together. He hadn't played fair. He knew studying was important to her. He turned around at the next corner. They headed back to his house. He kissed her every few steps.

Oswald tugged on the leash. He was the first up the steps and onto the porch. The first one through the front door, anticipating a further treat. Zane unhooked his leash. He left Tori in the entry hall and went to the kitchen for a raw carrot. Returned.

He held out the carrot, told his dog, "Veggie time. You've had enough snacks for one night." His neighbors had handed out treats like Halloween candy.

Oz sniffed the carrot, gave a grumbling snort. He eyed Zane with a *get real* doggy glare. Tori covered her mouth, tried not to laugh. A snicker escaped. Oswald turned up his tail and retraced Zane's steps to the kitchen. He sat down on the tiled floor, then looked up at the counter where Zane kept a large plastic container of treats.

"Ozzie," Zane coaxed, calling him back to the carrot.

A flicker of the dog's ears, yet Zane was ignored.

"Give him a cheese biscuit," Tory insisted. "One more won't hurt. He's a growing boy."

"He already weighs forty pounds. He's so spoiled. Always gets his way."

"So do you. Get your own way."

"Not with you, I don't."

"You get plenty."

Not nearly enough. But as much as she could give him, he knew. "I'm outnumbered," he muttered. Carrot in hand, he returned to the kitchen. Ozzie wagged his tail . . . barked wildly. Zane retrieved a biscuit. "From Tori, not me," he told the dalmatian. Oswald didn't gobble the snack as Zane had expected. He took it to his dog bed and ate it slowly. Savoring it. Zane saved the carrot in a Ziploc bag. He'd chop it up, put it in Oz's food in the morning.

He came back to Tori. "Ready?" he asked.

She kissed him on the cheek. "You're a good dog dad."

"Oswald is the family dog, but I spend the most time with him."

They left his house, took the steps to the shell walkway. He slowed, asked her, "Have you bought your grandmother flowers this week?"

"I will on Friday, payday. I alternate between carnations, sunflowers, and daisies. Whatever's on sale."

"I'll save you the cost. No flowers are as pretty as my mom's prize-winning roses."

She was taken aback. "Really? You sure? They are beautiful."

"No problem." He went around the corner of the house, heading toward the garage. "Let me get a vase and garden stripper. I'll remove the thorns."

The tool would make the roses safe for Nana Aubrey. Zane didn't want the older woman pricking her fingers. He returned with the thorn stripper along with an empty red coffee container. Label removed. "Sorry, not very fancy."

"It's perfect," she enthused, only to frown. "It's the thought that counts. Gram wouldn't know the difference between a coffee can and a crystal vase."

The corner porch light illuminated the garden. "Choose the colors your grandma would like," Zane requested. Tori knew her grandmother best.

She slowly strolled the outer edge of the rose beds, lightly stroking the colorful velvet petals. Breathing deeply of the fragranced air. Her eyes bright. "Your mother has a green thumb. Gram would love any one of them," she finally said. "Do you help your mother garden?"

He shrugged. "Mom's the expert. I've pulled weeds and spread topsoil and mulch over the years. I've learned a few plant names. Ozzie's a digger. He's quick. I've had to re-plant a few bushes."

She clasped her hands before her. "Help me choose."

She valued his opinion. He liked that. He passed her the coffee container. Then made his choices. "Gertrude Jekyll," he selected. Three pink, and gently perfumed. He carefully snipped the stems and sheered the thorns. Leaving a few leaves. "Two Sunsprite," came next. Yellow with a sweet scent. The fragrances intertwined.

He added, "Four Mr. Lincoln." Large, bold, red roses. Strongly scented, but not overwhelming. He scanned the garden, "A Fragrant Plum." Lavender was his favorite.

Lastly "Stainless Steel," sterling silver in color. Glossy. The coffee container swelled with blooms.

Tori swallowed down her emotion. "All gorgeous." Her tone was soft, appreciative.

"One for you too," Zane said. He took his time with the selection. "A Double Delight," he decided, reaching for the distinctive bicolored hybrid tea rose. The creamy white flower had rich, cherry-red edges. He didn't hand it to her directly; instead he gently caressed her cheek with the velvety petals. Brushed her lips, corner to corner. Stroked over her chin.

She closed her eyes. Breathed in the fragrance, sighed. "The scent of romance."

He leaned in, kissed her. "You are my romance," he whispered against her lips.

"You are . . . mine." Her eyelids fluttered open. "I love that you cut flowers for my gram. My heart thanks you."

He wanted her heart to love him. He placed the Double Delight in the middle of the coffee container. It was the rose with the longest stem. "Put the single in a separate vase when you get home. It's just for you."

She frowned. "We don't have any vases at the apartment, but I do have an empty grape Gatorade bottle. The rose will go in my bedroom. On my bedside table."

That worked for him. For now. Someday he'd buy her a vase. She still wasn't good at accepting gifts from him. He'd already formulated a pretext. Gatorade bottles would get recycled. A pretty vase was permanent.

The garden hose was nearby. He added water to the container. The blooms would fully open and live for a week.

She pulled a face. "Time to study."

He returned the garden tool to the garage, then met her at the Impala. He stared at her across the hood. Moon glow cast her in a silver halo. Starlight glittered on her hair, her face. His poetic soul embraced her. She was as soft as night air and prettier than the roses.

He'd been damn lucky Oswald had stolen her bikini top that day. He'd had girl friends, but never a special girlfriend. His parents liked Tori, but they felt she and Zane were too young to be so serious. His mom worried that his interest in Tori would shorten his attention span and hinder his academic progress. Fortunately his grades hadn't slipped. His dad insisted that a high school crush could weaken with college. Distance often stressed rather than strengthened a relationship. His older brothers Dune and Aidan believed in playing the field. His best buddy Race flipped his hormone switch with each pair of passing breasts.

He took note of everyone's opinion, and then formed his own. He listened to his gut. He and Tori were meant to be together. Nothing and no one would change his mind.

"Zane?" Tori raised an eyebrow, questioning his delay. She swept her hair behind an ear with her fingers. Dipped her head. Not coy, just shy. "You're staring at me."

He watched her often. He never got tired of looking at her. She should be used to it by now. She was not. "I like what I see," he said honestly.

She responded with a veiled look at him, and a hushed, "Back at you, Cates."

Nice to hear. Reassurance was good, even for a guy. They settled in the Impala. He keyed the engine, drove out the driveway. He took the long way to her apartment complex. She continued to clutch the bouquet to her chest. Buried her nose between the blooms. Inhaled deeply. The fragrance inspired her. Her imagination clicked, and she drifted into her world of design.

She spoke more to herself than to him. "A Victorian mansion. A lush antiquated sitting room. A color palette of porcelain-white satin, red-blush velvet, and sheer cream antique lace. The furniture calls out for human attention. A stroking of rich textures. The past curls up with the present on a glazed chintz fainting couch. The romantic warmth of a heavy brocade chair. Thick damask curtains drawn closed. Hiding secrets. A space all prim and proper, yet suggesting stolen moments of naughtiness."

He could see everything she described, felt he was living in her room. She deserved Pratt Institute. He was sure she would someday be a top designer. He believed in her.

"Home," she said when they reached the White Heron Apartments. "Walk me in?"

He'd driven from his house to her complex hundreds of times, but he'd been thinking about her, her career, and been on mental autopilot the last five miles. He pulled into visitor's parking. Cut the engine. They both got out, then took the cracked sidewalk to her door.

Once there, Tori handed him the bouquet. "I want you to give the roses to Nana Aubrey."

"Why?" he asked, startled. He didn't understand. He'd planned on a quick good night kiss before heading out. Not a flower delivery.

She tugged his elbow, drew him inside. Whispered, "I buy Gram flowers often. These are your mother's roses. They're special. You're generous to share. She'll sense that, I'm sure of it."

The apartment was quiet and dark. The television was turned to a low volume. Tonight her grandmother watched a gardening program. The roses seemed an appropriate gift.

"My parents are working," she told him. "She's alone."

Tori turned on a table lamp, then motioned Zane to

stand beside her at the front of the rocker. They blocked the TV. He saw the older woman blink, her expression confused. Tori was quick to say, "It's me, Nana . . . Zane's here too."

No facial recognition. Grandma was more inside herself than out tonight. Zane knelt before her. She stopped rocking. He settled the coffee container on her lap and steadied it with one hand. "My mother grows roses," he said. "From me to you—enjoy them."

Nana Aubrey lifted a shaky hand. Her fingertips trembled as she skimmed the petals on the lavender rose.

"Fragrant Plum," Zane told her.

She gave the stem a tug, struggled, but couldn't pull it from the bouquet. Zane removed it for her. She touched the rose to her nose, drew a breath, and her chest rattled. She released the air from her lungs, and the petals fluttered. Her brow creased. "Smells . . ." She couldn't find the word.

Tori helped. "Fruity, like a plum." She next selected a fragrant Stainless Steel. She held it for her grandmother. "Smells like citrus."

Her grandmother shifted slightly, and her arthritic shoulder popped when she reached for her photo album on the side table. Zane moved the flowers aside as she spread the album across her lap. Her fingers couldn't grip the pages, so Tori turned them slowly for her, one by one. Until Nana Aubrey laid her palm across one specific black-and-white photograph. Zane and Tori stared at the picture. 1953 was inked on the edge.

A couple stood on a narrow sidewalk before a stone church. "My grandparents," Tori softly recognized. "They would've been in their twenties."

Dressed for Sunday prayer, the man wore a dark suit. A dapper hat. Nana Aubrey wore a skirt suit, the jacket primly buttoned, the skirt draping her knees. A patent leather purse was hooked over her wrist. Her hand held a rose, high and against her heart.

"As many times as I've seen this photo, I've missed the rose," Tori confessed.

Her grandma pointed a finger at the flower. "Grande . . ." She mentally fought, but couldn't finish. Her brow furrowed.

Tori looked helplessly at Zane. "I don't know the name of the rose, do you?"

Grand Garden. Grand Lady. Not quite right. "Grande Dame," suddenly came to him. rose-pink in color. He quoted his mother, "'Grande Dame has been around a long time. A flowering antique. The fragrance epitomizes old world romance.'"

A fragile nod from Nana Aubrey. Her eyes were misty. A single tear trailed down her wrinkled cheek. Tori grabbed a tissue from the box on the table. Gently wiped it away.

Zane felt awful. "I'm sorry. I didn't mean to make you sad."

Little by little Nana Aubrey shook her head. The creak in her neck sounded painful. "Happy."

Tori lightly squeezed her gram's shoulder. "Roses are a good memory for you. No more carnations and daisies each week. I'll bring you a rose. Promise."

Nana Aubrey gave her granddaughter as close to a smile as Zane had ever witnessed. There was a softness to the older woman's face, as she bookmarked the page with the Stainless Steel bloom, then shut the album. She set her rocker in motion. Then closing her eyes, she relived the memory of her husband and the rose.

Zane pushed to his feet, placed the bouquet on the table. The scent of the roses drifted into every corner of the living room. He raised an eyebrow at Tori. "Walk me out."

They stood just beyond the door, left it cracked. She

stepped into him, and their bodies pressed to each other. She curved her hand about his neck and drew his face to her. "Thank you, Zane," she breathed against his lips. "My gram's response tonight was incredible. There was life in her eyes. In her smile." She kissed him with gentle gratefulness.

He didn't touch her, didn't walk her back against the outside wall and go for more. Instead he said, "I'll talk to my mom. Request a rose every few days. I'm sure she won't mind. Trust me."

She tilted her head slightly. Looked at him so steadily, so deeply, he felt her touch his soul. "I do trust you." It was the first time she'd admitted to having faith in him. Her words warmed his heart.

"I'll never give you a reason not to."

"You're one of the good guys."

"I try." To do the right thing wasn't always easy. "I have my moments. I'm far from perfect."

"You're perfect for me."

That surprised him. She'd never sounded so vulnerable, yet so serious. "You do it for me too." He'd said it before, and he said it again now.

"I . . ." Her declaration hung on the air between them. She licked her lips. Swallowed hard. "I love you."

Time held her words in place. They nearly stopped his heart. He'd fallen for her seconds after he'd seen her at the beach. He'd landed hard. He'd grown anxious. It had taken her months to accept him. To like him. To love him back. The moment was huge. Their relationship was no longer one-sided. They'd finally come together. A solid twosome.

"Hold that thought, Tori. Forever."

"That long, huh?"

"We'll work through whatever happens."

She sighed. "I'll hold you to it."

★ ★ ★

Once Tori allowed herself to love Zane, she took him into her heart, holding him close. Her grandmother and parents cared about her, but they'd never shown her the affection she received from Zane. She felt safe with him. Protected. Emotionally grounded. Despite the stability of their relationship, her life felt mildly disjointed. The end of the school year closed around her in those suffocating moments while she waited for the mail carrier. Her fingers were perpetually crossed for her acceptance to Pratt Institute. Meanwhile, Zane had yet to hear from the Air Force Academy. He appeared calm on the outside, but she knew him well enough now to sense his inner agitation. A jagged insecurity.

The senior prom was almost upon them. A charmed night for the two of them. She'd recently purchased a slightly used 2000 Camaro, a necessity if she was to function independently. Funds were tight. She didn't have the money for a fancy dress. Zane had generously offered to buy her one. She'd glared his wallet back in his pocket. She loved him but lived on her own terms. She bought what she could afford. Without anyone else's help.

She continued to bring her grandma a weekly rose. Zane's mother delighted in sharing her garden. Today Tori presented Nana Aubrey with an Heirloom. Nature at its most beautiful. The magenta double bloom spiraled open, revealing lilac tones. Its fruity scent blended apple, wine, and raspberries.

A fluted cranberry bud vase sat on the side table by Gram's rocker. A gift from Zane. Tori gave her the Heirloom, then went to put water in the vase. She returned to her grandmother's appreciative gaze. A sigh of a smile.

Her grandmother looked at her. "Face . . ."

One word, but Tori understood. The prom was heavy

on her mind, and she'd been frowning. Nana Aubrey knew her heart. Her moods. She was concerned for her now.

"Ch . . ."

"Cheer up?" Tori guessed. The older woman always seemed to sense her feelings. Tori told her secrets. Shared her happiness and heartbreak, never expecting a response. "I'm going to the prom with Zane," she confided. "I need a dress."

Her grandmother's brow wrinkled. "Help."

Her offer touched Tori deeply. "Don't worry. I'll figure it out."

"Store . . ."

"Most are too expensive. I'll shop secondhand and consignment shops next week. If I don't find something dressy, Zane's offered to ditch his tux and wear a suit or white shirt and tie. He'll go informal if I do." Extremely kind of him.

Nana Aubrey's face tightened. "Storage," took a great effort for her to say. She coughed afterward.

Storage? Tori was lost. "I'm not following."

Nana looked at her, as if willing Tori to read her mind. She drew a ragged breath. "Trunk." The effort wore her out. She rubbed her throat. Grew pale. Crumpled on the chair, eyes closed.

Distraught over how hard her grandma had worked to tell her something, Tori withdrew to the kitchen and brought her a glass of water in an emptied and washed Smucker's Grape Jelly glass. "Drink, Gram," she encouraged, holding the rim to her lips. Nana Aubrey's eyelids fluttered. She took a sip. Color slowly returned to her face. A second swallow, and she gripped the arms of her rocker and managed to say, "Bed."

Tori put it together. She figured bed meant bedroom.

Gram had her own sleeping space. It was small and narrow but allowed her some privacy. She asked for little. Tori was stumped. She wasn't aware Nana Aubrey had a trunk.

Her grandmother touched her arm. "Go."

Tori went to her bedroom, opened the door. Entered. The blinds were down. Shafts of light peeked between the slats. Her heart squeezed. Age had crept inside. Gram's walker was folded against one wall. A handicapped railing ran along one side of her metal-framed twin bed. A single pillow and basic white sheets. A gray and burgundy patchwork quilt.

Most telling were the empty face powder box and talcum powder tin atop a small two-drawer dresser. How long had they been empty? Tori wondered. Gram had never requested anything new. A hand-painted tea rose dresser tray held a small hand mirror and hairbrush. Nothing more.

After a full turn around the room, there was no sign of a trunk. The sliding closet door stood slightly ajar. She glanced inside. No hanging clothes. Her grandmother wore the same housedress day in and day out. It was washed once a week. Along with her nightgown and robe. No shelving overhead, but shoved in one corner was a trunk. Tori tugged it into the bedroom. Stared down on the leather-upholstered traveler with the brass closures. Presently used for storage. She didn't recognize the chest. Had no memory of it. Yet there it was, dusty, dented on the front left corner, and worn.

She knelt down, curious as to what might be inside. Decades sealed the closures. She needed all her fingers to pry them open. She broke a nail in the process. The lid stuck, and she gently shook it. A spring popped. Slowly, she lifted the lid. Despite her grandma's insistence that she view the items, she felt she was intruding. The feeling made her uneasy. She drew a breath and cautiously examined the contents.

Clothes. All flawlessly folded, as if preserved in time. She lifted, shook out the top piece, an elegant, vintage, Juilliard green wool coat, lined with satin. The designer label read CHRISTIAN DIOR. She draped it over her arm. The full-cut coat still had its lovely original buttons. Quality, Tori thought. Pricey in its day. She draped it over the lid.

A charcoal tweed suit came next. Partnered with black suede kitten heels, it would be retro and stylish. There was a blush-colored, full-length lace nightgown. Beneath, several framed photographs of Gram and her husband. Young, holding hands, gazing at one another. Tears filled Tori's eyes at this evidence of their heartfelt love.

She uncovered a Bible, a delicate petit point–embroidered evening bag with a floral chain handle, along with a golden brown velvet jewelry box. Inside were a strand of gray pearls and a cameo broach. Old and exquisite. A yellowed bankbook. A dog-eared page fell open, and Tori's eyes went wide over the amount of money once in the savings account. The account was long-closed with a zero balance. Her grandparents had been quite well off at one time. The older couple had been far different from her own mother and father, who lived from paycheck to paycheck. Drifters.

Her breath caught over the last item in the trunk. An incredible find. She held the formal dress to her chest. A sophisticated gown inspired by romance and an elegant era gone by. V-necked, sleeveless, the sheer mocha bodice was layered with a beautiful corded applique. Tori was taller than her grandmother. The navy blue chiffon skirt would've flowed about her gram's ankles. On Tori, it would sweep her knees. Graceful. A diversity of styles would be worn to the dance. The vintage classic was far prettier than any long mermaid style, layered tulle ballerina, or flirty mini.

Her heart warmed with a feeling of contentment. She had a prom dress now. She spread it on the end of the twin bed, then carefully repacked the trunk. She closed the lid and pressed down the closures, securing her grandmother's past. A strong push, and she put back the chest. She shut the closet door soundly. Nothing further would be disturbed. She returned to the living room, dress in hand.

She went down on her knees before her grandmother's rocker. Gram eyed her, the dress, and gave a small smile of approval. "Found."

Tori clasped one of her grandmother's hands. Gently held it. Emotion swelled her throat. "I had no idea you had the storage trunk. I don't know what to say. I'm so grateful."

Nana Aubrey's gaze softened. "Lo . . ."

"I love you too."

Her grandma nodded, and she closed her eyes. It was time for her late afternoon nap. She would sleep for an hour, her inner clock waking her for supper. Tori stood, kissed her fairy grandmother on the cheek. She was thrilled. Forever thankful. She would have the dress dry-cleaned. Her budget allowed for an inexpensive pair of navy heels at Shoe Mart.

She was going to the prom!

Her life would only be better if she heard from Pratt. Hopefully, she would get the long-anticipated letter soon.

The next day, Zane drove her home from school. They sat in visitor's parking and watched as the mail delivery truck entered the circular drive and slowed before the set of resident mailboxes near the front door. Tori had a mailbox key but hated to face another day of disappointment.

"Want me to check for you?" Zane offered. "Today could be your day."

"Could be . . ." She'd had months of could be. Might be. But nothing definitive. Her nerves were shot. She now sat in the Impala and watched as the mail carrier sorted out the mail, then climbed back in his postal truck and drove off.

Zane leaned in, kissed her lightly on the lips. "Let's do it together."

Together was good. He always comforted her. She welcomed his hug with each mail delivery. Letter or not. She questioned her own expectations. Unrealistic, perhaps. Maybe she wasn't good enough for Pratt, or the other two colleges where she'd applied. Disappointment crept up on her. Even with Zane beside her, it was difficult to shake.

They climbed from the car. He curved his arm about her shoulders as they walked across the lot. Their hips and thighs bumped. She loved the feel of him. Solid. Safe. Male.

Her mailbox and apartment keys were on the same ring. She slipped them from the front pocket of her jeans. *Be brave,* she told herself.

She keyed the mailbox, and the door fell open. Her pulse jumped. Stuffed in the box amid coupon flyers and bills was a manila envelope with Pratt's formal return address. Her hand shook as she withdrew it. Her heart nearly flatlined when she tore one corner wide enough to look inside.

Zane stood behind her, his hands on her hips. His strength supported her. He squinted over her shoulder. Read along with her. The words didn't fully sink in. Not until he dug in his fingers, squeezed, and whooped near her ear. "You made it!" He whipped her around, lifted her up, and gave her a rib-crushing hug. She could barely breathe. His mouth came down on hers. He kissed her fiercely, as happy for her as she would've been for him had their situations been reversed.

He leaned back slightly, let her slide down his body. He set her on her feet. "We need to celebrate. Wherever, whatever you like." He was a generous guy.

She considered, came to a decision. "I want to wait until you receive your acceptance too. A double celebration." It would be more meaningful.

"It could be a while, Tori."

"I'm in no hurry."

"Prom's in two weeks. We'll be in a nice restaurant. The dancing will be romantic. Afterward . . ." He trailed off suggestively.

"Afterward is home by midnight," she said, closing down their evening. Earlier than he would've liked. "My parents are flying to Key West for a job interview. A place called the Keys Tees is looking for a couple to manage their T-shirt and gift shop. I'm not certain they're qualified, but they want to give it a shot. I need to be home for my gram."

What would her grandmother do without Tori? Zane wondered. She was so responsible. She'd always been an adult, he realized. A grown-up without a childhood. But she was his girl. He would take care of her at the prom. Show her the best time of her life.

The dance was held in the ballroom at the Sandcastle, a five-star hotel on Saunders Shores, the sister city to Barefoot William. The two towns differed greatly. Affluence claimed the southern boundaries of Saunders Shores. There was no cracked cement boardwalk here; it was all cocoa brown brick. Tall glassed buildings. Sophisticated shoppers and carefree spending.

Couture fashions, gourmet dining, and designer boutiques. Waterfront mansions welcomed the rich and retired. Yachts the size of cruise ships lined the waterways. Private airstrips replaced commercial travel. The wealthy were a community unto themselves. Forbes listed The Shores among the top ten resorts in the world.

"A line of limousines," admired Tori, eyeing the slow-moving traffic as the rentals eased into the circle drive and let off their passengers. Most vehicles held several couples. Renting a limousine was expensive. The guys went in on the cost together. Zane had gone all out. They rode alone. For him, these private moments were important. The night was all about him, her, and their memories.

Tori leaned forward, tried to see through the window. "Isn't that your buddy Race Wallace in the limo ahead of us?"

Zane nodded. "Race and his two dates."

Tori blinked. "*Two* dates?"

"He's showing off," Zane explained. "He asked Blu to the dance, and she turned him down. Flat. Apparently she didn't go to her own prom and had no plans to go to his."

Tori grinned. "That sounds like Blu. So who's in the limo with him?" she asked.

"Khaki Davis and Rachel Coleman."

"Hmmm," Tori mused. "Both cheerleaders. Both popular. Both hot. An in-your-face challenge to Blu."

"I doubt Blu will even care."

"She has feelings."

"Just not for Race."

Tori rolled her shoulders, a noticeable shrug that had him asking, "Am I wrong?" Race was his buddy. Blu made him crazy. His crush on her had outlasted his girl-friend-a-month club.

"What's right?" she said, avoiding a real answer.

Not enough info. Unfortunately, their limousine now slowed, stopped, at the main door. He had no time to question her further. The doorman, whose name tag read TOM, was on the spot, opening their passenger door. Tom

assisted Tori from the vehicle, eyeing her with appreciation and interest. Zane understood. She was a total knock-
out, and all the males in the vicinity looked her way. His
date had momentarily stopped traffic.

As she eased aside so he could exit the vehicle, Tori
had no idea of the attention she was getting. Her hair was
shiny, swirling free about her shoulders. Her dress was
beautiful, like no other. There was an air about her, unaf-
fected and fine. Men continued to stare. When she finally
noticed, shyness overtook her. She slipped her hand in his,
seeking his assurance. He leaned toward her, whispered
near her ear, "You're gorgeous, babe."

She skim-gazed his black tux. "Looking good yourself."

Automatic doors slid open, welcoming them into the
hotel. Persian rugs covered hexagon terra cotta floor tiles.
Floor-to-ceiling mirrors reflected the guests. A wide impressive staircase wound to the second-floor ballroom,
where chandeliers cast prisms of light on the dance floor.
It was truly a red carpet prom.

He and Tori stood closely, just inside the door. He
glanced her way. She was wide-eyed, and worrying her
bottom lip. Her expression concerned him, but it didn't
surprise him. He knew her better than he knew himself.
She didn't feel worthy to be here.

"You belong, Tori," he quietly told her.

"Because I'm with you." *A Cates.*

"Don't sell yourself short," he stated. "You're strong,
smart, and your own person. You stand just fine on your
own."

She brushed his side. "I'd rather lean on you."

"You can always lean on me."

Race and his two dates soon approached them. "Hey,
prom king, music's about to start. Mind if I dance with
Tori?"

"I'm not prom king yet," Zane corrected. "It could well

be you, dude." Both their names were on the ballot. There were five names in total. Race would surely get the female vote. He flirted with them all. The other three guys were into sports and extracurricular activities. All but Zane had been accepted to college.

"How 'bout it, Tori?" Race asked her directly as the DJ stepped onto the dais and spun the first song. "Your boyfriend can dance with my girls."

Reluctance on Tori's part. Eagerness from Race. "Go ahead," Zane told her. One fast dance would not be a big deal. But when Race went on to claim a second dance it grated on Zane's nerves. Despite the fact he had two partners. Both girls wore bandage dresses, short and tight; the knit bands barely covered their butts. "I Want It That Way" by the Backstreet Boys seemed to play forever. Zane gave in to the two-step, while the girls gyrated around him. His gaze never left Tori. She moved gracefully.

The lights dimmed, and bodies pressed close for a slow number, "I Don't Want to Miss a Thing" by Aerosmith. Zane crossed to Race. His friend had two dates. Tori belonged with him. He stepped between them before Race could draw her close. "My turn," he growled, claiming her. Tori sank into him. He nodded left. "Khaki and Rachel? Remember them?"

Race grinned. "A slow-dance sandwich." He then squeezed in the middle of the two. The girls snugged him from the front and the back. A slow sway brought out his satisfied smile.

A fast song separated the couples, all but Zane and Tori. Holding her was the best part of the prom. He made it last. Zane glanced at Race. Somehow his buddy managed to dance with two girls and keep them both happy. No jealousy. He had charm.

"I missed you," Zane whispered near her ear. It felt good to hold her. She was so soft and beautiful.

Tori smiled against his neck. "We were only separated for two songs."

"Did Race hit on you?" It was a hard question for him to ask. He believed his friend was trustworthy, to a point.

"Jealous?" she teased him.

"Should I be?"

"He flirted a little and got hard against my hip."

"He did?" Zane asked sharply.

"Turned out he had a flask in his pocket. Vodka."

Zane chuckled his relief. Race had never crossed the girlfriend line. Tonight Tori stood out. Unique yet unassuming. She claimed male attention without trying. She could've tempted even a guy with two dates. Fortunately Race had honored their bro-code.

"Vodka loosens his tongue. He gets talkative," he said.

She updated him. "Between songs he asked about Blu. What she was doing tonight."

That didn't surprise Zane. "She's working your shift, right?"

"Eddie's short on help. He initially refused to give me the night off. Blu took my hours."

Zane would have to thank Blu next time he saw her. He was curious. "She's making pizzas?" He'd never seen her in the kitchen.

"Blu started out there, being paid an hourly wage. She twisted Eddie's arm and went on to waitress. She makes good money in tips. The regulars love her. She calls them by name, takes interest in their families—kids and pets."

"She's never paid much attention to Race."

"Ignoring isn't always indifference."

If that was so, perhaps Race had a chance with Blu. Four years down the road. Once he'd graduated from the Air Force Academy. Doubtful, but always a possibility.

Tori and he continued to dance while the dining room

staff set up the buffet. Couples soon drifted toward the food. The prom committee members had mailed the menu to the senior class. Tossed salad and fresh fruit. Chicken cutlet and sliced prime rib. Honey-glazed carrots and mashed potatoes. Chocolate cake and a build-an-ice-cream-sundae station. An open bar for soft drinks. Zane was pretty sure others beside Race had sneaked in booze. But they were discreet. The chaperones had yet to call anyone out.

Zane angled back. "Hungry?" he asked Tori. The DJ had taken a break. It was the perfect time to eat.

"Good by me," she agreed.

They served themselves, then sought seating at a large round table. Next to Race and his dates. Conversations centered on high school memories and college plans. Tori was congratulated on her acceptance to Pratt over and over. His classmates seemed genuinely thrilled for her. Zane got encouraging looks and pats on his shoulder. He was hoping for late acceptance. When his letter arrived, he and Tori would manage the four-year separation. They had been talking about marriage, but both were willing to wait until he graduated from the Air Force. *No spouse* was an academy rule.

The DJ returned to the dais. He spun a reverberating drum roll. The principal, Roger Abbott—known to the students as Roger Rabbit—joined him on the low stage, a microphone in one hand, two glittery crowns in the other. Abbott gave a welcoming speech that went on and on until Race shouted out, "Who won?"

Zane shook his head. His buddy lived up to his name. Always in a rush. The principal cleared his throat, went on to say, "The votes were nearly unanimous for our prom royalty. Both are long-standing students in the community. Both have high grade point averages and excel in extracurricular activities."

"All me," from Race. He slid to the edge of his chair, anticipating his name would be called.

"Your prom king has run marathons in support of numerous charities. He spent a summer in Birmingham, Alabama, building homes with Habitat for Humanity."

"Not me," Race shut down. He cut Zane a look. "I've got it narrowed down, dude."

"Your prom queen," Abbott praised, "opened her family's stables and established a therapeutic horseback riding program for special needs children. She did so quietly and without fanfare."

Applause echoed, even before the names were called. The principal held up a sparkling crystal crown. "Your prom queen, Nora Evans."

Zane stood along with his classmates. Nora was well liked. One of the nicest people he knew. Pretty and always smiling, she put others first. She did favors and gave second chances. She took the microphone and accepted her crown with a heartfelt "thank you."

"Your king—" Abbott raised a second crown, a high-pointed headpiece embellished with red and green rhinestones. "Zane Cates. Congratulations!"

Wild clapping, lots of female hugs, and guy punches to his arm. Thumps to his back. Exuberant Race pounded his shoulder overly hard. He knocked Zane sideways and into Tori. He caught her before more human dominoes fell. Through it all, Tori's smile meant the most. A path parted for him, and her happiness walked with him toward the stage.

He put the crown on his head, was handed the mic. He bowed to his classmates. Locating Tori across the room, he spoke directly to her. "It's been a very good senior year."

Whistles, woot-woots, and arm-pumps from the guys. Romantic sighs from the girls. Zane couldn't have been happier. The king and queen danced to Bon Jovi's "Livin' on a Prayer." Then parted as the music ended. They rejoined their respective dates.

Tori still stood where he'd left her. She hugged him. "Kiss the king," he breathed against her mouth. She willingly did so.

The DJ spun his next song, only to stop within seconds, his gaze fixed on the main door. Everyone craned their necks, jockeying for a better view. Zane was tall. He immediately caught sight of two sheriff's deputies, standing on the edge of the dance floor, looking formal and serious. He immediately sensed something was wrong. Very wrong.

The principal excused himself from the table of chaperones, all seated and enjoying dessert. He cut through the crowd and soon reached the deputies. Brief handshakes before their heads came together. A short conversation ensued.

Speculation ran wild among his classmates. Law enforcement didn't show up at a high school dance without good reason. Drugs or theft. A death. A foreboding chill spread between Zane's shoulder blades. Goose bumps chased themselves down his spine. He reached for Tori's hand. Held it tight. The news was slow in coming.

Principal Abbott wound back through his students, his gaze fixed on Tori. She stood as close to Zane as was humanly possible. Close as skin. He hugged her, offering safety and protection for whatever was ahead.

The principal reached them. He spoke quietly, calmly, a note of sadness in his voice. "The deputies would like to speak with you, Tori. There's an empty convention room down the hall. It will allow privacy."

"Speak with me?" Her words were barely audible.

"It's important. Zane can come with you," Abbott suggested as he guided them toward the door.

The seriousness of the situation had Zane removing his

crown. He tossed it to Race for safekeeping. He didn't care if Race wore it the rest of the night or not. Nothing seemed more important than the immediate moment.

A hush fell over the senior class. The enthusiasm of the prom died. Curiosity, concern, worry filled the ballroom. Heartbeats slowed. They stood still as statues.

Zane stuck by her side as the deputies led the way. Abbott hesitated, then followed. A disturbing silence walked them down the hallway to a corporate meeting room. The carpet muffled their steps.

Tori looked up at him, questioningly. Frightened. "What's happened? It feels awful."

"I have no idea," he told her. He prayed for the best. Feared for the worst.

Officers Barnes and Jacoby solemnly introduced themselves once they reached the room. Abbott turned on the lights. The room was cavernous. High ceilings and a wide open floor plan. Zane felt hollow. The space seemed to swallow them. Tori was offered a chair but preferred to stand. Jacoby's voice was deep, intense. His words echoed off the walls. "You're Tori Rollins, correct?"

She nodded.

"Can you verify that your parents Kyle and Marie Rollins flew to Key West today?"

She bit down on her bottom lip. "That's right. They went for a job interview."

Barnes took over next. He swallowed hard. "You're the next of kin. It is with deepest regard and regret that we inform you that your parents' plane malfunctioned. The commuter aircraft went down off the coast of Marathon. Rescue teams have searched the crash site. There were no survivors."

"No survivors . . ." Tori repeated, stunned. She paled. Her gaze was flat, unfocused, disbelieving. Zane supported her when her knees buckled. He held her upright. The moment seemed surreal.

"You're sure?" she whispered.

"They were on the flight manifest," Jacoby affirmed.

"Did they actually get on the plane?"

"Boarding passes were issued."

"Oh . . . no . . . no," escaped her. She went so still, Zane was afraid she'd stopped breathing. He rubbed her back.

"One additional question," requested Barnes. "You're eighteen? Legal age?"

"Yes."

"We will have a report to you once all details are fully reported and filed."

"M-My grandmother," Tori stuttered. "Does she know?"

"We stopped by your apartment. Knocked, but no one answered. A neighbor indicated you were at the prom. At the Sandcastle."

"Gram doesn't hear well. I need to be the one to tell her."

"Do you need a ride back to your apartment complex?" asked Barnes.

Tori shook her head. "Zane rented a limo."

Barnes locked eyes with Zane. "You'll see her home? Stay with her?"

Zane nodded. "For as long as she needs me."

The deputies reiterated their expressions of sympathy, then departed. Principal Abbott sheltered them from prying eyes as they left the hotel. The limo arrived, and Tori collapsed against him on the backseat. Death. Zane had been to funerals, but never had anyone close to him lose their parents. He was as numb as Tori. There were no words to bring her parents back. No words to ease her heavy heart. Still he tried. "I'm so sorry." The words were lame, insufficient. He just didn't have more.

"I–I'm sorry too." She stared straight ahead.

She trembled but did not cry as she informed her grand-mother of the accident. Her gram sat and rocked her chair, her expression blank. Tori continued to shake through the funeral, the senior graduation ceremony, and into June. He watched as she went on autopilot, going to work each day and taking care of Nana Aubrey. Tori's paycheck wouldn't cover their present apartment. They faced mov-ing to a smaller place.

Zane gave up on hearing from the Air Force Academy. He'd yet to receive admittance, and, with each passing day, his acceptance seemed less likely. Disappointment had tainted his dream. But his letdown was nothing compared to Tori losing her parents. Unimaginable. He started working part-time at Gray's Garage. Not his goal in life, but it kept him busy.

Then one Monday morning in mid-June, Zane's life took on new meaning. He was doing an oil change when a thought crossed his mind and stuck. He left work at noon and went by his parents' house first, to include them in his decision. To marry Tori Rollins. They were stunned and not nearly as supportive as he had hoped. They tried to talk him out of his future plans.

His mother cried. His father was deeply concerned. They believed him too young. The responsibility of taking on a grieving girl and her grandmother was enormous. Had his sympathy for Tori stolen his common sense? Couldn't they just live together? He answered their questions the best he could. Honestly. From the heart. Still they wor-ried. He stood firm. Tori's struggles were his struggles. He wanted to make her life better.

At the end of their conversation, his parents came to-gether and supported him. Albeit reluctantly. There'd be no division in their family. A small Cates cottage sat empty on the cul-de-sac of Palmdale Drive, two streets east. It had belonged to his aunt Mae, a retired newspaper photographer. She had never married. Upon turning sixty, she'd retired from the *Barefoot Sun* and made the decision to travel the world. She'd later met and wed a photo journalist in England. Acquiring dual citizenship, she'd moved to London. Zane left his parents' house with the key to the cottage in his pocket.

He drove to the White Heron Apartments. He'd called ahead, and Tori was expecting him. The door was unlocked. He entered. As always, Nana Aubrey sat in her rocker before the TV set at low volume. She was watching *Antiques Roadshow*. It was nearing the noon hour. Tori had made her lunch and left it on the side table. Half a ham sandwich and a cup of tea.

Gram heard him arrive. Her neck creaked as she looked his way and managed, "Bed . . ."

Tori was in one of the bedrooms. He needed to speak to Nana Aubrey before he located her. He narrowed the space between them, lowered himself on one knee beside the chair. He took the older woman's hand, wrinkled and cold. He held it gently. "I need to talk to you," he said.

She stopped rocking. She might not understand everything he said. Might not even respond. Yet she would listen. "I love your granddaughter," came first.

"Ferris . . ."

"Yes, we rode the Ferris wheel last fall." He was amazed she remembered their first date. Months ago. "Our lives have changed." Drastically. "I want to marry her."

A long pause. "Dad . . ."

He intuitively knew that she wanted him to ask Tori's father for her hand in marriage. Reality had faded for Nana Aubrey. Her daughter and husband remained alive in her mind. Zane wouldn't take that from her.

His chest tightened. "Okay by you?"

"What?"

He wasn't making himself clear. He didn't know how.

"Tori and I will marry." He spoke slowly, concisely. "A small family ceremony. We'll move into a cottage. You will live with us."

Bits soaked in. "Rocker?" seemed important to her.

"You'll have your rocker and TV," he promised.

She set the chair in motion and returned to watching specialists from the country's leading auction houses appraise antiques.

Zane located Tori in the bedroom her parents had occupied. Her back was to him as she packed up their clothes, robotically folding and sealing the boxes with duct tape. She wore an oversized man's T-shirt, no doubt her father's, and jeans. There was a tightness to her shoulders, to her spine. She held in her emotion. Her loss pushed deep, leaving her dazed. Numb. She had yet to cry. That bothered Zane the most.

He leaned against the doorjamb. Brought up the same question he'd asked her yesterday, and the day before that, "Anything I can do to help?"

He received the same answer. "I have to do the sorting myself. Alone. My parents didn't have much. One day I make a pile for the Salvation Army; the next day I change my mind. I have to make final decisions soon. It's . . . hard."

He crossed to her. Took her in his arms. Kissed the top of her head. "You're doing just fine."

"I'm trying, Zane." Her words were whispered against his neck. "It's so sad—I received a call from the owner of Keys Tees, where my parents were hoping to be hired. Their interview apparently went well. They would have gotten the job, had they lived."

A *would have* that was lost to the plane crash.

"I, uh—" Her voice dropped. She spoke with difficulty. "I called Pratt's admissions office. I canceled my scholarship."

She'd done the unthinkable. Given up her dream. Her pain was his pain. He hurt for her. He rubbed her upper arms soothingly. She sighed away her regret. Went on to point out, "One good thing, the apartment manager gave Gram and me an extra two weeks, rent free, to pack up and move. Move where, I'm not exactly certain. I will find us a place."

"I may have a solution."

She tilted her head. Chin up. "I don't expect you to fix our situation."

"The result benefits me also."

"You too?" Total surprise. "How so?"

"I have connections and know of a cottage," he told her. "A comfortable two-bedroom, two-bath. Rent free."

"No way."

"Way. It can be yours, but it comes with one condition."

"What might that be?"

"Me and a wedding ring."

Three

Wedding ring. Tori started. Her breath caught. Had she heard him correctly? "Come again?" she requested.

"I want to marry you, Tori Rollins." His expression was completely serious.

She eased back. Two steps. He lowered his arms. "Yes" would've been the appropriate answer. Instead, she asked, "Why?"

"Because I love you."

"Oh . . . Zane." She sighed heavily. His love was honorable. Protective. Heartwarming. He wanted to make her life better. She was grateful but also practical. They'd always been honest with each other. Truth was important to her. She spoke from her heart. "You are everything to me, but marriage won't fix me. I try to stay strong for Gram, but I miss my parents. They weren't always around, but I knew they'd return eventually. Now they won't come home anymore. That scares me."

She crossed her arms over her chest, shielding her emotions. She bit down on her bottom lip. She hated feeling vulnerable. Lost. She hadn't cried. Wouldn't cry. She'd face her problems, alone. As best she could. "There are times during the day that I shatter," she admitted. "I feel so fractured, all I want to do is curl up in bed and sleep for days. But I can't. Gram needs me, in her own way. I will always be here for her."

He stared at her. Took it all in. He then widened his stance, jammed his hands in the pockets of his jeans, and responded with, "We've discussed marriage, and you were all for it."

She remembered their talk. "At the time of our discussion, we were planning on college and four years apart. Then a wedding. My life changed on prom night. Pratt is out of the picture for me."

"I haven't heard from the Air Force Academy, and I doubt I will. Which means we're four years ahead of schedule. We can get married anytime."

His logic somehow grounded her. Her breathing calmed. Her heart felt lighter. She had to be sure that she was who he wanted. Truly wanted. Not just for the moment, but forever. "You are such a decent guy," she softly said. "But I don't want you to feel obligated. I plan to take care of Nana Aubrey. She would come with our marriage."

Not a blink. Not a frown. No hesitation on his part. "I'm committing to you both." He grinned. "I come with Oswald."

"Oz would live with us?" A small smile. That made her day.

Zane pulled a face. "You're more excited about him moving in than marrying me!"

She punched his arm. "Hardly." A significant pause. A moment of concern. "Have you spoken to your parents?"

He rubbed his chin, lips pursed. "We talked. Worked through it."

Worked through it. His parents were realistic and apparently not fully on board. She understood their apprehension. "They think we're too young. Taking on too much responsibility. Too disappointed that our lives have taken a detour. They think we're grasping at straws."

"Not grasping, Tori. We're not desperate, but we've reached a defining moment. My parents came through for us and offered a place to live." He told her about his aunt, retired and living in England.

"A Cates cottage." *Rent free* now made sense.

"I have the key," he informed her. "Care to see it? It stands empty, in need of a family and an interior designer."

Family first. Decorating second. He tempted her. Greatly. "You, me, Gram, Oz, quite the household."

"I like it."

"Me . . . too."

"So . . . you're accepting my proposal?"

"I do."

Zane took her in his arms, hugged her so tightly the air rushed from her lungs. His kiss was deep, thorough, promising so much. It was the kiss of a future husband more than present boyfriend.

He cupped her bottom, lifted her against him. Immediate body heat and desire. Touching, feeling, rubbing. Arousal and greedy need swamped them even with their clothes on. Her breasts grew heavy. Her nipples pointed. A quiver in her thighs. Damp panties. His erection pressed her belly. He was jacked. They kissed until their lips were numb. He then eased back, and she slipped down his body. She felt his strength. Every muscle. They smiled at each other.

"You do it for me, Tori. I'm boner-fide."

"You're always hard."

"Only with you."

She had little control around him. Her heart raced and her body hummed. "Our bodies like each other."

"You'll soon see just how much."

Lovers. Hot sex. Expectation.

"I could use some cold water," he said.

Her too. She crooked her finger. "In the fridge."

He followed her, asking, "How often does your grand-mother leave the house?"

Tori scratched her head, thoughtful, as she opened the fridge, withdrew a pitcher of water. She poured, then passed him a glass. "It's been ages." Nana Aubrey hadn't had the awareness or strength to attend her parents' funeral.

"Weeks? Months?"

"Months," Tori said sadly.

"She gets out today," said Zane. "I want her to see the cottage along with us."

"You do?"

"She's part of the family. Her opinion matters."

"She might not be responsive."

"Doesn't matter. Being with us counts."

Tori sipped her water. Zane downed his glass in three gulps, then eyed hers. She took one more swallow, then shared hers with him. The man was thirsty. He winked at her.

He placed the empty glasses in the sink. They walked to the living room together. "Can she walk?" he asked.

Tori realized that he'd only seen her grandmother in the rocking chair, watching TV. "She shuffles. Gram has a walker and a cane."

"One hand on the cane might be easiest," Zane suggested. "I'll support her other arm." Tori went for her cane, a wooden, quad-tipped model.

Nana Aubrey's hair was combed. Her glasses in place. She wore a floral housedress and quilted slip-on sneakers. She stopped rocking upon their approach. Tori gently touched her shoulder, and her grandmother looked up.

"We're going to move soon, Nana," Tori told her. "I want to show you our new home."

"Me . . ." A flicker of understanding.

Tori's heart squeezed. Her grandmother didn't want to be left behind. "We go together, Gram."

A faint nod.

Tori and Zane assisted Nana Aubrey to her feet. Tori positioned the handle of the cane in her right hand. Her grandma next took Zane's arm and leaned heavily on him. She was weak, her shuffling slow, unsteady. Starting and stopping, they took fifteen minutes to get from the rocker to the front door.

"We're doing great," Zane stated when they'd cleared the door. He paused on the threshold to give the older woman a moment to catch her breath. "Visitor's parking is close. Only a few more steps." They took them slowly.

Tori eyed her gram, anxious the outing might be too much for her. Summer sunshine warmed the afternoon. The air was still, the sky bleached white with patches of blue. Nana Aubrey made it to the Impala with assistance. Zane helped her into the car, fastened her seat belt. Her grandma closed her eyes, and, within seconds, was sound asleep.

Tori settled on the backseat. Zane slid behind the wheel. He cut her a look in the rearview mirror. His brow creased in concern. "Go, stay, what?"

"Gram's exerted herself and will nap for a short time. We'll wake her at the cottage."

"You want me to take the long way?"

"Give her fifteen minutes. Drive around your neighborhood."

The ride was pleasant. Tori rolled down her back window. She admired and respected Olde Barefoot William; it was a place where the Cates family history lived on. There was a sense of roots and stability. A permanence she'd never known. Enormous evergreens lined the narrow two-lane roads. Ancient moss clung to the cypress.

Sunlight splashed through the scarlet-flowered branches on royal poinciana trees at the street corners. The scent of plumeria, gardenia, and hibiscus was heavy on the air. Sprinklers on automatic timers kicked on, watering lawns. Summer was here, the ground dry, and the earth welcomed a good soaking.

Nana Aubrey yawned, blinked, as Zane parked the car in the cottage driveway. He killed the engine. Perfect timing. Gram stared ahead, unsure of her surroundings. The white cottage with the dark blue shutters sat back from the street, quiet, unassuming, and surrounded by foliage. Tall carmine-red rose bushes fronted the porch.

Her gram struggled to sit straighter. Zane unfastened her seat belt. Her lips moved, but words failed her. She drew a breath, sighed appreciatively over the beauty.

"Robin Hood roses," Zane told her. "They're growing wild now and need to be cut back. My aunt called them her blooming, living, privacy fence. They have long-lasting blooms and a light scent."

He touched her grandma's shoulder. "This fall, we can crack a window and let in the fragrance. We'll get an outdoor rocker so you can sit on the porch if you'd rather take in the scent firsthand."

Tori's heart warmed with his kindness. Rocking chairs and roses. A delicate balance. Her grandmother would survive the change in residence. Tori exited the Impala along with Zane. Her gram once again leaned on her cane and clutched Zane's arm as a lifeline. They carefully climbed two wooden steps onto the cottage porch. He removed the house key from his pocket, let them in.

They were greeted by a crescent moon hardwood entrance hall that gave onto an open-raftered, high-ceilinged living room. The honey-blush-colored walls were soothing. A wide bay window invited the sunshine in. The dark brown window seat below provided views to the outdoors, creating a sense of coziness and security. Zane guided Nana Aubrey to the cushioned niche and settled her there comfortably. Her grandmother sat perfectly still. She stared straight ahead.

"She'll be okay?" he asked Tori.

"She'll be fine," she assured him.

"Then let me show you around," he suggested. "It's a nice starter house."

Starter? She turned around in a full circle and felt immediately at home. She could live here forever.

They linked hands, and he led her through the living room. Off to the left, French pocket doors parted to reveal the two bedrooms. The master had a full bath and walk-in closet with built-in shelves. Nana Aubrey would sleep in the second bedroom. It was the ideal arrangement.

The kitchen unfolded at the back of the cottage. It featured an old-fashioned brown-and-white-checkerboard-tiled floor. Narrow refrigerator with bottom freezer, two-burner stove, and a mini-dishwasher. The countertops were a bamboo laminate. Natural and practical. The cream-colored kitchen cabinets had glass-fronted doors.

"Like it so far?" Zane asked.

Tori was captivated. "The cottage is perfect."

He moved their conversation outside. "The rear porch."

They walked through the back door and onto a private redwood sundeck. "We can get a barbecue grill. A double-wide hammock."

"Have you barbecued?" she asked him.

"Cooking with my dad I'm a master. By myself, blackened hamburgers and burned hot dogs. I'll improve." He gave her the once-over, slow and thorough. "How are you in a hammock?"

"Same way I am in a canoe," she admitted. "It flips over."

He grinned. "You can always land on me."

She sensed he would catch her whenever she fell. Still, she worried her bottom lip. "We're taking a big step, Zane."

"Big steps or baby steps, it doesn't matter as long as we're moving forward together. I want a life with you."

"I want the same."

He curved his arm about her waist and pointed beyond the deck. Butterflies swarmed an overgrown, unkempt garden. "My aunt didn't keep up the butterfly garden, but the black-and-white Zebra Longwings live on. They're attracted to the orange Mexican sunflowers and white asters."

Tori's spirit lifted. Her own heart took flight. "Their transformation from caterpillar to free-flying butterfly is so beautiful." She squinted against the sunshine. "Is that a gazebo in the distance?" A faded white outline against the deepening woods.

He cupped his hand over his eyes, blocked the sun. "I think so, but I haven't noticed it before now. Looks weathered and in need of repair. We'd have to cut a path, but it's worth exploring."

A thought formed. One she shared with him. "Wouldn't it be the perfect place to exchange our vows?"

"I'll need a lawn mower, hammer, nails, paint. I'll recruit Race and Rylan, but even so, it could take a few days."

"We have time."

"A lifetime."

So much to take in. Tori leaned into Zane's side, sighed heavily. Happily. The cottage was overwhelming, in a good way. The promise of stability touched her soul. Permanence prompted her smile. She tilted her head, kissed his neck, his cheek, the corner of his mouth. He angled down his chin, gave her full access to his mouth. They kissed deeply. Her scalp tingled. Her toes curled. She ached for him.

"My gram," she managed, coming up for air. They separated. "We should go back to the apartment. I need to fix her supper before I go to work. I'm scheduled at five."

Zane pulled a face. "Zinotti's. I'm not a fan of Eddie. Dude's sleazy."

"He's not well liked," admitted Tori. "However, he just gave me a raise. I'll stick around until I find something better."

"Wilbur Gray offered me full-time at the garage," he told her. "Which I'll accept after we're married."

"Married . . ." She still couldn't wrap her head around the idea of marrying Zane Cates. She was almost afraid to ask. "A small wedding?" He had a huge family. She didn't want to offend anyone.

He shrugged. "Works for me. My parents, brothers and sister, and Grandpa Frank. Your grandmother. I'll ask Race to stand up for me."

"I'll ask Blu."

"Decisions made. Next, when?"

"We'll need to get a wedding license," was the logical next step.

"Got it covered. They're issued by the clerk of the court. The license is valid for sixty days. There's a three-day waiting period after issuance unless we take the Florida premarital course."

Her eyes widened. "You know this how?"

"I had a good friend who got married last summer. I was his best man. I listened and learned." Pause. "I have an uncle who's a minister. He could marry us, unless you have someone else in mind."

She had no church. No minister. No religious affiliation. "Your uncle is fine. What about the premarital course?"

"A pass for me, unless you want us to attend."

"Pass for me too." They were in agreement.

He nudged her toward the door. They went back inside. He leaned a hip against the kitchen counter, asked, "Can you clear time tomorrow to go to the courthouse?"

"Anytime, actually. It's my day off from work."

He was all focus and forward motion. "I'm at the garage until noon. We'll go and fill out the paperwork after that. Afterward, we'll shop for our bed."

Their bed. Her heart raced with the changes in her life. She could barely keep up. "I'll prepare Gram for moving into the cottage."

"Electricity is on. Let's get the two of you settled before the weekend. I'll grab a couple guys to help with the heavy lifting."

She dipped her head. "We don't have much. The sofa's seen better days. The beds are lumpy. The drawers in the dressers don't fully close. I'd thought to have them hauled away. Nana Aubrey has her rocker, TV, and a traveler's trunk."

He scratched his jaw, noted, "I'm living at home and have no furniture to call my own. I'd like to buy a new bed. King-size for us. A double for your gram. After that, I want you to use your decorating skills. Make the cottage our home. I have some money saved."

Their home. Her design. Incredible. "We don't have to buy everything all at once. One piece here, one piece there."

"Just don't make me sit on the living room floor or stand up to eat in the kitchen for too long."

She gave him a thumbs-up. "Got it."

They returned to the living room with a plan in the making. Her grandma was still on the window seat. She no longer faced the main room but had swiveled slightly to look out the window. Her usual blank expression was now equally curious and concerned. As if she feared she'd been misplaced. Conceivably forgotten.

"We're here, Gram," Tori was quick to assure her. "This is our new home. Zane was showing me around. I didn't want to tire you. You'll get the tour soon too."

"Mov . . ." she began.

Moving. Tori understood. "Zane and I will soon be getting married. You and I will be settled here by the weekend."

Nana Aubrey was quietly accepting. Sunshine slipped through the bay window, warming her face, putting color in her pale cheeks. The roses drew her attention once again. She stilled and stared. Softly smiled.

Zane rubbed the back of his neck. "I need to fence the backyard for Oswald. Does your grandma like dogs?"

"She had a tiger cat named Chester for eighteen years."

"Oz can be rowdy, although he's learning to mind. Calming down. I'll have to be stricter. I don't want him jumping and scaring her."

"We'll be fine," Tori said confidently. "I have faith in Ozzie. Dogs have a sixth sense when it comes to detecting human frailty and emotion. He could pick up on Gram's depression and sadness and adjust his behavior accordingly. Becoming protective. He'd be good company for her."

"I never thought of him as a therapy dog."

"Because you two roughhouse. He's gentle around me."

"I'm not worried. It's all good."

She'd never have believed that anything good could've come from the death of her parents and Zane not being accepted to the Air Force Academy. She was strong in her own right, but peace came in having a partner. Here she was on the cusp of marrying her high school sweetheart. Her life was pulling itself together. Bit by bit.

Tori watched as Zane assisted Nana Aubrey to the door. Her gram clutched his arm, trusted him. Tori relied on him too. They were soon to be a family. She had a secret that she'd yet to share. She would before long. Time flew by, and she hadn't had the opportunity to address her greatest fear and ultimate relief.

For now she hid her concern. Feeling guilty and selfish. Small minded. Disappointed in herself. Her parents' accident had crushed her. They'd left her without warning. She'd held the pain inside and barely survived herself. Tragedy had practically paralyzed her. After their funeral she was scared stiff that Zane would leave her too. His possible career as a fighter pilot ripped her apart. She feared for his life. Quietly. Obsessively. Her dread was so deeply embedded, she couldn't shake it.

She felt little consolation that he hadn't received his acceptance to the Air Force Academy. His dream was denied. And she was torn in two. Half her heart hurt for him. The other half exhaled.

Zane drove her home in time to shower and change for work. Once inside the apartment, he seated her gram in her rocking chair, then turned on the TV. Located the weather channel. He next dragged the small sofa toward the rocker, sat on the arm. Tori's heart warmed when he offered to sit with Nana Aubrey while she ate supper. Tori fixed a lettuce and cherry tomato salad and a baked potato. Zane opted for a potato, no salad. She served them and headed toward the door.

He pushed himself up, walked with her. "Let's hook up at the courthouse at one tomorrow afternoon," he said. "Afterward, Sleep on It. The mattress store."

A bed. Her heart skipped. "I'll be there."

"Later then." He kissed her, so long and deep, his taste lingered on her lips long into the night.

Tori arrived at the Barefoot William Courthouse with love in her heart. She might be only eighteen, but she loved Zane Cates with all her being. She'd been an adult for much of her life. Growing up and raising herself when her parents had worked long hours, double shifts. She had helped take care of her gram whenever needed. Following her parents' deaths, she'd planned to move forward alone. Not so anymore. Life had taken an unexpected twist. She now faced her future with Zane.

She recalled the previous night. She would never forget the image that had greeted her after work when she arrived home. Zinotti's had been exceptionally busy, and Eddie kept the pizza parlor open beyond closing time. Business was business. Eddie was all about the money.

Once the last customer had left, Tori cleaned up and hurried home. She'd parked her Camaro in the apartment lot and been surprised to see Zane's Impala still in visitor's parking. She'd entered quietly to find the weather channel projecting seasonal rain for the Gulf coast. What she saw brought tears to her eyes. Her throat tightened. Her chest warmed. Before her, Zane lay on the short sofa with tousled hair and cramped legs. Yet one of his arms was stretched toward her grandma. His hand rested on the arm of her rocker. Nana Aubrey's own hand covered his. Her gram continued to rock. Her eyes closed. Her expression relaxed.

Tori had leaned over Zane and awakened him with a light, grateful kiss. Sleepy eyed, he'd smiled against her lips. Then, catching her off guard, he'd pulled her down atop him. He'd quieted her gasp with his warm mouth. She'd gone soft, appreciative, against him. He'd gently eased his left hand from beneath her gram's. Then wrapped both his arms about her. Snugged her close. Breast to chest. Their abdomens aligned. Their legs tangled. She rested her cheek against his shoulder. Breathed him in. A hint of fabric softener on his cotton T-shirt. Azure Lime cologne at his neck. His own male scent.

She sighed, exhausted from work.

"Long night?" he whispered near her ear.

She nodded beneath his stubbled chin. "Eddie's not one to turn away a customer. It got later and later. Blu ran her butt off."

He slid his hands along her sides, began to rub her back. "How did Blu react to us getting married?" he asked.

His massage deepened, relaxing her muscles. Her work stress faded. "Total surprise, then happiness. She agreed to be my maid of honor." She pushed up on her elbows. "Race?"

A flex of his shoulders, and she sensed his hesitation. He was slow to respond. His hands shifted. He pressed his palms into the small of her back. Finger-kneaded her butt cheeks. Zane had always told her the truth. He was honest now. "Race thought I was joking. He punched my arm. Laughed. I remained serious, and he got a grip. He asked if you were pregnant."

Tori rolled her eyes. Typical Race. He wasn't aware she was still a virgin. He thought everyone was doing it, just like him.

"Race likes you," he continued. "He thinks you're good for me."

"But he's hoped for years that you'd attend the Air Force Academy together. Fighter pilots, do or die."

He shrugged a shoulder. "More or less."

"What about you?" She had to know. "Second thoughts?"

"I can live without the academy. I can't live without you."

"Thank you," softly spoken.

"No, thank *you*." He kissed her neck. Her chin. Her mouth. "Race'll stand up for us. He just needs a date and time."

A date and time, which Tori currently mulled over as

she climbed the historic stone steps of the William Cates County Courthouse. Built in 1925, it was a formidable three-story building with narrow external windows spaced like sentries across the front. The timeless cast bronze grating on the main door resembled a bank vault and was nearly as heavy. There'd been minor renovations, but the building proudly displayed its age and legacy. Delivered law and order.

Once inside, she again focused on the wedding. There would be a three-day waiting period with the marriage license. She needed to sign off on the lease and close her apartment. Then concentrate on the cottage. Her excitement centered on decorating. Which came easy to her. She would furniture shop and pick pieces that would turn the cottage into their home. Items could be added in intervals. She had a lot to do in a very short time. The gazebo was Zane's project. To repair and to paint.

She took an elevator to the second floor, then slowly walked the hallway to the county clerk's office. She lightly patted her thighs. She hoped her outfit was appropriate. She hadn't been certain what to wear to fill out a marriage application. A big deal for her. It was silly to be so nervous, but she didn't want to embarrass Zane. She'd chosen a short-sleeve, muted gold Bohemian top with tiny mirror detail around the neckline. She'd matched it with a flowing brown skirt. Ankle-wrapped leather sandals. Small hoop earrings.

Zane stood just inside the office door. Spotting her, he swung it open. He grinned and greeted her, "You look great." He winked. "Cool, I'm reflected in your mirrors."

He looked pretty great himself in a collared, short-sleeve navy pullover and khaki slacks. Loafers without socks. He took her hand, and, together, they approached the main counter. Zane explained to the female clerk that they wanted to apply for a marriage license. The woman nodded and located the form in a tall filing cabinet. They stood at one end of the counter and filled it out. Tori's hands shook ever so slightly when they were asked to produce the required identification. Zane's hands were steady when he paid the processing fee. The woman disappeared for several minutes. Soon returned.

"Your marriage license has been officially signed and sealed." She placed it in a manila envelope and handed it to Zane. "Three-day waiting period," she reminded them. "Whoever officiates at your ceremony must return the license to the Recording Office, in person or by mail, within ten days of the ceremony. The license will then be recorded and a marriage certificate issued. Congratulations."

"Thank you," Tori and Zane simultaneously said.

The hallway was quiet on their exit. They barely cleared the office door when he caught her to him. His arms encircled her waist and he swung her around, then proceeded to kiss her soundly when he set her down. Her heart quickened. Lightheaded, she grasped his shoulders. She'd never been happier.

"Marriage license down." He appeared pleased. "We still need a wedding date. Any thoughts? We have to wait three days."

"We have quite a bit to do."

"I won't rush you." He dropped a kiss on her forehead. "I want everything right."

She did too. She ran a mental list of all that needed to be done, and she settled on, "Saturday, July seventh. One o'clock."

He slowly nodded. "Eleven days." He made it sound like forever.

"It's not that far away."

"Says you." He cocked his head. "Time to hunt down a bed."

A sexual safari. Goose bumps rose.

He took her hand and led her to the elevator bank. One car opened, and they stepped inside. No other riders. The elevator was old and moved slowly. Zane took advantage of their private moment together. He slid his hands into her hair, leaned in, and kissed her breathless on the ride down. She stepped out of the lift and caught her reflection in a window. She'd been aroused in a heartbeat. Reflected back in the glass was mussed hair, wide eyes, flushed cheeks, puffy lips. Weak-kneed, she bumped him twice on their way to the door. He grinned at her. Aware of his effect. She'd gotten to him as well. His own gaze was dilated. He held the manila envelope over his groin. Desire walked them out.

They'd arrived at the courthouse separately. Both their vehicles were parked in the government lot. He suggested, "Drive your car back home and check on your grandmother. I'll follow. We'll take the Impala shopping."

She agreed. Traffic was light, and they reached the White Heron Apartments within seconds of each other. Relief swept Tori when she spotted Doreen, the complex manager's wife, seated on the sofa next to Nana Aubrey's rocking chair. A surprising shift in TV stations. No weather report today. Instead they watched black-and-white reruns of *The Lawrence Welk Show*. Days gone by, when her gram had enjoyed big band music. "A String of Pearls" played loudly. Doreen reached for the remote and turned down the volume. She finger-waved at Tori and Zane.

A lump formed in Tori's throat. She swallowed hard. She valued Doreen's friendship. The forty-something woman was like family. A lifesaver, ten times over. Tori hated leaving her gram alone. The occasional, unavoidable need to do so always caused Tori great concern. Doreen had volunteered to keep an eye on Nana Aubrey while Tori prepared for her wedding. Tori was grateful. She constantly worried over her ability to care for her grandma. She would do her best. Fortunately, she and Zane would be working opposite shifts. He would be at the garage during the day. She worked the evening shift at Zinotti's. Not ideal, but workable. For now.

She went directly to her gram. "Zane and I are running errands," she told her. Tori never knew what she'd comprehend, what she would not. "I stopped by to give you a hug." She bent down and gently embraced her. "I'll be back before supper. Leftover baked chicken and ice cream."

"Straw—"

"Strawberry, yes." Her gram's favorite flavor. Tori glanced at the side table and noticed her grandmother's water glass was empty, along with her bowl of hard candy. She turned toward the kitchen, but Zane was one step ahead of her. He brought back the pitcher of water and a handful of individually wrapped butterscotch. He was considerate. Caring. Definitely one of the good guys. She loved him more and more.

Her parents had doubted his intentions toward her. Her dad had passed judgment the moment he'd met Zane. He'd called him a "rich kid." The Cateses had money. The Rollinses barely scraped by. Her father swore Zane would never take their relationship seriously. He had been wrong.

Zane was marrying her. For better or worse. They'd both faced sadness and disappointments. Tori hoped the worst was behind them.

She straightened and kissed her grandma on the cheek. "I love you."

Her grandmother managed, "You . . ." too.

Zane gently squeezed her gram's shoulder. "See you later."

"We'll be here watching television," Doreen assured her.

"Thanks again," Tori called to Doreen at the door.

Doreen waved them off.

Zane drove to the outskirts of town. To Sleep on It, the largest mattress warehouse in the county. Located between the local farmer's market and a used car dealership. Tori blushed on their walk in. They were buying their marriage mattress. Sleep and sex. Her whole body heated.

Once inside, the warehouse appeared to go on for blocks. There were mattresses everywhere. Discount banners draped the ceiling. Twenty percent off and half-priced bedding. Tori took it all in. The selections were overwhelming.

"Hello, I'm Don. How can I help you?" A man in a suit approached them.

His formal attire appeared out of place surrounded by beds. Tori smiled to herself. A robe, pajamas, and slippers would've been more appropriate.

"We're looking for two beds. A king and a double," Zane told him.

Don chuckled. "You've come to the right place. Mattresses and headboards. Our specialty. You have lots of options. Do you have a preference?"

"We've just started looking," said Zane.

"Feel free to look around. We have a test room toward the back. A full display of mattresses. I'll give you a quick rundown. Afterward you can lie down, try them out, and find the one most comfortable for you."

"Sounds good," Zane replied. He bumped Tori with his elbow, lowered his voice, "Go to bed with me?"

Color rose in her cheeks. "A test run?"

"With our clothes on."

The sales clerk directed them down a side aisle. They walked and walked. The warehouse was quiet. Only two other couples viewed the stock. They finally reached the floor models. They soon faced dozens of mattress and box spring sets. Headboards from plain to ornate framed the walls.

Zane debated where to start. Don was helpful. "Remember as you shop that you'll spend more time on your mattress than any other piece of furniture that you own." He then maneuvered them between the beds, stopping often and pointing out the differences. "We have all the up and coming styles, just released: firm, plush, or pillow tops. Those custom-made have adjustable firmness, temperatures, and some vibrate. We also have several waterbeds. A few sofa beds and futons." He stepped back. "Additional manufacturer descriptions and prices are on the mattress tags. I'll give you a chance to test whichever ones appeal to you. I'll return shortly."

Zane cut his gaze to Tori. She stood wide eyed, worrying her bottom lip. He didn't want her apprehensive or nervous. He lightened the moment. Snagging her wrist, he dove onto the nearest bed. A California king with a black leather, diamond-tufted headboard. Massive and masculine. He landed flat on his back, and she sprawled across him. All twined limbs, laughter, and disarrayed clothing. His pullover twisted, baring his abdomen. Her skirt crept up her thighs, flirted with his khakis. He lost a leather loafer. A slight shift of his hips, and their body parts aligned. Man to woman.

Tori glanced toward the door, nervous they'd be discovered. "Someone might come in." She tried to wiggle off him.

He firmly flattened his palm on her back, held her down. "Mm-mm, this feels nice."

She narrowed her gaze on him. "Me or the mattress?"

"You on me on the bed. I like."

She pushed up, elbowed him in the side. "Let me go. What if Don returns?"

He grunted. She had sharp elbows. "We're *testing*. Beats the backseat of my Impala."

Still she squirmed. Her knee connected with his thigh, nearly bumped his balls. He jolted, released her. She crawled off him, then reversed onto her back. Their fingertips barely touched. She swooshed her arms and legs, made snow angels. Blew out a breath, said, "This bed is huge."

"Room for Oswald to sleep at the foot," he pointed out, including his dog. He rolled toward her, lay on his side, facing her. Teased, "Our bedroom would be wall-to-wall bed." She blushed, as he'd expected. He stroked a finger down her cheek, across her lips.

She reached for the mattress tag, read, "Six by seven feet. Our bedroom measurements are slightly larger. Yet there wouldn't be much room around the edges to change the sheets. What about a dresser?"

He pulled a face. "You're being practical. We could hang our clothes on the shower rod in the bathroom. Fold our clothes over the towel rack."

"You're being ridiculous."

"I'd make adjustments for this big boy." He pointed toward a small black box on her side of the bed. "Flick the switch, turn the dial." She stretched, did so. The mattress slowly began to vibrate. He fell back. Grinned, "Nice. A firm bed with a sexual buzz."

"Zane . . ." She scrunched her nose. "Let's look farther."

"You look, I'm taking a nap."

She punched his shoulder. "No sleeping."

He sat up, flung his legs over the side of the bed. Stood. He tugged down his pullover and slipped on his missing shoe. "Where to then?"

She rose too and straightened her skirt. "Once around the room at least."

"One time, then back to the California king."

"It's not our finish line," she said firmly, then emphasized, "We're not racing. Keep an open mind."

He smiled to himself. She knew him as well as his family did. Better even. She'd already guessed he was partial to the California king. Still he conceded, "Let's see what else is here. Although, in my opinion, this bed is hard to beat."

He took off ahead of her. Glancing left and right as he checked out the floor models with record speed.

"No jogging." Tori followed at a more leisurely pace.

He pulled up, gave more attention to the beds.

She slowed at a plump, pillow-top queen mattress with a stark white lacquered headboard. "Clean lines and romantic," she called to him. She tapped her finger on her chin. Thoughtful. "Colorful sheets and a vibrant comforter would jazz it up."

"Is it adjustable?"

"No."

"Does it warm?"

"No."

"Vibrate?"

She shook her head. "No . . ."

"Selling point then?"

"It will fit our bedroom. Comes with a low matching dresser." There was a pause in their conversation as she read the manufacturer's tag. "It's a discontinued brand. The last one in stock. On sale."

He crossed the storeroom. Eyed the bed set. The white was pure, virgin innocence. Like Tori. Her brow furrowed, and he understood her concern. He hooked his arm about her waist. "Price doesn't matter. I have money saved, and I want to invest in a bed. *Our* bed. One that fits us both."

She broke away and lowered herself onto the queen. She planted her palms and leaned back, looking up at him. Her sigh was one of pure pleasure. "Comfy as a cloud."

He didn't mind soft. Although he preferred adjustable. He glanced toward the California king. A man's bed. Tori was his woman. She deserved his consideration.

She slipped off her sandals, tucked her skirt beneath her knees, and scooted back on the bed. "Try it, you'll like it," she encouraged.

He heel-toed his loafers. Left them next to her sandals. The toes kissed. He rounded the foot of the bed and closed in on her. She lay full out, her gaze veiled. Gently smiling. He joined her and was immediately cocooned in softness. He felt spineless. The additional padding cushioned every bone in his body.

Don showed up as Zane rolled from side to side. The salesman hovered over them. "How do you like the pillow top?" he asked.

Tori propped herself up on her elbows. "It's like sleeping on air."

"This mattress is therapeutic." Don gave his sales pitch. "More likely to contour itself to the body and relieve aches, pains, and pressure points. No stress."

"Durability?" asked Zane.

"Normal wear and tear. Rule of thumb, people should change their mattresses every six to seven years. This style will definitely last that long."

Tori eased off the bed. She slowly returned to the California king. She skimmed her fingers over the mattress. "Sturdier than the pillow top?" she asked Don.

"Not necessarily sturdier," said Don. "Being adjustable, definitely firmer. The king comes with a vibrating massage. The best mattress for someone with back problems."

Tori eased down a second time. Zane watched as her body relaxed and she closed her eyes. No smile on her lips, as there'd been when she'd lay on the queen-size. The bed dwarfed her. They could stretch out to their heart's content. There would be room for two additional people between them. He didn't want to have to reach for her. He wanted her near. Snuggled against him. Sleepy-eyed, her warm breath on his neck. She'd wrap her arms around him, never letting him go.

Don cleared his throat, his expression hopeful. He awaited their decision, anticipating a sale. "More time?" he offered them.

Tori blinked, inhaled deeply.

Zane squared his shoulders.

Their decisions came simultaneously.

"California king," said Tori.

"Pillow top," from Zane.

"*What?*" Their words rolled over each other.

Silence suspended their decision. Until she popped off the bed and approached him. He met her halfway.

"I–I don't understand." Her voice caught. "You wanted the big bed."

"The queen fits us better. Brings us closer."

She was at a loss for words. "Only if you're absolutely sure."

"I'm sure of us." He then nodded to Don. "We also need a full-size mattress."

"Medium firmness," added Tori.

"Headboard?" the salesman inquired.

Tori considered the selections that framed the room. Minutes later she'd found the perfect one. "Contemporary style in pale sunbeam yellow. I want Gram's bedroom comfy, soothing, and inviting."

"We'll take both beds," Zane told Don. "You deliver?"

"Free of charge."

"Write them up," Zane finalized. "We're good to go."

They left the warehouse for Sweet Dreams, where they

shopped for bedding. Sheets, blankets, pillows. The store was packed, the salesclerks spread thin. They grabbed a cart and browsed on their own. He instructed her to buy whatever she wanted. Still she was cost-conscious. He nudged her beyond the reduced and two-for-one sales bins. Then pushed her past the displays of cotton sheets.

"Satin," he told her.

She hesitated, frowned. "Too expensive, Zane."

"But worth the price. Trust me." He was a tactile guy. He liked to touch, feel. While cotton was nice, satin was better against bare skin. It took sleeping and sex to the next level. Naked and his wife went together perfectly. The color meant little to him. He could make love to her on any hue.

Her mental debate continued. Thrifty or pricey? He came up behind her, softly kissed her on the neck. Nipped her earlobe. Whispered, "Silky, shiny." She shivered and went with satin. He eased back to let her work her decorative magic.

She soon held up several sheet sets, pillowcases included, seeking his opinion. "Platinum, gold, burgundy, dark plum, chocolate, zebra, or solid black?"

He'd always leaned toward the basics. Black, white, and gray. Tori saw life through a kaleidoscope. Flashes of brilliance. Vivid and bright. Even though she consulted him, he noticed that she clutched the plum against her chest. Her preference. He agreed. "Plum."

Her smile was worth his decision.

They proceeded to the down comforters on display in the center of the store. Tori brushed aside the pastels and florals. Then lingered over the chevron, paisleys, and geometric prints. All colorful. He liked the inverted V, zigzag-patterned chevron in deep purple and pale green. Their body heat would keep them warm most months.

However Florida had the occasional cold winter night. A quilted down comforter would be cozy.

She came to him, the chevron comforter in her arms. "It'll go great with the sheets."

He nodded his approval. "We're on the same page."

She went with mauve-colored sheets and a matching comforter for her gram. Standard rectangular bed pillows came next. One for each of them.

The cart was filled by the time they headed to checkout. Zane caught Tori unzipping the clear plastic packaging for the sheets. She reached in and felt the satin. Her expression softened. Her gaze dreamy. He could picture her naked and needy. Heightened moans and holding him close. His body reacted. Damn boner. He snagged a pillow from the cart and covered his groin. He was still semi-erect when he reached for his wallet and paid.

He glanced at his watch in the parking lot, noted, "Getting close to suppertime."

"Gram will be hungry."

"I'm starving too."

"You don't need an invitation. Join us?"

"It'll be eat and run."

"I don't mind."

"I asked Race to meet me at the cottage at seven. We're going to check the damage to the gazebo. Decide on repairs."

They reached the Impala, and she helped him unload the cart. Tossing most items on the backseat. "I'll shelve the bedding in the linen closet."

He then passed off the cart to a customer headed toward the store. They climbed in the car and drove to the White Heron Apartments. Dinner was quick, and while Nana Aubrey enjoyed her second scoop of strawberry ice cream, Zane took off. Tori followed him to the door. He had wanted to kiss her all day, and he did so now. With pent-up need and frustrated passion, he pinned her between the wall and his body. He took her mouth, and their tongues tangled. She curved her calf about his thigh, secured him to her. Ignited teenage hormones. They pressed and rubbed and nearly came undone. Her fingernails dug into his shoulders. He was painfully stiff. They were both breathing heavily when they finally broke apart.

He slapped his palms against his thighs. "Tomorrow?" He left it open-ended. "I work in the morning and will catch up with you in the afternoon. I'll sit with your grandmother while you're at work."

"I'm furniture shopping early," she said. "I'm going by the flea market, then stopping by one storage unit sale and two estate auctions."

He tilted up her chin with his finger. Looked her in the eye. "We have money, Tori. There's no need to buy secondhand."

She narrowed her gaze. "You telling me how to decorate?"

He held his hands high, palms out. "No way. You're the expert."

"Glad we agree."

They both grinned.

A final kiss, and he left her. It was difficult leaving. His heart missed her, even for a short time. Being apart sucked. He wouldn't see her until tomorrow afternoon. He had a lot to accomplish before then.

Race was punctual. "Hey dude," he called to Zane from his black Range Rover, a graduation gift from his mom and dad. He was an only child. All he had to do was show interest in something, and his parents bought it. He didn't have a summer job. He dated and partied off his fat weekly allowance.

He climbed from his SUV in a faded T-shirt scripted

with *I Meant to Behave but There Were Too Many Options* and jeans torn at both knees. "Where's your girl?" he asked.

"Home with her grandmother."

"Nana Aubrey. Tori comes with a ready-made family." Zane's dark stare had him apologizing. "Sorry, man. I'm your friend and call it like I see it. I'm worried about you."

"Concentrate on yourself."

"I like thinking about me."

"You're an ass."

"You're getting married." Contemplative pause. "Show me the cottage."

Zane gave him the tour. Afterward they stepped outside. The grass and vegetation were high, and they stomped a path to the gazebo. An octagonal structure, it had weathered and tilted over the years. The seats on the custom-fit benches rippled. An empty bird's nest perched inside the roof. Spiderwebs were spun high in one corner. They stood on the lowest step and assessed the repairs.

"Holy crap," from Race. "I'm not a carpenter—"

"No, you're not."

"But this place is unsafe. Tear it down. Rebuild."

Zane refused to be discouraged. He lay down on the ground and looked beneath the gazebo. "The base appears strong. No cracks or wood rot."

"Snakes?"

"Only the one by your foot."

Race sidestepped. No snake. "Dumbass."

Zane pushed himself up, surveyed further. "The steps are broken."

Race snorted. "No joke. You don't want anyone falling through."

Hands on his hips, Zane made a list. "We'll replace two of the four main posts, along with the six wall panels of latticework. A fresh coat of paint. Fortunately the gazebo is open air. No windows to install."

Race looked up. "Does the roof leak?"

"Not a clue. Let's hope it doesn't rain."

"Buy a tarp." Race blew out a breath, swore. "This is more than a two-person job."

"I'll get Rylan to help."

"If you can drag him away from the batting cages."

"Maybe . . . my dad."

"You need a full crew."

"I believe in our abilities."

"I question your sanity."

Zane rolled his tongue inside his cheek. "I love her."

"Yeah, I know. I've never felt what you're feeling."

"Then don't judge."

"Not another word on your wedding."

"Blu will be there. She's Tori's maid of honor."

"News to me. Blu hasn't said a word."

"You two talk often?"

"I talk, she ignores."

"You'll miss her when you leave for the academy."

"I'm dating, doing just fine without her."

"You'd be better with her."

"She's sarcastic. A total smartass."

"So are you."

"Whatever."

Zane rubbed the back of his neck, gave the gazebo one last look. "So you'll help me?"

"Yeah, you need me. I'm better with a hammer than you."

"Bullshit." Still he grinned.

High fives started the repairs.

Zane and Tori were apart more than together over the next few days. Doreen at the complex stayed with Nana Aubrey as the two of them put the cottage in order. The beds were delivered. Set up. Zane walked by the master bedroom with his eyes closed. His imagination ran wild. He envisioned Tori naked on the satin sheets. He had an endless erection.

The cottage came alive under Tori's designer's touch. She put her stamp on every inch. She painted the living room a rain-washed blue. Peaceful and soothing. She attended storage unit and estate sales. She became friends with the auctioneers. They gave her quality tips on the best values. A few offered her early previews. Her choices were colorful, quaint, and quirky. New or gently used furniture at affordable prices.

Each pass through the living room made him smile. He *felt* Tori's presence. The velvet, striped, brocade sofa in blue hues reflected her eyes. They lightened and darkened depending on her mood. An apricot, knitted tweed throw was draped over its back, portraying her warmth. Her contentment was evident in the two lavender fabric over-stuffed chairs. Solid and sturdy. The geometric-patterned rug in cream and black would soften the rocking of her grandmother's chair.

Her kaleidoscope eye replaced the cushion on the window seat. Switching out the brown for a nugget gold. Zane attached cottage-style indoor shutters in tango orange. A refurbished tripod table accepted keys at the entrance. A catchall.

A neighbor on the block tore down a stark-white picket fence. Tori broke off a section, brought it home. She tacked it to a living room wall. She restored vintage photos of roses, representing different varieties from tea to cabbage roses. She fit them in antique frames. Then hung the pictures above the pickets. An imaginative garden effect.

She creatively put together a large wall mirror from smaller mirrors of different shapes. Squares, circles, rect-angles, and triangles made up an amazing hexagonal reflecting glass. Decoratively fractured, yet whole. It was freakin' amazing.

Time passed, and the weekend came and went. On Saturday, Zane moved the rocking chair and TV from Tori's apartment to the cottage. They placed the rocker near the window seat. Sunshine filtered in, a warm welcome. His girl and her gram settled in. Zane wished he could share the bed with her that very night, but he held off. They'd be together in a week.

Sunday was a big day for them. Tori and he introduced Nana Aubrey to his dalmatian Oswald. He let Oz run off steam in the yard, then brought him inside on a short lead. Ozzie sniffed every corner of the cottage, including the rocking chair. The dog nudged Nana Aubrey's knee with his nose. No response. Her attention was fixed on the weather channel.

"Be good, Oswald," Zane instructed as he unhooked the leash. He sat with Tori on the sofa while Oz made a second sweep of the cottage, all on his own. Zane patted his calf on Oz's return. "Lie down now."

The dalmatian dropped next to Zane's feet for less than a minute, then belly-scooted over to Nana Aubrey's rocking chair. She nearly rocked on his tail. "What's he doing?" Zane wondered aloud.

"It appears he's checking out my gram."

"I don't want him scaring her."

"He's not jumping. No playful biting. He's just . . . staring at her."

Zane had no reason to believe Oz would hurt the older woman. His dog had been around the elderly, including his grandfather. However, Grampa Frank was robust, coherent, while Nana Aubrey was fragile and living in her own world. Oswald's nails had been recently clipped, yet one accidental raised paw could break her crepe-thin skin. Zane held his breath. Willed Oz to behave.

"Ozzie," Zane warned when his dog kicked out his back legs and inched closer to Tori's gram. "Behave."

Tori slowly stood. "I've got this."

Zane watched as she crossed to the rocker and knelt down. She laid her hand over her grandmother's own and spoke softly, "I want you to meet Zane's dog, Oswald. The dalmatian will be living with us after we're married."

No change in her grandma's expression. Her words had not sunk in. Ozzie surprised them all by introducing himself. He sat up, then dropped his head on the woman's knee. Whined for her attention. Nana Aubrey tensed slightly but didn't push him away. Tori took her hand and placed it on Oswald's neck. Her gram's fingers flexed. Oz licked her wrist. All wet tongue and louder whine.

A marginal roll of her shoulders and Nana Aubrey peered down on Oz. No fear in her eyes. Just minor confusion. "Where's Ches-" She wasn't able to finish her question.

"Chester, your cat." Tori's voice was low, compassionate. "He aged and passed away. You gave him a good life, Gram. We have a new pet now. Zane's dog Oswald."

Hearing his name, the dalmatian wagged his tail. It thumped Nana Aubrey's calf.

"Os . . ." she attempted. And Ozzie answered. A low bark.

The end. No harm done. Nana Aubrey went back to rocking, and Oswald flopped down beside her. A yawn and he soon snored.

"An easy adjustment," Zane noted.

"My grandma will get used to him. As long as Ozzie doesn't crowd her. Leave him with us overnight. Let's see how it goes."

The dog slept well. His *crowding* came in sleeping on the end of Nana Aubrey's bed. Zane lost his dog to the older woman. Oz adopted and adored Tori's gram. Zane wasn't always certain that she knew Oz was around, but Ozzie kept his eye on her. Vigilant, protective, loyal, he followed her around. Never darting ahead or bumping her side. Her canine bodyguard.

Their wedding came together better than Zane expected. His father and his brother Rylan assisted with the gazebo. Repairs were made and, following two coats of dove-white paint, the structure welcomed their exchange of vows. Zane proved a better carpenter than Race. He walked away with only a scratch. Race's expertise with a hammer ended in a string of profanity and two black fingernails.

Tori and he had agreed on a small wedding. The guest list totaled ten. His parents and Nana Aubrey. His three brothers and sister. Grandpa Frank. Race and Blu. The minister would preside over the ceremony, then return to his church to prepare for his Sunday sermon. He would file their marriage license with the Records Department at the courthouse on Monday.

"You nervous, dude?" Race asked Zane on his wedding day. He'd arrived on time, casually dressed in a khaki sport coat and navy slacks. Zane wore the reverse outfit. Navy jacket and khaki slacks. They stood in the kitchen, awaiting Tori and her grandmother. His parents, brothers, sister, and granddad were already seated in the gazebo. The minister would arrive shortly.

"I'm cool," he told his buddy. "Life is good. I'm marrying Tori."

"I still wish we were attending—"

"Don't go there. We're not." Zane cut him off. Race sucked air. Despite his earlier disappointment, he was happy for his friend. "When are you leaving for the academy?"

"Two weeks. I'm going out early. I want to check out Colorado Springs before initiation and classes start."

"Before you have to get serious?"

"I'll buckle down."

"You damn sure better, bro. You're there for both of us."

A moment of silence before Race handed Zane a wrapped package. "You requested no presents, but my gift to you is a box of condoms."

Zane grinned. "Thoughtful and appropriate."

"To be shared with Tori." Race next presented him with a bottle of champagne. Expensive for even his allowance. "My parents kicked in. We're cousins, but they've always considered you a second son."

They were as close as brothers.

Blu arrived shortly thereafter, a wedding bouquet of pink roses in one hand and a boxed wedding cake in the other. She set the flowers on the triangular table inside the door, then slapped Race's wrist when he peeked in the box and swiped a fingertip of frosting. "Hands off," she said.

"Hands off you and now the cake. You're no fun, Blu."

"You're fun enough for us both."

Zane rolled his eyes. The two constantly sniped at each other. It was never-ending. "Kitchen." He herded them down the hallway. There, Blu leaned against the counter.

Race propped himself against the back door. His best friend openly admired Blu in her pale pink sheath. Her hair was streaked red. Race said, "You clean up good. No pizza smell. Nice perfume."

"Your approval means the world to me." Sarcastic Blu.

"Someday it just might."

"Don't hold your breath. I don't like you," bluntly said.

Race had the balls to smile, as if he knew different. So cocksure and annoying.

Zane shook his head. "Cool it," he said when the doorbell rang. The minister had arrived. His uncle Joseph. Introductions were made all around. His uncle was an older man with a strong church following. Zane was glad to have him officiating at their wedding.

Blu soon gave them a nudge. "You guys get ready," she said. "Go out to the gazebo. I'll check on Tori. We'll join you shortly."

Zane led Race and his uncle Joseph to the gazebo. The fresh white paint reflected brightly in the early afternoon sunshine. Their wedding day was blessed by eighty-five degrees, lemony sunshine, and angel-wing white cirrus clouds. Tori's color wheel sensibility had rubbed off on him. His world had brightened considerably.

A few moments of conversation passed before he heard Oswald bark. His dog had taken on the role of wedding attendant. He trotted through the back door ahead of Tori, Blu, and her gram. The dalmatian then slowed and waited for Nana Aubrey. Zane never would have believed how strongly and quickly his dog had bonded with the older woman. Though he still took Ozzie for a morning and nightly run, the dog always beat him home. Oz seemed to know that Tori's grandmother needed him.

He'd been knocked sideways with surprise when Tori told him that her grandma now responded to Oswald's whining to go outside. It was the first sign of active engagement from the older woman since the stroke. Her gram would cautiously rise from her rocker, cane in hand, and shuffle with Oswald to the side door. She'd then release him to the newly fenced yard that flanked the garage. She would wait for him to return. This development was totally amazing to Zane.

Still more astonishing than Oz and Nana Aubrey was his first glimpse of his bride. He was rendered speechless. She and Blu walked on either side of her grandmother, supporting her to the gazebo. Tori had bought her gram a simple dress in dove gray, pinned with an antique cameo broach. There was life in her grandma's eyes. She appeared attentive.

Tori came to him in an ivory lace shift, a similar style to Blu's own dress. She'd added her gram's long strand of pearls. Her cheeks were as flushed and pink as the roses in her bridal bouquet. Her heart shone in her eyes. With love for him.

He welcomed her. There was nothing traditional about their ceremony. He took her in his arms and held her close. She hugged him back. Her pearls dangled between them, hanging from her neck down to his groin. Zane had the insane image of her naked on their bed, wearing only the pearls. His dick stirred. He did a quick silent countdown—twenty, nineteen . . . one—and got himself under control.

The minister cleared his throat, and they separated, turning to face him. Zane heard her shaky intake of breath and reached for her hand just as Tori reached for his. She trembled. He squeezed her fingers reassuringly. Her breathing softened.

His uncle Joseph modified their ceremony to fit their lives. He spoke of youth and the strength of young love. He believed in Zane and Tori. He blessed their union and wished them happiness. Before he could request their responses, they went off script.

"I do," they both declared together. Zane's voice was strong. Tori's tone as watery as her eyes. Emotion overtook her. He slipped his arm about her waist and held her close while they exchanged rings. They'd decided on simple sterling silver bands. Hers narrow and feminine. His wider, more masculine.

"I now pronounce you man and wife," the minister intoned, closing their ceremony. "Zane, you may kiss your bride."

He curved her to him, held her gently. He slid his hands into her hair, and she looked up. He looked deeply into her eyes. The color would stay with him forever. Bride blue. Dark and devoted. They kissed, lightly. Passion would come later.

"Mrs. Cates." Race was first to congratulate them. A man-hug for Zane. A tender embrace for Tori. "Take care of my best friend," he told her.

"We'll take care of each other," Zane reassured him.

His family cheered his future. His parents were happy for them, despite believing they were too young. He'd prove them wrong.

Tori tossed her bouquet to Blu.

Blu fumbled and nearly dropped it. Race stepped in, caught the flowers against her hip before they hit the gazebo floor. Their hands brushed. Race stroked his thumb over hers. She started, pushed him away. "I've got it."

"I've got you."

Irritated, Blu stared a hole in him.

Race took it as interest.

Zane shook his head. His cousin took every opportunity to taunt Blu. Their heightened tension would end in sex or in Blu knocking him out. Zane was betting on Blu's sucker punch.

Blu collected herself and announced, "Cake and champagne inside."

Everyone trooped toward the cottage. Zane and Tori assisted Nana Aubrey to her feet. He couldn't believe Oswald had sat beside the older woman all during the ceremony, quiet and calm. He took his protective status seriously. Zane swore Oz kept one eye on her, even in his sleep.

"He-" Gram said, her way of calling the dog to heel. Ozzie understood. He followed closely. The dog's early training was paying off beautifully.

Everyone waited for them in the kitchen. Once inside, they seated Nana Aubrey on a café chair. Oz dropped beside her, his head on her knee. Blu located a knife, paper cups, and plates. It was a modest celebration. Tori cut the cake and Zane poured the champagne. There were toasts, good cheer, and lot of hugs.

The minister took off after his second piece of cake. Before leaving, he took Tori and Zane by the hand. "Be faithful to each other and fall deeper in love each day." He picked the marriage license up off the counter. "I'll file with Courthouse Records on Monday. Your certificate of marriage should arrive by mail within a week."

The kitchen grew quiet when his father and mother presented them with a wedding check graced by a lot of zeroes. Zane was their son; no matter his age, and despite his having taken a wife, they would forever see him as their baby boy. It was only natural for two such loving parents. They would always worry and be protective of him. Zane loved them fiercely. And was grateful for the money.

His parents' words resonated between the bride and groom. "We are here for you always, in whatever capacity you may need."

Tori kissed them each on the cheek, more appreciative than she could say. With her own parents gone, she hoped one day to have a close relationship with Zane's mom and dad.

His family soon departed. Race sipped another glass of champagne, then started to pour a third. Blu took his paper cup, intervened. "Time to leave."

"Leave with you?" He raised one eyebrow. Expectant.

"Leave the married couple alone."

Zane grinned, agreed. "Sounds good to me. Tori?"

"We were crazy-busy before the wedding. I barely saw you. It's time. I'd like my husband all to myself."

Zane tugged her close, kissed her temple. "I'm yours, wife."

Blu and Race took off. She walked fast. He kept up. The front door opened, closed, and Zane commented, "Idiot cousin. He's dating three different girls at the moment. Yet he's pursuing Blu like she's the only one for him."

"Maybe she is."

"Doubtful. There's no commitment in Race."

"What about you, Zane Cates?" she softly asked. "Will I be enough for you?"

"More than enough. I ache for you." The rise of his erection showed her how much.

"I will relieve your pain," she quietly promised. "First, my gram. Let's get her settled in the living room."

They turned to assist the older woman, only to see her shake her head, manage, "Ca–cane."

"I'll get it," from Zane.

"By her rocker," Tori remembered.

Zane retrieved the cane. They assisted Nana Aubrey to her feet. He heard Tori swallow hard, saw worry on her brow. She held out a hand. "Let us help you, Gram."

"No." There was a startling strength in her voice. She moved forward on her own.

Zane and Tori held their collective breaths as she shuffled from the kitchen, Oswald by her side. Zane snagged the box of condoms off the counter, wanting to be prepared for the afternoon ahead. They then trailed closely behind Nana Aubrey. Tori with her hand over her heart. Anxious. Zane ready to lunge if Gram wavered or started to fall. He felt intense relief when she finally lowered herself onto the rocker. The television remote was reachable, left on the window seat. Nana Aubrey turned on the TV. Viewed the weather station as always. Ozzie stretched out by her side. Slept.

"She made it," Tori choked out. She went to hug her grandmother. Her eyes glistened with tears. "Love you so much."

"You too. And Za-" Her voice gave out. Still, it was the longest sentence she'd spoken around Zane. Remarkable.

"Zane and I are going to spend some time together," Tori told her. "I'll see you at supper."

He gently touched Nana Aubrey on the cheek, saying, "Thank you for your granddaughter. I love Tori with all my heart."

A nod and soft smile from her grandma.

Oswald snored on as they left the living room.

Zane swept Tori high against his chest just outside their bedroom. She circled his neck with her arms. He carried her across the threshold. She gasped as he closed the pocket door behind them. Inside, he kissed her slowly as she slid down his body. His wife. All warm and womanly. The backseat of his Impala was not a wedding bed. Over the past months, they'd fooled around and brought each other to climax. Hot and quick. All heavy breathing, tousled hair, twisted clothing, yet restricted satisfaction.

Today Tori deserved romance. He might be only eighteen, but he was her man. Her husband. He would give her pleasure. A slow peeling away of her clothes and plenty of foreplay. She liked to kiss. He drew her close. She looked up as he glanced down. Their kisses started light as air, then deepened. They kissed until his lips lost feeling and hers were swollen. They eased back to breathe. He tenderly ran his thumb over her plump lower lip. Her pulse quickened at the base of her throat and her nipples puckered. He was throbbing hard. And couldn't hide it. He didn't even try.

"You are so beautiful, Tori Cates," he admired.

She smiled, sighed. "Tori Cates." Her married name sounded good on her lips.

He angled left, aimed, then tossed the box of condoms on the bedside table. He paused and let her set the pace. "So . . . here we are."

"So . . . what should we do next?"

"You tell me." He needed her to want him as badly as he wanted her.

She told him what he most needed to hear. "I love you, Zane Cates. Let me fit your condom."

Relief warmed his chest. He broadened his stance, situated her between his legs. He began to touch her. Every inch of her. She felt soft, feminine, amazing. He ran his fingers over her shoulders, down her ribs, with infinite care, then with increased craving.

Tori wasn't the least bit tentative. She ran her hands through his hair, then drew her thumbs across his cheekbones. She skimmed her fingertips along his jawline. She initiated removing his clothes. She took her sweet time. Easing off his sport jacket, then unbuttoning his shirt. She feathered her fingers over his chest, scraped a fingernail over his abdomen. He inhaled sharply. The once pressed cotton wrinkled beneath the grip of her hands. She shoved the button-down over his shoulders and then stripped it down his arms. He stood bare chested before her. She stared. Licked her lips. Then flicked her tongue over each male nipple. Smooth, moist licks. Followed by a nip, light sucking, and then a tug of her lips. He nearly came out of his skin.

His wife was sexy as hell and unbelievably bold. He liked her initiative. She flattened her palms over his ribs. Finger-traced each rise and indentation. Then arrowed down to the waistband on his dress slacks. She unbuckled his belt, gave a swift yank, and slid it through the loops. Let it drop to the floor. She worked his pants open, revealing a V of boxer briefs.

She flashed a grin. A seductive parting of her lips. He gritted his teeth in frustration. Went on to fist his hands when she reached behind his zipper. His dick bumped her hand, begging for attention. He sucked air when she

shoved down his pants, along with his My Package underwear. He kicked his loafers across the room, all the way
to the closet.

She had her way with him. Rubbing and squeezing his
length. He was more than ready. Fear tightened his balls
that he'd come in her hand. He sucked air. Stilled her
hands. "Give us a minute."

He slowed things down. Pinning her arms behind her
back, he cuffed her slender wrists with one of his big
hands. He then started on her, needing to even the sexual
score. Slow and sane, he slid the back zipper of her wedding shift several inches down. The neckline loosened,
the lace sketching her breastbone. Tori had beautiful skin.
He wanted to see more of her. He took the zipper all the
way to the base. Then stripped away the narrow straps.
Her dress fluttered over her breasts, her hips, and folded at
her ankles. She slipped out of her ballerina flats. Her bare
feet were small, narrow, her toenails painted a pale pink.
Her silky white bra and thong soon disappeared. Her body
was now naked, except for her strand of pearls and wedding band.

Time slowed, allowing memories to be savored all their
lives. Their bodies were hot and flushed, and they communicated through their chemistry. Deep kisses and wander-
ing hands. Rapid heartbeats. Stirring souls and heightened
arousal. Husband and wife.

He cupped her bottom, and their teenage hormones
walked them backward to their wedding bed. Her calves
bumped the wooden footboard. She fell backward, and he
followed her down. The soft-top mattress caught them.
Indulgent and lush. The plum-colored satin sheets shimmered around them.

He appreciated her nudity. He stroked her wet. He det-
onated beneath her touch. His gaze never left her as he
reached for the box of condoms on the bedside table. He

removed a silver packet and tore it open with his teeth. He passed it to her, lay back, said, "All yours."

A momentary fumble, a restart, and she sheathed him. "All mine." Her voice was husky.

He centered himself over her. His knees sank into the mattress as he sank into her. A slow slide, and she gasped, stiffened. She felt a moment of faint pain; then it was over. Her body accepted him. A sigh of longing escaped her lips. His sign to continue.

He shifted his hips, rocked gently, thrust slowly. He found a rhythm that she could accept. She began to move with him. Elusive sensation built. Lifted them both. A pulsating high. She climaxed first, color flushing her cheeks and her body trembled. One last stroke, and he followed her to the end.

But the end became the beginning in a very short time. They made love twice more before they showered and dressed for supper.

That evening they ate roast beef sandwiches and cole slaw, visited with Nana Aubrey, and then returned to their wedding bed. The sex between them was both physical and emotional. Devotion and discovery. They got little sleep that night. They were too into each other.

They slipped into a routine. One that pleased them both. Zane would go to work each morning, come home at noon; then he and Tori would spend the afternoon in bed. Up until she left for Zinotti's Pizza. Nana Aubrey had a newfound strength. She got around the cottage without their assistance, using her cane or walker. Her body grew stronger though speech was still difficult for her. She had gone as far as to sit outside on the front porch, enjoying the roses with Oswald by her side.

They had been married seven days when he arrived home and collected the mail at the curbside postal box on his way into the house. He carried the stack into the kitchen. He dropped onto a chair, and Tori scooted onto his lap. She always seemed to fit there perfectly. They sorted through the letters together. They opened bills, flipped through retail catalogs, and circled daily specials in the grocery flyers.

Two letters caught their eye. The first being a manila envelope from the courthouse. It held their marriage certificate. Notarized and official, emanating a sense of future and permanence. Perfect timing on their one-week anniversary. They grinned and kissed. Happy.

The second envelope stole their smiles. The return address on the envelope nearly stopped Zane's heart. The forwarded mail was from the United States Air Force Academy. He looked at Tori. She appeared as surprised and baffled as he. He held on to the letter for a long time, afraid to break the fastener.

"Open it, Zane," she said, her voice soft and unsure.

There was no reason for his hands to shake, but they did. He carefully flicked the clasp with his thumb and slowly removed the letter. He couldn't believe the words. His breath caught, his chest tightened, and he found it difficult to focus. Tori had read along with him, and she processed the news first.

She cleared her throat, noted the high points. "It's a late acceptance letter. You've received an appointment to the United States Air Force Academy, as a member of the Class of 2004. You're a replacement candidate. Some initial appointees declined their appointment offers, and other qualified candidates were selected to fill those vacancies." There was a pause as she skimmed over the acclaim and congratulations. Her expression was wooden, her tone stilted as she finished with, "Please accept or decline this offer by phoning our admittance office or by completing the form and returning to the above address within five days."

Zane lowered his head. He covered his face with his hands. He found it hard to breathe. "Oh . . . wow." He'd been offered his lifelong dream.

Tori tucked herself into him, molding her life to his. "What are you going to do?" Her question was barely audible.

Reality kicked hard. Exhilaration, obligation, and disappointment collided. Splintered in his chest. He shrugged. His voice was raw when he spoke, "Not much I can do. The academy accepts single cadets only. I'm married now."

Four

"Zane and Tori are getting a divorce," Blu Burkhardt hissed at Race Wallace. "He's leaving her for the Air Force Academy."

"She doesn't seem upset," Race replied.

"She's devastated. A broken heart isn't always visible, asshole."

"Don't swear at me."

"You're here, and I'm angry."

Race sat in a back corner booth at Zinotti's Pizza. All kicked back and relaxed. She stood at his table, glaring down at him. Fire in her eyes. He'd spent an hour sipping his soda. There was no reason for him to drag things out, yet he was doing just that. Owner Eddie Zinotti had locked up and handed her the key.

Over the last year, Race had become a steady customer. Eating for an army. Eddie didn't boot his regulars. He cut them slack and left it up to his waitresses to nudge them out the door. Race had ignored her hints to leave, so she began cleaning up around him, wiping down the tables with a damp, soapy sponge. She knew she smelled like pizza sauce and bleach water.

Race finished his soda with a straw-sucking slurp. Totally annoying. He held up the plastic glass. "Top it off."

"Hell, no. You've had five refills. More than enough."

"Eddie would give me one."

"I'm not Eddie, jerk face."

"Again with the name calling. Not pretty, Blu. It will be reflected in your gratuity."

"Screw you." He drove her to swear. Obnoxious and irritating. Race might be a good tipper, but tonight she didn't care. She was dead on her feet and wanted him gone. She couldn't wait to get home, to take a hot bubble bath and enjoy a glass of wine. Unfortunately she still faced an hour's worth of side work. "Forget the tip," she growled. She pointed toward the door. "Just leave. I have plans."

A muscle jerked in his jaw. "A date?"

"Plans don't always mean a man."

"So what are yours? I'm in a listening mood."

"I'm not of a mind to share."

He sat deeper in the leather seat. Frustrating her. He wasn't going anywhere, anytime soon. "Don't make me physically toss your ass."

"Watch your mouth, Blu. I like sweet talk."

She didn't feel the least bit sweet. She tossed the dishcloth from one hand to the other. "We're done talking. I've work to do."

"I could help, if you asked nicely."

He'd exhausted her store of nice. She was on a rant and threw the towel at him. It hit him square in the chest, dampening his navy T-shirt scripted with *You Couldn't Handle Me Even if I Came with Instructions.* She had no desire to handle him. However, he did have two perfectly good hands. So she directed, "Wipe down the remainder of the tables."

"I'm wet," he grumbled as he slid from the booth. He pulled his shirt away from his chest, shook it out with his fingers. "You could've handed me the cloth."

"Could have." But she had not. It felt good to chuck it at him.

He picked up his empty glass and walked to the recycle bin at the end of the counter. "What are you going to do while I'm cleaning tables?"

"I'll be in the storeroom. Replenishing the waitress station. Napkins, straws, plastic silverware, and glasses."

"I could join you there."

She shook her head. No way. "I'll manage." As she left him, she listened on the off chance that he would follow. No footsteps. One person could barely turn around in the small storage space. Two people would collide. She didn't need to be bumping bodies with Race. He was a solid guy. Not bad looking either with that unconventionally long dark hair, those incredible amber eyes, and slashing cheekbones. A mature face for eighteen.

She had already turned twenty and considered him young. Their age difference bothered her but apparently not him. He was all fun and games and she had life experience. Still he pursued her with an intensity that should've worn her down. Yet she refused to let him get to her. She remained indifferent. Unresponsive. He was unfazed.

She entered the storeroom and collected all the items, then returned to the dining room, her arms loaded. Quickly, she set about restocking the waitress station. She was surprised to find Race still working. He'd finished wiping down the tabletops and had moved to the counter. He made large swipes with his big hands.

He cut her a look, asked, "What's next?"

"Really? You want to continue?" Surprising. "You're not getting paid."

"Payment isn't always money."

"I've nothing else to offer you."

"The reward is your company."

"Get real. *Nothing*, Race."

One corner of his mouth tipped up. All sexy and shrewd. "We'll see."

No, they would not see. "Wipe down the soda machine next," she suggested.

Race did so. He growled when he pressed too heavily on one of the nozzles and got sprayed with Coke. All over his front. Sweet and sticky. "Damn," he muttered.

She couldn't help but smile.

"Not funny, Blu. You could've warned me. This is one of my favorite shirts."

His frown prodded her to say, "Wet a napkin with club soda, dab the stain."

He did more than dab. He jerked off his shirt and spread it on the counter. Bare chested, he filled a small glass with club soda and poured the carbonated beverage from neck to hem. He grabbed a handful of napkins and scrubbed the front. Hard.

Blu stared. Race was impressively fit. He obviously worked out. Muscles flexed across his shoulders. Roped sinew lined his arms. A fan of chest hair darkened his torso. She had pinned him as a horny kid until that moment. She now realized his body had very adult possibilities. However, there was no loyalty in him. He charmed countless girls. Tori had mentioned that he'd taken two girls to the prom. Apparently he'd decided to double the pleasure after Blu declined his invitation to the dance.

Race soon shook out his shirt. Fully drenched, the fabric snapped with the excess club soda. He looked at Blu. Her gaze held his. The air between them was charged with awareness.

He narrowed his eyes. His expression tightened. His body was visibly tense. He balled his T-shirt and lobbed it on the counter. She sensed his desire to kiss her. Instead, he stayed the impulse. Clenching his fists. Controlled.

She'd gone physically slack. Embarrassingly so. Her pulse skipped. Her stomach softened. She swallowed hard. Against her will, she desired him. Unsteady, she drew a breath and pulled herself together. "Let me get you a Zinotti's tee," she offered. She wanted him covered up. "You're—"

"Exposed?" he taunted. "A turn-on, Blu?"

"Don't flatter yourself." She hurried past him. Shivered. With no other customers, the air-conditioning had cooled the empty restaurant. His nipples now puckered. There were goose bumps on his ribs. She returned to the store-room and located the stack of T-shirts. She guessed his size. An extra-large. The shirts in stock were women's medium. Snug on a big guy. At least he'd be covered.

Partially covered, she soon realized, as he poked his head through the opening, rolled his shoulders, and squeezed into the tee. The cotton defined his chest, yet came up short, exposing his navel and four inches of his abdomen. He lifted his arms and stitches stretched along his sides.

He grunted. "Perfect size."

"Best I could do. It will get you home."

"Home, once we finish here."

"You still want to help?"

"For a few more minutes."

"I'll wash the greasy plastic baskets from the meatball subs." Pause. "You can stack the chairs on the center tables. Then sweep and mop. Everything you need is by the back door. That should wrap it up."

It took her all of ten minutes to soak and scrub the baskets. Race's tasks took longer. She fixed herself a soda, slid into a booth, and watched him work. He put his back into it. Muscles rippling. Fast and thorough.

He dipped the mop in the soapy water bucket, leaned on the handle, and eyed her suspiciously. "Thought I was helping, not doing it all."

She sipped her drink. "I'm taking a break."

"Me too." He came toward her. Dropped down across the table. He reached for her glass and drank from the side. Not from her straw. They'd shared. A little too intimate for her liking.

Race rested his elbows on the tabletop, steepled his fingers, and returned to their earlier conversation. "Divorce is bad, but don't get your thong in a bunch. Zane and Tori will work through their issues. It's none of our business."

Thong in a bunch? What an idiot. "Tori's my friend. I'm there for her."

"Zane and I are cousins. I side with family."

"You're on the wrong side, dude."

"We grew up together. Airplanes were our first toys. We've wanted to attend the Air Force Academy for as long as I can remember. Zane even more than me. He lived and breathed becoming a fighter pilot. We set our goal and stuck to it. I was admitted, and he got late acceptance. Our dreams were realized."

"But Zane's dream was realized *after* their wedding." Race was such a moron. "Or have you forgotten standing up for him in the gazebo? They exchanged vows. Now he's broken them."

"Only for four years," he adamantly defended. "They can marry again when he graduates, following his commissioning."

"Insensitive ass," she accused him. "She'll be a different person by then."

"How so?"

"No one goes into marriage thinking they will get a divorce," she explained. "Tori and Zane were married for one week. It was a short time, yes, but dissolving that bond is going to be stressful, hurtful. I know Tori well. She feels like she's losing another loved one. She's never had stability in her life, until Zane. He grounded her, gave her permanence, only to take it away."

"Yeah, the timing couldn't have been worse," Race admitted. "His late acceptance to the academy was unexpected. It surprised us all. Then one thing just led to another. No one was meant to get hurt."

"But Tori did."

"Zane's not feeling so great either. They talked and talked. Deadlocked."

"Words mean little," Blu grated. "Zane made up his mind with the acceptance letter."

"You're wrong."

"Bullshit," she shot back. "Tori instantly knew that he would resent her if he didn't go."

"Yet *she's* resenting *him* now for leaving her."

"Can you honestly blame her?" Blu demanded. "She recently lost her parents, now she's losing Zane. That's a lot in a very short time."

"They'll recover."

"Don't bet on it. She'll grieve. There are stages of emotion in the grieving process. All crippling. Sadness, panic, loneliness and depression, then anger. Anger lasts the longest."

"What makes you an expert?"

"Been there, done that. Won't happen again."

"Never?" he asked.

"Not for me, but, given time, Tori has a chance. She'll work through it, for the sake of her grandmother. But I doubt she'll ever return to Zane."

"That would kill him."

"Choices, consequences, neither of them will benefit."

"Pretty callous, Blu."

"Truth is harsh."

Their throats were dry from the heated debate, and they simultaneously reached for the glass of soda. His hand covered hers. Big and rough against her smaller, softer one. He rubbed his thumb over her wrist. Her pulse jumped. An automatic response. He seemed pleased. She was not. She withdrew her hand from under his. Glanced at her watch. Time closed in on the midnight hour. She collected her glass and slid from the booth. "I need to finish up."

He took the hint and finished mopping. Afterward, he returned the broom and mop to the kitchen, all on his own. He emptied the bucket by the back door. She heard the water running and knew he was rinsing it out with a hose. The click of the lock secured the door. He'd done his duty.

She heard his footsteps on his approach. He located her behind the counter, near the cash register. "All done."

She nodded but refused to look up. He stood too darn close. She felt his gaze on her as she refilled the condiment caddies. Adding packets of salt, pepper, and sugar. She refreshed small, lidded jars with red pepper flakes and peppercorns. Both customer-requested.

She straightened, and they bumped shoulders. She wanted to tell him to leave, but the words wouldn't form. She'd never been tongue-tied in her life. Race stared at her, his amber eyes dark and searching. She couldn't look away. She was unexpectedly drawn to a guy she'd avoided at every turn.

They stood so close, they were barely a breath apart. She glanced left, right, until he tipped up her chin with his finger and forced her to hold his gaze. She seldom blushed, but at that moment her cheeks grew warm beneath his stare. Her chest rose, her breasts felt heavy. He leaned in, and his scent seemed to touch her. Earthy and sinful. Clean and sexy. Challenging and dangerous.

His mouth hovered over hers when he said, "I'm going to take off now, unless you want me to stick around."

Stick around and do what? "Bye," was safest.

He smiled. "A mental tug-of-war, Blu. You like me but are afraid to admit it."

"I don't date younger men."

"Because of the jerk who burned you?"

Race was intuitive. "Maybe." She refused to share her past.

He eased back. "I'm not him, Blu."

"You're close enough."

Still he persisted. "One date?"

"We wouldn't have a good time. All we do is fight."

"You start it."

Perhaps she did. "We have nothing in common."

"We both like pizza."

She rolled her eyes.

"We have Zane and Tori between us."

"We're on opposite sides with them."

"We could work at bringing them together again."

"Zane's leaving for the academy before long," she pointed out.

"So am I," said Race. "Doesn't mean we won't be back for holidays and vacation."

They were both from Barefoot William and would eventually return. Blu felt an odd sense of missing Race already. She shook it off. Ridiculous. She nodded toward the door. "Let's close up."

"No reward for my cleaning?"

"I won't slam the door on your ass when you leave."

"Such a mouth on you." His gaze held on her lips.

She almost expected him to kiss her. Almost. He was that near. He had a very sexy mouth. Instead he backed away, scooping his wet T-shirt from the counter and walking toward the door. She followed more slowly.

He finished the night with, "It's late, but I plan to stop and see Zane. He moved out of the cottage and is back at his parents' house."

"I was on my way to see Tori. She's returned to the White Heron Apartments."

"Zane never asked her to leave, you know. He pleaded with her to stay at the cottage."

"It was her call. She rejected his offer. How could she stay after the divorce?"

"But she was the one who fixed up the place."

"And Zane tore her down."

Race rubbed the back of his neck. "Zane checked to get his family's permission, and he's leaving Oswald with her grandmother."

Which was thoughtful and kind, something to ease the pain of their divorce. Nana Aubrey and Oz needed each other. Ozzie's companionship had gotten Tori's grandma on her feet. The dalmatian was a calm and well-behaved dog, devoted to her gram. It would have been a shame to separate them.

"The apartment manager lifted the 'no pet' rule for them," Blu told him. "My condo lease is up next month. I've offered to move in. We plan to share expenses. Cut the rent in half."

"Tori never has to worry about money. Zane's family will take care of her."

"She's too proud. She won't take a dime."

"Bills add up," he reminded her. "The two of you will barely make ends meet, working at Zinotti's."

"We'll manage."

"Good luck." He bumped the door open with his hip. Left. A guy with broad shoulders in a too-small T-shirt. Gone.

Alone, Blu felt suddenly cold. She rubbed her arms. Race was bad for her. He made her crazy. They sparred and sparked. He was hot. Holy-hell hot. Still she held off dating him. Her loss? Perhaps. Live and learn. She'd never repeat her past mistake.

Blu walked back through the pizza parlor, turned off all the lights. She left minutes behind Race. She'd parked her dark blue Mustang with the white racing stripes in the alley, beneath the only corner spotlight on the building. A police patrol car sat close by at the curb. Law enforcement kept a sharp eye on the street as the late-night restaurants and bars closed. There'd be no disturbing the peace. Barefoot William had a low crime rate. She pulled from the alley and blinked her headlights at the deputy. Her signal to him that she'd wrapped up and was headed home. He waved out the window.

Traffic was light as she headed to the White Heron complex. Tori was her best friend; they were nearly close as sisters. Blu would do anything for her. They could talk or they could sit in silence. It mattered little to her.

Blu had called Tori from Zinotti's before she left. Tori met her at the door. She was wrapped in a faded yellow robe and scuffed slippers. Her face was pale, with dark circles under her eyes. Blu sensed her sadness and vulnerability, and she suffered along with her. She immediately gave Tori a sisterly hug. One that attempted to take away Tori's pain and shore up her strength. Tori's sigh was heavy, her soul bruised. Her healing would not come overnight.

They separated. Tori stepped back. "Come on in," she softly invited. "Gram's in bed. Oswald too."

Blu entered. The apartment was bare bones. The television was turned off. There was hardly anyplace to sit. "You take the rocking chair," she told Tori. "I'm fine on the floor." She found a spot amid the dog toys. Sat crosslegged.

Tori settled on the rocker. She drew up her knees and hugged her legs to her chest. Protectively. "Thanks for coming by," she said gratefully. "I've yet to settle into a routine, and I'm feeling off. Nana Aubrey is holding it together better than I am. I've always fixed her meals. But today she made me a tuna salad sandwich for lunch. Then heated us chicken pot pies for supper."

"What can I do?" Blu asked.

"Make small talk. Nothing too heavy. I'm not ready to sort out my feelings. I'm merely attempting to exist."

"Breathe deeply. You'll find a way to get through the day."

"Eddie called me," Tori said, referring to their boss. "He told me to take a few days off. A week, if needed."

Blu startled. "Eddie has feelings?"

"It seems he's been divorced three times. His marriages lasted a year, six months, and a week. I can identify with the week."

Blu rubbed the back of her neck. "Damn, girl. I'm really, really sorry. I wish things were different for you."

"Yeah, me too," Tori admitted.

"How's your gram doing?"

Tori grew thoughtful. "I'm not sure how much she realizes or understands. We moved from this rundown apartment to an amazing cottage, then returned here again. Gram shuffles, and I'm taking baby steps. She needs me, and I, more than ever, need her."

"You can count on me, anytime, anywhere."

"You offered, and I want you to move in with us," Tori decided. "If you don't mind living with a teary-eyed divorcee."

"I'll bring tissues and furniture."

"Appreciated." Tori turned the conversation to the pizza parlor. "Has Zinotti's been busy?" she asked.

"Packed, from dinner to closing," said Blu. "One lingering idiot even after closing."

Tori managed a small, tight smile. "Race."

"He doesn't know when to go home."

"He likes you."

"He's a pain in my ass."

Tori's smile became a yawn. Her eyes closing.

Blu understood the emotional toll the divorce had taken on her friend. She pushed to her feet. Stretched, cracked her spine. "Get some sleep. I'll see myself out. See you tomorrow."

"Thanks, Blu."

"Welcome."

"You're welcome to leave anytime," Zane told Race. He lay in the dark, sprawled across the living room couch. "My family is out for the evening. I want to be alone."

"Alone isn't always good, dude." Race dropped onto a leather La-Z-Boy recliner. "Let's talk."

"We have nothing to discuss. Not the cottage. Not Oswald. Definitely not Tori."

"How about the Air Force Academy?"

"No comment. Can't concentrate. All I can think about is that I hurt my wife."

"She's technically no longer your wife."

Zane flipped him the bird. "You're such an ass."

"Blu has the same opinion of me."

Zane side-eyed him. "When did you see Blu?"

"At Zinotti's."

"You're haunting the place."

"She works a lot. It's the only time I get to see her."

"Does she want to be seen?" Zane asked.

"I'm making progress. When the restaurant closed tonight, I helped her clean up."

Zane snorted. "She couldn't resist your janitorial skills."

"Whatever it takes."

"Don't get too involved," Zane cautioned.

"Can't. We leave for the academy in a few days."

Zane pushed himself to a sitting position. He bowed his head, asked, "Did Blu mention Tori?"

"Yeah . . ."

"And . . ."

"Thought you didn't want to talk about her."

"I don't. I . . . do."

"Make up your mind."

His voice hitched. "Do."

"I don't know much."

"Tell me what you do," Zane demanded.

"Blu protects Tori like family. She dislikes you at the moment."

"Expected."

"Blu stops by Tori's apartment and checks on her each day. Tori's taking time off. She goes back to work next week, after we've left town."

"How's she doing?"

"How do you think?" Race retorted. "I haven't seen her, but she couldn't look worse than you. You look like shit." His cousin's hair spiked in every direction. His face was drawn. Scruff darkened his jaw. He wore a wrinkled T-shirt and board shorts. "Something a dog dragged in."

"Oswald's not here."

Race commiserated. "You did a good thing by giving Oz to Tori's grandmother."

"Ozzie took to Nana Aubrey. They belong together."

"You can visit Oz when you're home on leave."

"We'll see. Tori's pretty much closed the door on me."

"She'll come around," Race said as if to give Zane hope.

Zane wasn't so sure. "I broke her."

"Even Humpty Dumpty was put together again," Race pointed out.

"Shut up. Not funny."

"Sorry."

Zane pressed his palms into his eyes. "I'm hurting, man. I'm questioning my decision. My family is on my side. They believe the academy is right for me. Why does it feel so wrong? I'm stressed as hell. I love Tori, yet I'm leaving her."

"I'm leaving Blu."

Zane rolled his eyes. "Not the same."

"She'll miss me."

"You're delusional."

"We'll see."

Zane rose from the couch. "Want a sandwich?"

"Whatcha got?"

"Grilled cheese or barbecued beef."

Race rubbed his stomach. He'd eaten a pizza and meatball sub earlier. He'd ordered, kept the food coming, so he could watch Blu work. He liked the way she moved. How she interacted with customers. How she still called him "Table One." Her short spiked hair with the new pink streak was sexy. She might resist his advances, but he saw through her. Her words told one story, her light green gaze another. She wasn't as averse to him as she pretended. He was sure of it.

Race slid off the recliner. He wasn't ready to leave. He wanted to spend more time with Zane. He could manage another sandwich. "Barbecued beef. You have those deli dill pickles?"

"Two left in the jar."

"I'll have both."

"You never were good at sharing."

"I'll save you a bite."

"Bite me, Race," Blu ground out. It was four thirty in the afternoon. She'd just arrived at work. Her daily schedule didn't fluctuate, but she didn't have to be on the floor until five. He'd waited for her in the alley, wanting to talk.

He cornered her by the car door. "Biting's good, but I'd rather have a kiss."

"Not going to happen."

"I'm leaving in two days."

"I'm supposed to care?"

"You do care. Admit it."

She glared. "You're head-tripping, dude."

He didn't want her mad at him, so he played nice, changing the subject. "I've seen my boy Zane three nights in a row," he said. "A part of him regrets his decision to attend the academy."

"The other part?" snottily asked.

"Reminds him that the Air Force has been a lifetime goal."

"And Tori lasted only a week."

"She's on his mind every waking moment," he insisted, keeping his voice even. "Be realistic. How far could he go at Gray's Garage? Not a great living. The Air Force will provide a solid future for both of them."

"You sound like a recruiting poster."

"Accomplishment is important."

"So is love and loyalty."

His jaw locked. He picked his words carefully. "I don't want to fight with you."

"But we do it so well."

"We could find something better."

She shook her head. "Best is walking away."

"You don't mean it."

"Don't tell me what I don't mean."

"Damn, you're difficult."

"Stop swearing," she said snidely.

"You swear."

The air sparked between them. "Because—" She bit her lip.

"I've gotten to you." That pleased him greatly.

"Don't pat yourself on the back just yet."

"If not now, then when?"

"You are so pushy," she complained.

"Only with you."

"What do you want from me, Race?" she asked bluntly.

He was honest. "A chance to know you."

"I already know enough about you."

"That would be?"

"You're charming, a flirt, and date a lot of girls."

"All superficial. I'm also smart, focused, and serious."

"Modest too."

He looked her in the eye. "I'm also patient. I wait for what I want."

"You want me."

He pulled a face. "Less and less by the moment. You're mean to me."

"Poor baby," she mocked. "We're not meant to be together."

He disagreed. "We're going to be together, whenever we think about each other. You will be thinking about me a lot. Hourly. Daily. You will miss me."

"Don't be so sure."

"I'm positive, babe."

He edged closer to her. Backed her against the car door. His body hemmed her in, but he gave her an inch of space, purposely not allowing their bodies to touch. He said what he knew to be true. "You were burned by another guy, and you hold him against me. I'm not him."

He tilted his head so that their lips were a hairbreadth apart. His breath warmed her mouth when he spoke. "This is it. Right here, right now. I won't be back later tonight or tomorrow. I'd wanted to kiss you good-bye, but I won't."

Her eyes widened. Dilated. Her body heat touched him.

Still he held back. He'd chased her for nearly ten months. She'd constantly blown him off. At that moment, he could've kissed her, slow and deep, and she would've responded. Man to woman. They'd have heated the alley. Hotter than the summer sun.

But afterward he'd walk away, and she'd shake off their kiss. He wanted her to remember him. So he breathed in . . . as she breathed out. The air between them shimmered with sexual want. Anticipation, ripe. Her eyes slowly closed. Her lips parted. Awaiting his move.

His move came, and it wasn't what she expected.

She would be ticked. All anger, angst and arousal.

He gave her what she'd given him from day one—nothing.

Nothing often led to something.

Someday.

Five

Time passed. Years in fact. Sometimes life moved forward. Improved. Other times it stood still. Memories could hold a person in place. Hearts didn't always heal. Zane Cates still felt the pain from his teenage decision. He'd broken Tori Rollins's heart.

He presently stood in the parking lot behind Zinotti's Pizza. The streetlight had long burned out. The sliver moon cast eerie shadows across the cracked pavement. The restaurant had closed an hour earlier. Owner Eddie Zinotti and two kitchen employees had left soon after midnight. Only one person remained to lock up. His ex-wife, Tori. Eighteen years had passed since their wedding day. Now he was back in Barefoot William for good. As he waited for her tonight, he felt protective, in spite of their divorce. So long ago. He wanted to be sure she made it safely to her car.

He crossed his arms over his chest so the script on his gray T-shirt that read *Fly into the Center of the Storm* was barely visible. He leaned a blue-jeaned hip against the hood of his 1967 Impala. Crossed his booted feet at the ankle. He was visible should she look his way. He was in no hurry. He had all night.

The back door of the pizzeria creaked open. Old and off one hinge. Tori body-slammed the heavy, warped wood to get it closed. The click of the lock broke the stillness. The screen door banged next. She leaned against the jamb, and her shoulders sagged. She blew out a breath. Her bangs fluttered on her forehead. Exhaustion claimed her.

Zane's chest tightened. Overworked and underpaid, she'd lost weight. He knew she'd been busting her ass, clocking a seventy-hour week at the pizza parlor. He wondered when she'd last eaten a decent meal. Something other than pizza. Slenderness had stolen her curves.

No matter their situation, he'd always wanted to make life easier for her. He had offered her several career opportunities over the years, and she'd turned each down. Flat. Time and again. He was a Cates heir. His relatives were a reliable grapevine of news. Through phone calls, then texts and emails, they shared news of Tori's life with Zane. They kept him up-to-date. Her struggle was his struggle. Always would be. Despite their separation.

So he knew her situation at Zinotti's sucked. Tori was loyal to a fault. She worked steadily, without complaint. She'd never called in sick or taken a vacation. Sleazy Eddie had promised her a partnership but had yet to deliver. He took a sizable amount of money out of her paycheck each month, claiming it was being put toward a financial buy-in. Yet she had never received a bonus, any benefits, or owner recognition. The guy was a dick as far as Zane was concerned. Rumor had it that Eddie was dodging taxes and that he was under investigation. An audit in his future. Zane wanted Tori out of there, far beyond IRS scrutiny.

She presently walked in profile to him as she proceeded to her car. She was thirty-six and she still drove her high school Camaro. The vehicle had gotten old. Beat up too. It had faded paint, bent windshield wipers, bald tires, and was held together by rust. Gray duct tape wrapped a segment of the bumper. Zane had mechanical skills. Once, he'd offered to repair her Camaro. She'd declined. No surprise. His suggestion of a new car only irritated her. She'd turned him down flat. Obstinate woman. She had once needed him. Not so anymore. She was too independent for her own good.

Despite her denying him, a part of him admired her strength. They'd once been strong together. That was in the past. A past that lived with him still. They both carried emotional baggage. Weighty and dragging them down. Tonight was no different. Nothing had changed. They'd never moved beyond their short-lived marriage and the pain of their divorce. He'd left her and never regained a footing in her life. He hadn't a clue how to make it better between them. His stomach sank. He might never have another chance with her.

Tori suddenly sensed him. Amid the darkness. Awareness slowed her near the trunk of her car. She tilted her head, as if listening. No more than twenty feet separated them. He scuffed his boot on gravel, alerting her to his presence. She turned and faced him fully. All wild auburn hair, narrowed blue eyes, and raised stubborn chin. Tomato sauce spattered her white cook's shirt and red jeans. Her full lips flattened against her teeth. "Stalking me, Zane?" she asked sharply.

"Evading me, Tori?" he countered.

"Dodging a bullet."

Bullet. His Air Force fighter pilot tactical call sign. A nickname given him by his squadron in a show of camaraderie. He would have taken a bullet for any one of his team. Tori, however, took *bullet* as a shot to her heart. A painful wound. One that had never healed. Despite his best efforts.

He had entered the Air Force through the Total Force Integration program that allowed active-duty pilots to fly in the Reserve and Air National Guard units after ten years of active service commitment. The nickname *Bullet* had followed him into the reserves as a hurricane hunter. Then into civilian life. A reminder of his career.

She took a step, blew him off. "Leaving now." *Like you left me.* The accusation was unspoken, but lingering.

"Stay, give me five," he requested.

"I've no time."

Which he had expected. Over the years, he'd gone out of his way to fix their relationship. He pursued her, and she pushed back. Total avoidance. A glimpse of him a block away, and she would turn on her heel and head in the opposite direction. The visits he scheduled with Oswald and her gram at the apartment were awkward. He would arrive and she'd leave, allowing no more than an uncomfortable pass at the door. On the rare occasions he'd cornered her and attempted conversation, she had darted around him. Disappeared. He was left talking to himself.

Not so tonight. They would converse like adults. Or so he hoped. "Make time. I have something to tell you."

She took a second step away from him. "Not interested."

"I think you will be."

"Nothing about you interests me."

That hurt. "This might. I'm back in town."

She shrugged. Unfazed. "Nothing new. You come and go. How long this time?"

Longer than she would like. He'd often taken military leave in Barefoot William. A week's vacation, sometimes two. This time was different. His next words would impact their lives from here on in. He braced himself for her anger. "Permanently. I've retired."

Her stunned silence hung on the air, as heavy as the humidity in July. The night clutched eighty-eight degrees and wouldn't let go. The heat was oppressive and smothering.

It took her a moment to process his words. "You're home? For good?" She was incredulous. "I thought you were a lifer."

"I considered reenlisting," he told her. "I gave it a lot of thought. The Air Force has given me a great life, yet it's time to come home. I want to be closer to my family." Nearer to Tori too. Despite her holding him at arm's length.

"I've been warned." Agitation and aversion crept into her voice, along with a hint of despair. He picked up on it. He'd once known her well. Every nuance in her tone had been an expression of her heart back then. Was it still? He heard misery there now. Damn.

He'd made a decision at eighteen that had affected every moment of his life over the years to come. He'd been young. Conceivably even selfish. Perhaps he could've handled things differently. Hindsight was twenty-twenty. His career as a pilot had greatly benefited him but crushed her. She blamed him still. No forgiveness. No do overs. She disliked him immensely.

They faced a rough road ahead. Despite their difficulties, he still loved her. He was desperate for a second chance. Whatever it took. However long.

She hesitated, asked him, "Where are you staying?" She'd steer clear if she knew his location.

"Granddad Frank's stilt house." It was situated outside town, ten miles from the beach. His gramps had kept his finger on the pulse of the family businesses for much of his ninety years, even while distancing himself from the tourist trade.

"A customer at Zinotti's mentioned that he'd moved to the retirement village after a bad fall. Cleaning the porch gutters, I believe."

"That was his second fall, actually. The orange grove became too much for him. Upkeep and daily chores around the house were more than he could manage. The gated community suits him well."

Tori shifted, but stayed. "I've heard it's a nice place."

"Pleasant and welcoming. Being a widower can be lonesome. He's fortunate to have friends at the village—those old-timers who grew up locally. Many have roots as deep as the Cates family." He paused, waited for her to get into her car. She did not. So he kept talking. "The facility is self-contained. Anchored by a small grocery store. A gift shop, hair salon, pharmacy, and library are also open for business. There's a medical team on staff and a hospital close by. There are lots of activities too. Gramps plays bingo and shuffleboard." Zane went out on a limb. "You should visit him sometime. He was always fond of you."

"Fond of me as your teenage bride."

"My family still cares about you."

"Don't go there, Zane."

"Sorry, but there are things we need to discuss. We have to deal with our cottage. Nothing has changed. It stands as we left it." Neither of them had been back, as far as he knew. The memories weighed heavily on his heart. The cottage reminded him of what had been, and might never be again. He hadn't been able to let it go.

She paled. "Does someone want to move in?"

"Not right this second, but eventually. Right now, all the Cateses are settled in their own homes. The cottage could sit for a while longer, I suppose, but I'd like to tackle it fairly soon."

"Soon is for your convenience, not mine."

The air sparked. His heart squeezed. They stood on the edge of an argument. He didn't want to fight with her. He held up his hands, palms out. A sign of peace. "It was merely a suggestion."

"A poor one."

"My timing's not always on target."

"An understatement, Bullet."

She reached for the door handle of her car. She'd had enough of him. He sensed she was about to leave. He quickly dug into the pocket of his jeans, retrieved a key. "Here," he called out, drawing her attention just before she ducked inside the Camaro. He held up the key, then tossed it to her. She caught it. "To the cottage. For whenever. Take what you want. I could help you move—"

"Out, like you once helped me move in."

He swallowed. "I'm sorry, Tori."

"For what, Zane? Marrying me? Leaving me? Tying up loose ends?"

"For hurting you." Hell, he hurt too.

"I survived." She climbed into her car. Shut the door. The engine turned over and she backed from the parking space. She pulled dangerously close to him. The right rear tire edged his boot. It was not a great first meeting, but it could've gone worse. She couldn't run over his foot.

She rolled down the window, warned, "I'd move next time if I were you."

"Or you'll what?"

"Don't chance it."

It was late. "I'll follow you home." For safety's sake.

"There's no need."

"I feel the need."

His peace of mind tailed her to the apartment. He let

his muscle car idle in visitor's parking until she cleared the front door. She didn't look back, not that he expected her to. He took himself home.

Only to return to Tori's apartment early the next morning. It was an important day. He was willing to face Tori's disapproval. He climbed from his Impala. Stretched. He bumped the door shut with his hip, then walked around the hood to the passenger side. He removed two items. Held them behind his back. Then took the sidewalk to the door. He knocked instead of ringing the doorbell. He figured Nana Aubrey would be up—she was an early riser. He looked forward to seeing both her and Oswald. Tori should still be sleeping. She'd put in a long shift at Zinotti's.

"Happy birthday," he wished the older woman when the door creaked open.

Nana Aubrey stood before him in a floral robe and bedroom slippers. She leaned heavily on her cane. She stared at him blankly for several heartbeats before her eyes brightened. She gave him a small smile. "Zane." She remembered.

Ozzie found his way to the door too. The dalmatian was slow moving. His vision was cloudy, yet he never forgot Zane. He gave a low bark and wagged his tail. Zane patted him on the head. Scratched one ear. Content, Oz returned to his orthopedic dog bed next to Nana Aubrey's rocking chair. The bed had therapeutic benefits, providing support and comfort for his arthritic joints. Zane believed Ozzie lived to protect Gram. He was her bodyguard even in his old age.

"In," Gram invited. Her speech was still minimal, but her comprehension had improved over the years. She shuffled ahead of him into the living room. The TV was tuned to the weather channel. That hadn't changed.

Zane took a moment and looked around. Race had told him that Blu had once shared the apartment with Tori and Nana Aubrey, following the divorce. She'd stayed for a year, then moved into her own apartment in the same complex. Blu was close enough if Tori needed her, but not underfoot. Blu had generously left several pieces of her furniture to fill the emptiness. Zane had always felt it a shame that Tori hadn't cleaned out the cottage. He'd offered her everything. She hadn't taken a thing.

He crossed to the older woman and withdrew his hands from behind his back. Keeping his voice low, he said, "Roses for the birthday lady from Tori and me." He set a tall crystal vase with a dozen long-stemmed, coral-red roses next to her on the narrow rectangular table. He selected a single Fragrant Cloud and handed it to her. The scent was rich and lasting.

Nana Aubrey drew in the fragrance, sighed. "Lov-"

"Lovely? Love it?" he guessed.

She managed a short nod.

He next presented her with a decorative tin of hard candy. "Butterscotch, peppermint, lemon, and cinnamon."

"Thank-"

He gave her a gentle hug. "You're welcome." He'd debated including his ex as one of the gift givers, and decided it best. Tori had appeared tired and stressed last night. She might not have had time to shop for her gram.

He looked toward the kitchen and wondered if Nana Aubrey had eaten breakfast. He had no idea what was in the refrigerator or breadbox. Still he asked, "Hungry?"

She pursed her lips, thoughtful. "Toast," she managed.

"Coffee or tea?"

"Coff-"

"Can do." He moved quietly across the room. No sign

of Tori. He sure as hell didn't want to wake her up. She would not be happy to see him. Of that he was certain.

The smell of coffee soon blended with the scent of burned toast. The toaster was old and the timer selector knob broken. He removed the charcoal-blackened bread and tried again. He watched carefully this time, toasting the next slices perfectly. He plated the lightly buttered toast, then poured two cups of black coffee. He snagged a segment of paper towel, a substitute napkin. He went over to join Nana, for a few minutes anyway. He delivered her breakfast, then lowered himself onto the end of the gray-and-black-plaid couch. The sofa had seen better days. The fabric was faded, the cushions lumpy, with an uncomfortable metal bar across the back. Luckily no springs poked him.

Nana Aubrey reached across the side table and touched his arm with her arthritic fingers. An appreciative gesture. Afterward she slowly ate the toast and sipped her coffee. She seemed to enjoy his breakfast efforts.

Zane was about to offer a refill on her coffee when the bedroom door opened. The master bedroom, he remembered, which wasn't that much bigger than the second bedroom. Tori appeared, all sleepy-eyed and mussed hair, in a white tank top and matching boy-short panties. One strap on her top hung off her shoulder. The hem gapped inches from the waistband on her shorts. Her mouth formed a what-the-hell frown. No words—yet.

"Coffee?" he inquired before she could pick a fight.

She stared at him, as if he was insane. "Why are you here?" she sharply asked.

"My bir-" Nana Aubrey attempted to explain his presence. "Gifts," took a great effort to say.

Tori glanced at her grandma. She took in the bouquet of roses and tin of hard candy. "Your birthday . . ." she said, deflated. She side-eyed him and kept her voice low. "You bought—"

"We bought Nana presents. You've been busy. I had time and stopped at the florist and store." His tone dropped below the volume on the television. "You owe me half."

Tori was overtaken with emotion. Tears pressed her eyelids. She sniffed and blinked them away. Nana Aubrey was the most important person in her life. How had she forgotten her eighty-sixth birthday? She felt awful.

Enter Zane Cates with his phenomenal memory. She'd once known him to be kind and considerate, and purchasing gifts for her gram placed him in a good light. Even if she did owe him half the money. She looked at him now, standing over Nana Aubrey, offering to top off her coffee cup. Gram enjoyed a two-cup morning. She nodded.

He walked past Tori on his way to the kitchen, giving her little notice. She took him in. She had every right to stare. He was in her home.

Time had favored him. Undeniably. He'd gotten even better looking over the years. His features looked sharp and focused beneath his military haircut. The boy had met the man in the Air Force, and he'd fully filled out. He looked muscled and strong beneath his blue button-down with the sleeves rolled up to his elbows. He packed his jeans just fine. New Nike tennis shoes.

She didn't let herself dwell on his looks. Handsome was a heart breaker, she knew. Their divorce had taken her soul. She had not healed with time. Pain held her captive. She might never pull herself fully together. There was no good to come from Zane dropping in unannounced, in spite of her grandmother's birthday. It couldn't happen again.

He gave her the once-over when he next passed, returning to the living room. A corner of his mouth tipped up, amused. She set her jaw. What was he grinning about? Realization snapped its fingers. His grin was because of her. She stood in a skimpy tank and boy-leg briefs. Bed-tossed hair. Unshaved legs. He seemed to take perverse pleasure in her appearance.

She had not slept well. She'd tossed and turned after speaking to him in Zinotti's parking lot. She'd been anxious and upset that he was back home. *Permanently.* He had then shown up at the apartment at first light. Before her alarm had rung. She'd heard voices in the living room and imagined it the TV. Zane was the last person she'd expected. Damn the man. She was dying a slow death.

She appeared calm on the outside, but her heart hammered on the inside as she returned to her bedroom. She glanced in the mirror over her dresser and cringed. Dark circles under her eyes, sleep in the corners, and a pillow crease on her cheek. Her face was surprisingly flushed. An aroused pink. She undressed and took a shower. She shampooed and scrubbed with a strawberry bath gel, then thoroughly rinsed. Only to repeat the process. Procrastinating and squeaky clean. She finished with a spray of cold water and display of goose bumps. She toweled off and debated what to wear.

Zane had always liked her in an oversized man's T-shirt and leggings. The shirt gave him plenty of room to feel her up. He would slip his hands under the hem, slide his palms over her ribs, and then cup her breasts. Finger foreplay. The memories left her breathing heavy and her nipples hard. She refused to dress for him today. She opened her closet door. Stared for a long time. She had several Zinotti's kitchen uniforms, but few casual outfits. She and her gram seldom had company. Tori lived in her tank tops and boy-shorts before and after work. They were comfortable.

She sighed heavily. Her kaleidoscope vision had dimmed following the divorce. The colors in her life no longer popped. She selected a sleeveless blue top and jeans. Red flip-flops. She ran a brush through her hair, tamed it. She'd taken her sweet time. A half an hour had come and gone. She drew a breath, set her features, and went to face Zane. How much longer would he stay?

He had left. She sensed that he was gone the moment she opened the bedroom door. His presence lingered, but the room was empty. Her gram and Oswald had also disappeared. They'd no doubt returned to her bedroom for a short nap, which was part of their morning routine. Up at dawn, breakfast and the weather forecast, then back to bed. Day after day.

Tori was alone.

She felt strangely lost. Hollow.

Zane had left a huge hole in her life.

The void only widened with him back in town.

She went to the kitchen and poured herself a cup of coffee. She preferred it with cream, but cream was a luxury. She'd learned to drink it black. She rested her hip against the kitchen counter and contemplated her day. She didn't have to be at work until five. Free hours loomed. Zane's request to clear out the cottage came to mind. A stab to her heart. Sadness settled bone-deep. The cottage represented what had been, but would never be again. Perhaps it was time to fully let go of her past. However difficult it might be. She would do a little at a time. Sort, dismantle, and save those memories that didn't gut her.

She finished her coffee, rinsed out the cup in the sink. Then wrote and left a note for her grandmother. She set it on the rocking chair. She promised to be back by noon to fix them lunch, and to bring a special birthday dessert. A piece of chocolate ganache cake from For Goodness Cakes. A delicious splurge.

She locked up the apartment and drove her Camaro to the cottage on Palmdale Drive. Once there, she parked at the curb. Her hands were clammy on the steering wheel. Her legs betrayed her. She couldn't move. She was slow in getting out of the car.

She breathed in the scent of freshly cut grass. Someone had recently mowed the yard. Trimmed rose bushes thrived along the front porch. She climbed the steps. Stood before the door. She inserted the key in the lock. Shivered. Déjà vu walked her inside and took her back in time. She was riveted by lost dreams and broken promises. Misplaced hope. Marriage failure.

Her hands shook when she opened the tango orange indoor shutters for a better look. The sun streamed in. Someone had tossed white cotton sheets over the living room furniture, preserving the fabrics. She lifted one corner on the sofa and peeked beneath. The velvet striped brocade appeared brand new. The two lavender overstuffed chairs hadn't a mark between them. No wear showed on the arms; there were no butt indentations on the cushions. Dust had accumulated on and around the edges of the geometric patterned rug. It needed a good vacuuming.

She ran her fingers along the section of picket fence tacked to the wall. White paint chips fluttered to the floor. The once shiny photos of roses in antique frames were now cloudy. The garden effect was lost. She gazed across the room and caught her reflection in the large mirror assembled from smaller ones of different shapes and sizes. Her happy younger self had fragmented, supplanted by a woman struggling to survive.

She had lost weight. Not on purpose. Constant stress stole her appetite. Life had left her cheeks gaunt. No smile on her lips. No laughter in her heart. No fervent stomach flutters. She realized in that moment it would not have mattered if she'd returned to the cottage a year following their divorce or after fifty. She would've felt the same way as she did today—unbearably sad.

She couldn't face the bedrooms, especially the master, so she wandered into the kitchen. She opened and shut the cupboards. Pulled out the drawers. Zane and she had started out with so little. Orphaned glasses and dishes sat upon the shelves. Along with mismatched silverware. None of it had mattered when they were young and in love. It didn't matter now either, as they lived separate lives.

She stood at the window over the sink and looked out. The outside redwood deck had aged naturally. It deserved a barbecue and hammock, which she and Zane hadn't had time to acquire. She tried not to look, but the gazebo drew her. It was once again sun bleached and weather beaten. Ill fated.

A shadowed movement on the far side made her blink. A raccoon? Deer? A play of light? She left the kitchen for the porch, in search of a better view. Another shadow, wider and on all fours. A bear? Not dressed in a white shirt and jeans. The person pushed himself to his feet. Brushed off his clothes. It was a man. Zane Cates.

She slowly stepped back, only to have the plank creak. A loud sound in the stillness. Zane honed in. His stare caught her, held her. He wouldn't let her leave. "A nest of bunnies," he said, raising his voice just enough to be heard. "Come quietly. They're really small."

He had her at baby animals. She couldn't resist. She kicked off her flip-flops and cautiously walked toward him. "Check it out," he whispered on her approach. "Look under the edge."

Under placed her on her hands and knees. The sight that met her gaze was well worth grass-stained jeans. "They *are* tiny." She was both mesmerized and concerned. "Their eyes aren't even open. Are they abandoned?"

Zane shook his head. "Mom's nearby. I saw her. She won't sit on her nest after the babies are born. She distances herself, acting as a decoy, to keep predators away from the kits. They only nurse once a day. Mamma Rabbit wakes them up for mealtime."

He was an encyclopedia on nature and wildlife. She'd admired that quality early on. He took to animals, and he recognized both the common and scientific names of most flowers and trees. She inwardly sighed. Now was not the time to remember what she'd rather forget. Zane was no longer a part of her life. Not ever again.

She rose, leaned a shoulder against a wide beam on the gazebo. "Why are you here?" She needed to know.

He jammed his hands in his jean pockets and widened his stance. "Same reason as you, I imagine. It's been a while. I wanted to look around."

Her curiosity got the best of her. "What's a while?"

"I've dropped by now and again, when on leave." His eyes darkened. "You won't talk to me, ever, so I come here to feel your presence."

Feel her presence brought an unexpected lump to her throat.

He paused. "How about you? Last time you came here?"

"Eighteen years."

He ran one hand down his face. "That says it all."

She hadn't driven near the Cateses' neighborhood. Simply couldn't bear to. The cottage represented what she'd had and lost. That included Zane. They had loved and laughed, until he'd turned her inside out. She was no longer the same person.

No more heart on her sleeve.

No further willingness to love again.

No looking back once they'd cleared the cottage.

It was time to go. She'd seen enough for one day.

She turned to leave without saying good-bye.

He said it for her. "Catch you later, Tori."

"Doubtful."

"Suppertime, and there's always room for pizza."

Why wouldn't he leave her alone?

Seeing Zane three times in one day was three times too many. Zero would've been better. There was no reason for their paths to cross. Yet of all the pizza parlors in town, he'd chosen Zinotti's. Tori gritted her teeth. Not fair.

He arrived around eight, following the hungry families. It was summertime, and parents and their children ate early, then headed to the boardwalk to watch the sunset. No photograph or painting could fully capture the torchlight of gold, orange, and red. Or the last breath-stealing flash of color on the horizon before darkness claimed the coastline. Spectacular and vivid.

"Guess who's here?" asked Blu as she swung through the kitchen door. "A blast from your past. He's wearing an Air Force Academy T-shirt."

"Yeah? Well, *your* past just joined Zane at Table One."

"Race?"

"None other."

Blu groaned. Her expression looked pained. "No damn way. It's high school all over again. I'm not walking down memory lane."

Tori plated an Italian sub for Blu to deliver to a customer. "Didn't you go out with Race when he was home on leave, two or three years ago?"

"More like six. Supper at Molly Malone's Diner. Mistake and regret."

Tori grinned at her friend. "You had a great time, but—"

Blu held up her hand, warned, "Don't say it. I thought he was into me, after all his emails, phone calls, and texts. He begged for that date, and, against my better judgment, I agreed. Our age difference no longer mattered. He was a hot fighter pilot. I thought he'd grown up. Prick was a punk."

Tori couldn't help herself. "You finally wanted him, and he withheld sex. He took you home after the meal. No kiss, no fooling around."

Blu frowned. "Remind me not to take you into my confidence and share my frustrations."

"I can keep a secret." The women were best friends. Confidantes. "I'd never tell Race—"

"Never tell me what?" Race strolled into the kitchen as if he owned the place. A male force to be reckoned with. He wore a black T-shirt with five white stars across his chest. Scripted beneath: *755,288 Reviews.* The man was cocky.

Tori recovered quickly. "That you can't be in the kitchen."

"I just walked in."

"Walk out," Blu stated. "No customers allowed."

Race spoke directly to Blu. "I'm hunting down my waitress—you. We're ready to order."

"Be patient. I'll be with you shortly."

"When's shortly?"

"In good damn time."

"Still bitchy, Blu?"

Her jaw shifted, a comeback on the tip of her tongue.

Tori intervened. "You bring out the best in her."

He had the balls to wink at Blu. "I do, don't I?" He left her fuming.

Blu looked ready to pull her hair out. These days it was spiky blond with a hint of hot pink at the tips. "He got to me. All six hunky feet of him."

"He is hot."

"He knows it."

"So do you."

"Whose side are you on?" Blu grumbled.

"Yours," Tori assured her.

Blu glanced through the serving window. "The guys aren't lacking for company."

Tori peered around her friend. Her stomach sank. Two women were now seated at a table within inches of the guys' booth. There was arm-touching, flirting, and smiles.

"Bet Race picks up more than their tab," observed Blu. "Zane seems attracted to them too."

Tori removed her apron. Tossed it in the laundry bin. "I'm not going to watch it unfold." She then tapped the older lady who worked with her on the shoulder. "Vera, there's only one booth and two tables seated," she said. "Mind if I take off early?"

"Eddie cut out a few minutes ago. Go, girl," she allowed. "I'll be fine."

Blu caught the second shift waitress as she handed in an order. "Stephanie, I'm calling it a night. The remaining tips are all yours."

Stephanie brightened. A college student home for the summer, she would put the extra tips toward off-campus housing. Blu slipped her an extra twenty. "You never saw us leave."

Steph grinned. "Were you even here?"

"Back door," Tori suggested.

"Right behind you."

The two friends left together. Sneaky and silent, they kept to the shadows in the parking lot. Blu was quick to get into her new MINI Cooper and sped off. Tori exhaled slowly once seated in the Camaro. Her life was about to get difficult with Zane in town. He'd be hard to avoid. Hiding wasn't a realistic option. He would find her, by some means. Anytime, anyplace.

She cracked the driver's window. Let the night air clear her head. She then fished the car key from her red jean uniform pocket, ready to run. She turned the key. Gave the car gas. One faint tick, then nothing more. *No, no, no.* She clutched the steering wheel in a chokehold. This couldn't be happening to her. Not during her great escape. She frowned. What to do?

"Bad starter or dead battery." Zane appeared at her window, larger than life and staring at her. He made no offer to help. He waited for her to ask him for assistance.

"Something you can fix?" She hated to ask.

"Could, with the right incentive."

She scrunched her nose. "What might that be?"

"Explain why you snuck out of Zinotti's."

"My shift was over," she lied.

"Bullshit, Tori." He knew better. "I checked the work chart when I cut through the kitchen after you. You were scheduled 'til eleven."

Caught and cornered. "How could you possibly see me leave when you were—?"

"What?"

"Otherwise involved."

"The brunettes?" he guessed. "Race called them over to tick off Blu."

"He succeeded. We left together."

"Were you jealous too?"
"Dumb question."
"Answer me."
"I have nothing to say."
"I'll wait until you do."

Six

Zane waited for Tori's response. A stalled car might not be to her liking, but he was damn glad the Camaro hadn't turned over. He'd been drawn to see Tori tonight. He was back in town, and despite her resistance, she remained a part of him. He felt her in his soul. He was desperate for a second chance with her.

Race could be a real jerk sometimes, notwithstanding his good qualities. He'd no more than smiled at the two brunettes, and they'd taken it as an invitation to join them. Fortunately they hadn't crowded into the booth. Their table was close enough.

Zane had nodded at the ladies, then tuned them out. He'd kept one eye on the service window and watched Tori in the kitchen. She was his priority. The brunettes had come on strong, but he hadn't weakened. They'd wanted more than pizza. A suggested tour of the bars and, afterward, a nightcap at their place. They were eager to show off their new beach house. The offer of sex was unspoken but heard. Zane wasn't attracted to obvious women. He'd always found shy and subtle far sexier.

Race had shown interest in the brunettes, but only to irritate Blu. He was watching her as closely as Zane was eyeing Tori. The guys were older now, but Race still acted like a teenager at times. Angering Blu would do him no good. She would carry a grudge.

But then so could Tori. Her resentment went deeper. It held as much hurt as anger. He was out to fix them. If only he knew how. He nudged her now. "Talk to me."

She dipped her chin, weighed her words. "You have to care about someone to be jealous. I'm . . . indifferent."

Wrong. He believed she cared, deep down. He held tight to the thought. Otherwise he'd die a slow death. Her face had fallen when she'd noticed the brunettes. He had caught a flicker of sadness in her eyes before she'd looked away. More pain. He kicked himself for allowing Race to play the I-can-date-anyone card. Zane didn't want just anyone. He wanted his ex-wife. But he was doing a damn poor job of winning her back.

"Fine." He let her indifference slide for now. He tipped up her chin with one finger. "I'll get my jumper cables. A low or dead battery can be charged. If it's the alternator, you'll need a tow to Gray's Garage."

"Gray's . . ." Her words trailed off.

He'd held a part-time job at the garage during high school. He liked working on cars and trucks. Antique vehicles were his specialty. He had yet to tell her of his future plans. Tonight was not the time. Perhaps down the road.

She closed her eyes. He assumed she was sending a silent prayer to the battery gods. A new battery would be less expensive than rebuilding or replacing an alternator. He crossed the parking lot, moved his Impala close to her Camaro. He left his car running. Got out and popped both hoods. He next retrieved the jumper cables from the trunk and proceeded with the hookup.

He circled back to her open window, said, "Corroded terminal. Give it a few minutes to charge. Even if the battery turns over, consider a new one. This one's old. You don't want to get stuck somewhere."

Her eyes opened, and she sighed heavily. Stillness settled around them. "Another expense," she muttered under her breath.

Still he heard her. "Wilbur Gray would sell you a battery at cost."

"He's a nice man," she agreed. "I had a flat tire not too long ago. He patched it and didn't try to sell me a new one."

"He has the reputation of being fair."

"He's older. I hope he doesn't retire anytime soon."

"Wilbur's seventy, healthy, and likes to stay busy," he told her. "Should he sell the business, he'd still stick around and work part-time."

She glanced at her watch. "Can I try the battery?" It had only been five minutes. Tori was itching to take off. She had an aversion to spending time with him.

"Give it a shot, but—"

She turned the key without letting him finish. Nothing. She hung her head, disappointed. "So . . . ?"

He rested his palms on the window ledge, leaned in. Close. "Can you handle ten more minutes?" he asked.

"Do I have a choice?"

"Some batteries need to charge overnight."

She exhaled sharply. "Great, just great." She rested her head on the headrest, stared at the ceiling of the Camaro, and became quiet as the night.

Companionable silence was one thing. A hostile hush quite another. He could hear her fume. Her unhappiness affected him too. He would repair her car and get her back on the road. He didn't, however, know how to fix the two of them.

He turned, gave her his back, and propped his hip near

the side-view mirror. She craned her neck. "I can't see around you."

"You're not moving. You don't need to see."

She flicked her wrist at him.

"Back, front, where do you want me to stand, Tori? I can't leave. Our vehicles are attached." By jumper cables. "Your Camaro is sucking power from my Impala." Sounded sexual, but he didn't care. His ex was unappreciative. He didn't expect her to fall in his arms with gratitude. She could, however, be a little nicer.

A small plane flew overhead. A car horn honked nearby. Tori sighed, heavy and dejected. He pushed off the Camaro, went back to his own vehicle. Got inside and pressed on the gas pedal. Increasing the current.

Another minute and he stuck his head out the window and shouted, "Start your car."

Tori did. A hesitant chug, and it turned over. Only to stall out. Then it caught once again. Fully fired. He returned to her. She covered her face, her shoulders sagging, visibly relieved.

She soon looked up, asked him, "Am I good to go?"

His chest clenched. She couldn't get away from him fast enough. "Once I unhook the cables." He proceeded to do so. He shut the hood on her Camaro, added, "The charge should get you home. Get a new battery, soon. I may not be around to jump you next time."

Jump her. All in the interpretation. He hadn't meant it to be suggestive, but she took it that way. She bit down on her bottom lip, blushed. He stepped away from her car, expecting her to leave. Pedal to the metal. She backed up, then braked. Her fingers flexed on the steering wheel. Tension, indecision.

She glanced his way. Managed a soft, "Thank you."

He nodded. "Welcome."

A second's hesitation before she drove off.

He watched her go until her taillights disappeared.

He wished she would turn around. Not tonight. Maybe not ever.

Zane got a decent night's sleep. Surprising after his encounter with Tori and the dead battery. She'd held him at arm's length the whole time. He needed a way to get closer. He'd figure something out. After a shower and shave, he toweled dry, then finger-combed his short, damp, military haircut. No brush was needed. He planned to let his hair grow out now that he'd retired. He drew old clothes from his dresser drawer. A worn black T-shirt and white-at-the-seam jeans. No belt. Next came athletic socks and steel-toed boots.

He left his bedroom and walked down the hallway to the kitchen. His grandfather's stilt house was old, but it never smelled musty. It had a lived-in feeling that took him back to his youth; back to family cookouts, games of hide-and-seek in the orange orchard, and lazy afternoons on the porch swing. His grandmother had once squeezed the best lemonade.

He stood in the living area and looked around. There was a hominess in the blue-and-green-braided rugs scattered over the hardwood floor. A hutch in one corner still held his grandmother's commemorative and collectable plates. Time had stopped for the grandfather clock. Both hands on twelve. An upright piano sat quietly. It hadn't been played in years.

The wicker papasan chair was his favorite piece of furniture, large and bowl-shaped with a discolored gold cushion. The L-shaped long sofa and matching side-sectional were reupholstered in durable brown fabric. His gramp's one-time biggest splurge had been a seventy-five-inch television. Four split-screens brought the family together to watch sports.

Everyone could track their favorite team.

His grandpa Frank had encouraged Zane to take over his residence. He preferred that the place not sit empty after his move to the retirement village. Zane had taken the older man up on his offer, making the stilt house his home.

Breakfast was easy. He juiced hand-picked oranges from the orchard. Toasted a rye bagel. He walked outside and surveyed the morning from the front porch. Clear sky. Static air. A hot day ahead with seasonal afternoon showers. It was six thirty, and Zane was headed to work. A new day. A new job. With light traffic, he arrived in twenty.

Gray's Garage was located on a busy corner, three blocks from the beach. There were two entrances. Zane entered the lot from the east, just as Tori in her Camaro drove in from the west. Business was good this morning. Three mechanics were already at work in the bays. The parking lot was nearly full of vehicles in need of maintenance or repairs. He motioned to Tori, pointed to a space nearest the office. She pulled in. He protected his Impala by choosing a spot between the security chain-link fence and the tow truck. Snug, but safe.

He cleared the car door seconds before she rounded the front bumper. She looked damn good in the morning. Always had with her braided ponytail, fresh face, and soft mouth. He liked her white top with lace and beads at the neckline and her pinstripe shorts. What he didn't like was her stiff-fingered poke to his chest. Annoying.

He grabbed her by the wrist, slowed her assault. "What's with you?" he asked.

Her blue gaze sparked. Her color was high. Her lips pinched. "With you, don't you mean?" Her voice was as stiff as her spine. "I'm here. You're here. I came for a new battery, as you recommended. There's no need to check up on me. I'm at Gray's and no longer need your help. Go away." She jerked her hand free.

Her assumption amused him. It was a mistake that he didn't immediately rectify. She brought passion to her anger. Her breathing was uneven. There was an indignant rise and fall of her breasts. Her nipples visibly puckered within the cups of her bra. Sexual agitation shifted her hips. She tapped her foot. He let her simmer. She was good at it, especially when it came to him.

He sidestepped and shut the car door. They stood so near now that they almost touched. A further inch, and they would be right up against each other. His body reacted with flexing fingers, itchy palms, a tightening of his abdomen. Spiraling heat and uncontrollable arousal, inspired by their closeness. Significant boner. He was a goner.

The rise in his Levis startled her. Her eyes widened. Her throat worked. Uncertain, flustered, she stumbled in her retreat, causing one thong strap on her purple flip-flop to break. She barely managed to stay upright. She collected the rubber sole and continued across the parking lot, one foot bare. She entered the office without a backward glance.

Zane gave his dick a moment to chill. He then strolled behind her. He passed through the bays, acknowledging the other mechanics with a nod or thumbs-up. He would personally take the time to speak with each man once he'd dealt with Tori.

A line had formed inside the office. Zane kept off to the side, concealed by a stack of retread tires. Wilbur Gray and the counter girl, Annie Harper, listened to the customers' concerns and filled out the necessary paperwork. The jobs were then divided between those repairs requiring no more than an hour and those in need of an entire day. The garage had a full schedule ahead. Zane liked being busy.

The line crept forward. Tori fidgeted. She kept glancing out the window. No doubt hoping he'd split. He stood within ten feet of her now. She unzipped her wallet and removed her checkbook. She flipped it open, scanned the check entries. Apparently her balance was low because she deflated on a sigh.

Annie left the counter for the storeroom, hunting down a pair of windshield wipers, while Wilbur conversed with a man holding an accident report, seeking an estimate.

Wilbur caught sight of Zane. The older man recognized Tori and marked Zane with a look. "You a silent or working partner?" he asked. "Care to help the next person in line?"

That would be his ex.

He circled the tires and got behind the counter, face-to-face with Tori. Her expression was disbelieving. His partnership rattled her far worse than his boner.

"What can I do for you?" he politely asked her.

"You, nothing." She was resolute. "I'll wait until Mr. Gray is free."

Wilbur overheard her. "Sorry, but it's going to be a while. I have to assess damages for an insurance company."

Disappointment clouded her eyes. She was stuck with Zane. "I need a new battery, as if you didn't know."

He knew, all right. Still he treated her like any other customer. "Model and year of your car."

She drew a breath. "A 2000 Camaro."

He nodded, then worked his way down the counter to the computer. He searched the inventory. "Six- or eight-cylinder?"

Really? Her look said it all. "Six."

He knew her Camaro as well as his own Impala. He had tinkered with the engine in high school. He'd kept

the Chevy running smooth. The car was older now. Lots
of wear and tear. Repairs would be more frequent. Today
a new battery. Tomorrow an alternator. A radiator leak in
a month.

The computer produced the info. He glanced her way
and found her staring a hole in him. He'd provoked her.
Lady was unhappy. The garage was known for its cour-
teous and prompt service. For its repeat business. Zane
upheld the policy. He smiled, said, "We have a range of
batteries. From our best-selling Duralast at two hundred
twenty-one dollars, warrantied for three years, to a less
expensive Econocraft, priced at sixty-nine ninety-nine,
with a three-month warranty. Both are in stock."

She went silent over the cost. She rested her elbows on
the counter and clutched her hands together. Her cheeks
heated. She was embarrassed by her lack of funds.

He was presently part owner of the garage and would
soon own it outright. No one would question his decision. He suggested, "Open an account, and charge the
Duralast. It will pay off in the long run. Twenty-minute
installation and you'll be on your way."

Still she was hesitant. She didn't want to owe him. But
she had little choice. She had to think of her grandmother
and couldn't afford to get stuck at work again.

She justified the cost with, "Half down now . . . half on
account."

He saw Wilbur's nod of approval from the corner of his
eye. Zane felt good about his decision. He would have
given Tori the battery, for free, but she would've pitched a
fit, claiming she could take care of herself.

"Don't forget her discount," Wilbur added. "Ten percent for locals."

"Got it." Zane was grateful to the older man. Wilbur
had just made the battery even more affordable. Zane rang

up the sale. "No need for the credit application," he told her. "We know you. You're good for the balance."

She wrote out the check and handed it to him. Their fingers brushed. A fire touch. Electricity zapped. An intimate engagement. Friction and foreplay. An inseparable fusion. The interaction was quick but undeniable.

She shivered.

He radiated heat.

He took a long filling breath.

Her own breath left her on a rush.

Wilbur cleared his throat. He gave Zane a knowing look. Customers were now crowded into the office. The single line had expanded to three, six deep, from door to counter. Zane resumed the transaction. He placed her check in the cash register. Preoccupied, he nearly slammed his fingers in the drawer. He pulled himself together.

An intercom connected the office and the bays. Zane called out to his mechanics, requesting a battery installation. Middle-aged Wiley Litton responded: all the bays were full; all the technicians were elbow deep in car engines.

"A do-it-yourselfer," came from Wilbur. "Tori's parked close. Grab the new battery, needed tools, and change it out in the lot."

Zane eyed Tori. "Can do, unless you'd rather wait for another mechanic."

She glanced at her watch. "Go for it. I'm working the lunch shift at Zinotti's today. I've errands to run before my shift."

"The customer waiting area is standing room only, but it has soda and snack machines. Otherwise you can watch me work." He gave her a choice.

"Will my watching make you go faster?"

"A good mechanic doesn't rush a job." He left her and

went to the storeroom, where he loaded the Duralast onto a small cart. Back to the shop for battery pliers, a combination wrench, and a wire brush to clean the corrosion from the battery cable connectors.

Tori had retreated to her Camaro. She'd popped the hood and now leaned against the front fender. He proceeded to remove and replace the battery. She watched him closely. Too closely, as if she were afraid he'd screw her over.

The morning heat made his brow sweat. He rubbed his forehead on the shoulder of his T-shirt. He met her gaze with a look to back her off. "I've done this before, once or twice."

"Not on my car."

As if he'd make a mistake.

She kept right on staring, up until the arrival of his sister Shaye on her turquoise Beach Cruiser bike. The bicycle had wide white-wall tires and a padded seat. A perfect ride for coastal cruising. Shaye climbed off, set the kickstand, and then gave him a hug. She would always be his baby sister, even at thirty-four. All four older brothers remained protective of her, and she of them. With the Cateses, it was all about family.

"Hey, kid, nice of you to stop by," he said.

"I came over to wish you well. This is your first day as co-owner, and Wilbur has you replacing a battery in the parking lot?"

"The bays are all full, and the lady's in a hurry."

Shaye looked beyond the hood and spotted Tori. "I thought that was your Camaro."

"Old, but still running," Tori returned with a smile for her former sister-in-law.

"I gave up my car for a bike," said Shaye. "Fresh air and exercise. Plus I can stop and visit with tourists. Welcome them to town."

Shaye was sociable, outgoing, and married to Trace Saunders. She was the president of Barefoot William Enterprises, and her husband was CEO of Saunders Shores. They were a power couple. Since their marriage, the two cities had often joined forces on projects that benefited both municipalities.

Zane sensed Shaye's curiosity, along with Tori's slight withdrawal. The two women had always gotten along. They'd never been as close as sisters, but they had upheld a friendship over the years. Though somewhat distant.

"What's up?" he asked Shaye while he made sure the cable connections were properly tightened. The new battery was secure. All good. All done. He dropped the hood.

Shaye looked from him to Tori, then back to him. Her gaze narrowed. "You missed the family meeting yesterday evening."

"I went out for pizza instead."

"We had pizza at the beach house."

"Not from Zinotti's."

"So that's how it is," said Shaye.

"It isn't what it seems," Tori quickly inserted.

"Yes, it is." Zane was straight with his sister. "I'm back in town and wanted to see my ex. Even if she didn't want to see me. She left work and had car problems, a dead battery, which I charged. Enough said."

Shaye's lips twitched. "Swear, not another word."

Their exchange left Tori uneasy. Zane had implied his desire to see her last night. Shaye now knew too. But Tori couldn't afford his pursuit. Her heart wouldn't survive another round with this man. Pain from their divorce still followed her everywhere. Now the man himself was on her heels. It was time for her to leave.

She tugged open the car door, only to have Shaye stop her. "Hold on, Tori," she appealed. "I want to share my idea for a new beach promotion with both of you."

It felt odd to be included in Cates business. Tori reminded herself that Shaye had never done anything to hurt her. Tori's letdown had come from Zane. It would be rude of her to gun the engine and speed off. So she leaned against the door and listened.

"Picture this—" Shaye paused for effect. "I want to convert the lifeguard tower shacks into boutique hotel suites. Two-story dream suites for the beach lover." Shaye's eyes twinkled, her smile was bright, and her enthusiasm contagious. "I'd like to refurbish, redecorate, and roll out rooms situated on the sand. We already have the lifeguard shacks. They're spread up and down the beach, built on short stilts and buffeted by the waves. All we have to do is paint them with whimsical designs and cheerful colors, then fit out the interiors, taking advantage of those unobstructed ocean views. Tourists would just love to be able to spend a night in one."

Zane scratched his jaw. Reserved his judgment. Even though his expression was dubious.

Tori, however, was captivated. She thought it was a wonderful idea. Innovative and creative. The lifeguard shacks would become memorable landmarks to turn heads.

Shaye could barely contain her excitement. "The East Coast resorts started the trend," she continued. "Trace and I drove to Miami Beach last weekend and checked them out. The lifeguard stations were unique and amazing. So cool. One tower resembles a lighthouse with red and white stripes. Another, inspired by *The Jetsons* cartoon, was round and hot pink. A third resembled a Mardi Gras float painted green, purple, and yellow."

Zane took in her descriptions. Still unconvinced.

Tori, on the other hand, could already picture the boutique accommodations. Vividly.

"Guests staying in the suites could be beachside casual

by day, enjoying the ocean and the boardwalk in their bathing suits, yet when night falls, there could be formal evening room service at the individual towers, a sleep-tight massage, along with luxurious bed linens." Shaye tilted her head. "Family vote. What do you think?"

"How did the others respond?"

"They're in, but I want to make it unanimous."

He slowly relented. "I think you've already made up your mind. You'd debate me to death until I agreed with you."

"Yeah, pretty much so."

Tori smiled to herself. Shaye was smart. Barefoot William benefited from her business savvy. She knew how to finagle her brothers. The final vote would be in her favor.

"Your contractor?" Zane wanted to know.

"Cates and Burke."

Tori recognized the company. Zane's brother Aidan and his partner Mike were well established throughout the state. They'd put up office buildings, restaurants, hotels. Locally they'd built the Richmond Rogue Spring Training Facility. Several years ago, Aidan had presented Shaye and Trace with an amazing beach house as a wedding gift. She'd driven by the outside but had never seen the inside. The back of the house faced the street; the front gazed out at the ocean. An ancient banyan tree spread its branches across much of the grounds and formal garden. An enormous dolphin fountain spouted water.

"What about the lifeguards?" Zane went on to ask. "Where will they relocate?"

"Dune suggested that we don't convert all the stations, just the biggest ones," she explained. "There will be plenty left for the lifeguards to use."

Tori liked Dune. The oldest Cates brother had played professional volleyball. He'd retired and married Trace

Saunders's sister Sophie. Dune ran volleyball camps for as-
piring athletes. Sophie was now curator of the Barefoot
William museum. She showcased the history of the town.

"Further concerns?" Shaye inquired.

Zane's gaze was on Tori, although he directed his question to his sister. "Interior design. How will the firm be
chosen?"

Tori's heart skipped. She was curious as well.

Shaye grew thoughtful. "I'll form a committee. We'll
advertise the project. Get media coverage. We'll review
portfolios and put a premium on creativity. I would want
detailed layouts. We'll be converting five towers, and I'll
hire five different designers. Diversity is important."

Shaye was two years younger than Tori. High school
was ages ago. Shaye wouldn't have remembered Tori's
passion for design or her acceptance to Pratt Institute.
Tori kept quiet and didn't jog her memory. There was
no point. What she did do was take the information to
heart. She'd lived a colorless existence since her divorce.
Participating in the tower renovation would give her life
purpose and meaning. Realistically, she wasn't qualified.
No experience in her mind to speak of. No portfolio. No
credentials. No hire. Shaye would choose an established
designer, not an unknown. That left Tori out of the picture. Disappointing.

It was time for her to leave. "Good luck." She wished
Shaye well with the project. "Appreciate the replacement
battery," she mumbled to Zane. He had missed a family
meeting the previous evening to eat at Zinotti's. To jump
her car battery. A small part of her was grateful for his
help.

Shaye waved her off.

Zane's stare was reflected in her rearview mirror.

Tori turned onto Spoonbill Boulevard. Brother and sister went back to their discussion.

Time had gotten away from her. She entered the apartment to find the manager's wife sitting with Nana Aubrey. Doreen was a lifesaver. Tori made sure the woman had a copy of her weekly work schedule. In case of an emergency. Doreen came and went, still protective of her grandmother after all these years. Oswald looked up on her arrival. The faithful companion wagged his tail but didn't get up. Old age and tired bones left him lazy today.

"I came home to fix Gram lunch before heading to Zinotti's," she told Doreen.

"I was just leaving," said Doreen. "I'll check on your grandma mid-afternoon. Offer her a snack."

"There are Fig Newtons in the cookie jar. Gram's favorite."

Doreen gave a thumbs-up on her way to the door. "Got it."

Tori crossed to the rocking chair, where she gently hugged her grandma about the shoulders, then kissed her on the cheek. "Lunchtime," she announced. "It's early, but I work the noon shift today. What can I get for you? A tuna salad or sliced turkey sandwich?"

"Tu-" Nana Aubrey struggled.

Both words started with tu. "Nod for me," Tori requested. "Tuna?" Nothing. "Turkey?" A short bob of her gram's head. "Spiced apple rings?" The older woman gave a small smile.

Tori prepared her grandmother's lunch in record time. She delivered the plate, then treated Oswald to a Milk Bone. He still had quite an appetite and an even bigger appreciation for snacks. It disappeared in seconds.

A quick change into her work clothes, and she left the apartment. The Camaro turned over with ease. She was indebted to Zane. Seeing him was tough, yet it was twice as difficult knowing that he was now part owner of Gray's Garage. He wouldn't be leaving Barefoot William anytime soon. He'd always loved flying and mechanics. But now planes were behind him. Cars ahead of him.

His future was in a good place.

She had yet to dig herself out of the past.

She arrived at the pizza parlor with five minutes to spare. She'd worked for Eddie for nearly two decades. He still scowled darkly whenever she cut it close. Blu often arrived right on the hour. A human blur, sprinting through the back door and into the dining room. Today was no exception. Tori tossed Blu her order pad when she flew by.

"Talk later," said Blu.

Later would be four thirty, once their shift ended and the dinner crew punched the time clock. Eddie always ran a lunch special, and this afternoon Tori cranked out chicken parmesan subs until her fingers cramped. There was a rapid turnover of booths. Two soon opened, and Zane sat down in one.

Awareness quickened her pulse. Reflection squeezed her chest. There was no denying Zane was a good-looking guy. Female customers openly admired him. There was something solid and sexy about a man who worked with his hands. He was a fine mechanic. He was also a heart breaker. To which she could attest.

She didn't want him showing up every day. So she took off her apron and wore her attitude as she left the kitchen for the dining area. Eddie was nowhere in sight. She could confront Zane without her boss breathing down her neck. She crossed to his booth, looked down. He was slow to look up. His expression surprised her. Always self-assured, he appeared hesitant now. The expression was fleeting, yet not lost on her. A blink of her eye, and he returned to his old self. Strong and confident. His gaze warmed, connecting with hers like an invisible embrace. Searing and unbreakable. She fought the urge to sit down and join him.

With great effort, she managed to step back. To distance herself by a foot. She swallowed hard, stood firm.

She kept her voice low, asking him, "Why are you here?"

"It's my lunch hour."

"You could've chosen a restaurant closer to the garage."

"I wanted pizza."

"You ate pizza last night."

"Call it a craving."

He wanted her. It was apparent in his eyes, his tone, and, when she glanced down, his erection. Damn the man. Too little, too late. His attempt to win her back would be unsuccessful. She'd once loved him with all her heart, with an all-consuming passion. She refused to weaken now.

She turned away, informed him, "Blu will take your order."

"Can't I just tell you what I want?"

"Blu has the order pad."

"You can't remember a medium pepperoni pizza from here to the kitchen?"

"I remember much, Zane," she stiffly said. "Memories that will stick with me forever. Your pizza order is forgettable."

His face fell. "Ouch."

She left him then, returning to the kitchen, her spirits low. Within minutes, Blu stuck his guest check on the orders wheel in the service window. She rolled her eyes. Mouthed, *Man likes his pizza.*

Her meaning wasn't lost on Tori. He was a Cates with an extensive reach around town. Yet he couldn't touch her. She had to be sure he understood that fact. They needed to talk. Seriously. No more hot pursuit.

He ate and left before she could schedule a meeting with him. Blu flashed a Ben Franklin through the order window. "Damn, girl. From Zane to you, a one-hundred-dollar tip. He enjoyed the pizza. Compliments to the chef."

She was stubborn. He couldn't buy her. "I don't want it."

"Zane thought you'd say that. He suggested you could make a payment on your new battery."

How thoughtful of him. He grated on her nerves. She disliked having him circling around her, giving her money to close out her bill at his garage. She would pay off her bill in good time. With her money, and not his.

Still she pocketed the bill with every intention of returning it to him when their paths next crossed. Their shift came to an end, and the women walked out the back door together. They crossed to Blu's MINI Cooper and leaned against the hood.

Blu yawned, said, "That was one hell of a long shift."

Tori agreed. "It felt like a double."

Blu cut her a look. "So what's the deal with Zane?"

"He's coming onto me."

"You're off him?"

"I can't go back."

"Never?"

"Never ever."

"He's going to be a hard man to resist."

"I have to put my foot down. He needs to back off."

"Like he'll listen."

Tori sighed. "He has to."

"Good luck with that."

"I should be fine. Mercury's not in retrograde."

"You and your astrology."

"You believe fortune cookies."

"At least the messages are always positive."

"*A hot man is coming toward you,*" Tori intoned, pretending to quote a fortune.

"Where?" Blu whipped around and was confronted by

Race Wallace. He stood directly before her, deep in her space. So close, in fact, that one of his knees parted her thighs. "Crap, it's you."

"I'm glad to see you too."

"What are you doing here?" Blu always had it together. A tough girl with a smart mouth. Yet today she seemed flustered.

"I texted you earlier."

"I haven't checked my messages."

"I'm here now."

"Why?"

"We're no longer teenagers. Man to woman, date me, Blu."

She snapped her fingers. "Just like that?"

"You've been waiting for me."

"Have not."

"Have too. We have unfinished business." Sex.

Blu never blushed, but she did now. Heat crept up the back of her neck and colored her cheeks. "Tonight's not a good time."

"We'll make it good. Give us a chance."

Tori shook her head. Their chemistry would heat up anyone in their proximity. It was time to head out and let them privately settle their evening plans. She waved. "Tomorrow, Blu."

"Unless I stop by later tonight."

"You won't," Race predicted. "Your night is with me. Breakfast too."

"Smug bastard."

"I'm not arrogant, just confident."

Tori reached her car, climbed in. Out of earshot. She silently wished Blu well, on whatever outcome they decided upon. She drove home to fix supper for her grandmother. Meat loaf and mashed potatoes. Scoops of strawberry ice cream for dessert.

She cleaned up after dinner, but restlessness claimed her. She was anxious, fidgety, and too keyed up to watch television. She needed to move. The summer evening would be light outside until nine o'clock. A walk, some fresh air, would ease her tension. She needed a place to think.

The Barefoot William Pier came to mind. She had walked its length nightly following the divorce and after Zane left town. It was one of the few places she felt she could breathe. She changed clothes, opting for a blue halter-top and jeans. She called Doreen and asked the apartment manager's wife to look in on her grandmother at least once while she was gone. She would be out no more than ninety minutes. She promised Gram a basket of fried Oreos.

Florida was hot during the summer, and the tourist trade slowed. Tori parked near the entrance to the pier. She exited the Camaro and strolled across the boardwalk. She was in no hurry. Every step drew a memory. Many were good, others not so happy. Forgive and forget: that was her motto. She had tried so very hard to forget Zane and move on with her life. Sadly, she was stalled in the past. And she was still too broken to forgive him. Blu had suggested she date. Numerous men had asked Tori out. None were Zane. That was the problem. Her first love lived on. A fact she couldn't shake.

Years later, the same kiosks continued to sell sunglasses, boomerangs, and baskets of chili fries. The Ferris wheel circled and the merry-go-round turned. Her favorite wooden horse raced by. Purple with a gold saddle and amber eyes. Next to the carousel, the bumper cars were activated. Metallic black with white racing stripes. Drivers accelerated, brushed and bumped each other. Cheers and laughter echoed on the air.

She passed Shades, the sunglass kiosk. She'd kept the

two pairs of sunglasses Zane had once bought her. They were wrapped away in her dresser drawer. The Boomerang Hut was the busiest of the pier concessions. She could still picture Zane tossing six at a time and catching each one. Such a pro.

Dusk crept in. The sun dropped like a golden ball. A countdown to nightfall. She closed in on the end of the pier. Benches flanked the sides. She sat down and stared out over the Gulf. Waves peaked, then broke against the cement pilings. A light breeze stirred, lifting the hair at the back of her neck, right before her skin prickled and goose bumps rose. Only one person prompted that sensation. Zane Cates. She dipped her head, closed her eyes, and prayed he'd walk away.

He did not. The scent of lime and man reached her first. Followed by his weight on the bench as he dropped down beside her. So near they touched from arms to thighs. "Come here often?" He kept it light when her heart was heavy.

She blinked her eyes open. "Not often enough."

"The pier's a great place to clear your head."

"Which I was attempting to do."

"Before I showed up and darkened your thoughts."

He had that right. "How did you know I was here?" she wanted to know. Doreen wouldn't have told him. So who?

"The Cateses are a grapevine of news," he answered her. "Two relatives saw you and texted me."

"Spies?" She was not pleased.

"They know that I care and am concerned for your well-being."

"Don't be," she said firmly. "You left your concern behind years ago. I"—she drew a breath—"need you to leave me alone."

"You don't mean it."

"We're older now. You have no idea what I mean and what I don't."

"I used to be able to read your mind."

"Trust me, you don't want to know what I'm thinking now."

"That bad, huh?"

"Worse than you can ever imagine."

"Damn." He grew silent, eventually saying, "I know we're worth saving."

"Time changes people."

His expression tightened. "You feel nothing, absolutely nothing, for me?"

"Nothing." A whopper of a lie.

A muscle jumped along his jawline. "I need one last chance with you before I live with your decision."

One last chance sounded ominous.

"I want us to attend couples counseling," he initiated. "I've researched Glen Glade, a highly recommended retreat located in the middle of the state. The therapists provide on-site, three-day, individualized sessions. Once there, we attempt to work through our issues. It's a weekend of gut honesty. Whatever the result, I will honor the outcome."

"Even if it means we're over?"

"I'm hoping for a new beginning."

"I'm looking for closure."

"Either way, will you give it a shot?"

She'd never heard Zane plead. His appeal touched her. He sounded desperate. She sighed. They'd been broken for so long. Therapy was only a Band-Aid. She held little hope for more.

But her heart engaged before her mind. "I'll go if Eddie will give me time off and I can find someone to stay with Gram."

"I have a cousin who owns Care and Compassion, a private live-in and overnight nursing service. I'll ask Karen to personally stay with Nana Aubrey. Don't sweat Eddie. You work seventy-hour weeks. He owes you time off."

Tori gaped. Zane had covered her bases. He was steps ahead of her. She couldn't allow him to take full control. She slowed him down. "I'll think about it."

"Think yourself into my Impala at noon on Friday. Glen Glade is a two-hour drive. I'll schedule the weekend and cover all costs." Instructions given. The end. He stood, leaving her and any further resistance behind.

Bossy man. She watched him walk away. Her ex-husband. Tall, wide shouldered, tight butt. He had the notable strut and swagger of a Cates. Her heart squeezed when he disappeared into the crowd.

Out of sight, but not out of mind.

Seven

Lettuce Eat was an off-the-beaten-path vegetarian cafe. Seven o'clock in the evening, and Race Wallace sat beside Blu Burkhardt at a table for two, outside on the screen-enclosed brick courtyard. He'd suggested inside air-conditioning and atmosphere, but she'd preferred fresh air. Hot, humid air. The furniture was stylish but uncomfortable. Cast iron chairs in antique copper. No seat cushions. Not even the thin ones.

Eighty-five degrees was too hot for a sport jacket. So he shrugged off his tan suit coat and hooked it over the back of his chair. Tonight was all about impressing Blu. He wanted her to like him. Regrettably they had yet to connect. On any level.

Instead he sweated bullets. He unbuttoned the top button on his white dress shirt before rolling up the cuffs to his elbows. His Rolex flashed. He went on to loosen his brown and silver silk tie, then ran his fingers beneath the collar and tried to relax.

Difficult to do since his ass was numb and his feet had fallen asleep. Even his dick felt limp. He rolled his hip and stretched out his legs, restoring the circulation. This was not the scenario he'd pictured when he'd asked her out. He was not having a good time. The date was stressful. A total suck. Definitely not what he'd envisioned.

Earlier that afternoon, he had made a mental list of the five-star supper clubs on Saunders Shores, Barefoot William's sister city. He'd carefully narrowed his choices down to three. The Pier House for seafood. Angus J's for steak. Island Sunshine for Floribbean—a combination of Floridian and Caribbean cuisine. The restaurants all extolled fine dining, elegant atmosphere, and excellent service.

Blu had dismissed each one, then countered with rabbit food. He couldn't believe she'd talked him into patio dining. Lizards climbed the palm trees, and wild Quaker parrots perched on branches beyond the enclosed courtyard.

His earliest opinion of Blu was that she was feisty. She had a banging body. He was attracted to her smart mouth. She gave as good as she got. He had busted his balls to date her. He'd dressed up for her. Had gone all out with a haircut and polished wingtips. He wore his lucky boxers. Black silk.

Meantime, she'd dressed down for him. The spikes in her hair were now flattened against her skull. No makeup. Her gray blouse and black slacks were as subdued as her mood. She wore plain flat shoes, when she had the legs for stilettos. She was quiet, almost reserved.

He was good at reading people. Always had been. Yet there was little resemblance between his date and the hot waitress from Zinotti's. He certainly had misjudged her.

They'd barely spoken since he picked her up at the White Heron Apartments and seated her in his new black Lexus. The car was expensive and impressive. She'd hooked her seat belt and stared out the windshield, as still as a mannequin.

Awkwardness had him now asking, "Are you feeling okay?"

"Couldn't be better."

"Are we having fun yet?"

"The best time ever." Her expression was closed.

Who was she kidding? Certainly not him. "Yeah, me too."

A waiter in a khaki jumpsuit brought them glasses of iced water with lemon and lime slices and one-page laminated menus. "I'm Sean," he introduced himself. "I'll give you a few minutes to look at the dinner specials, then return to answer any questions."

Race was a speed-reader. He scanned the menu in seconds. He called Sean back before the young man got too far. "Where's the beef?" he asked.

Sean looked horrified. "Vegetarians don't eat meat, fish, or poultry."

That Race already knew. He wasn't stupid. Oftentimes a server would provide a discreet suggestion for those diners preferring something other than the selections on the actual menu. An accommodating special, prepared by the chef. He took a chance, was civil. "What can you offer a non-vegetarian?"

"A different restaurant."

Snarky dude. Race pursed his lips and let it pass.

"Give us a bit," Blu requested. Sean walked off, and she eyed Race. "I would be happy to offer suggestions or order for you."

"Do you eat here often?" He was curious.

"Often enough."

"I didn't take you for a plant-eater."

"You don't really know me, do you?"

True, not beyond the pizza parlor. That's why he'd asked her out. He thought she was hot and wanted to know her better. He went on to scan the menu a second time. He'd had his heart set on a thick, juicy steak. The hummus grilled pita and barbecue tofu sandwich weren't for him. Shit.

"Tell me about yourself," he tried. She just might spark to life, if he could get her talking. He wanted more than her stiffness and stare. Always before, there had been sexual fireworks in the air between them. Tongue in cheek, he tried, "What color panties are you wearing?" The question was intimate, and totally off the wall, but he was seeking a reaction.

"Who says I'm wearing panties?" she said straight-faced.

Testy, but nice. "You're flesh-toned then. My favorite color." He then gave her a chance to question him. "Your turn, ask me anything."

"Were you in the military?"

Really? That was the best she could do? She had to be joking. "You know I was in the Air Force, and subsequently a hurricane hunter, same as Zane." He too had just retired.

"Slipped my mind."

She made him seem forgettable. That pained his ass.

The waiter circled back to their table, his order pad in hand, just as Race asked her, "Your favorite drink?"

"Organic carrot juice. We'll take two large," she informed Sean.

Carrot juice—what the fuck? He rested his elbows on the table and leaned toward her. It was a small table, and they were nearly nose to nose. "You're ordering for me?" he asked.

"I only thought to be helpful."

She was not. He had never walked out on a date . . . he was too much of a gentleman. However Blu was not Blu tonight. She was a stranger to him, both bland and boring. Thus far their date was one sided. There'd been few pleasantries. One suggestive innuendo. No teasing exchanges. She'd left her personality at home. She wasn't even trying to make conversation.

He eased back an inch and yet remained close enough to see the gold flecks in her green eyes. Blank stare. No sparkle. "You on medication?" he chanced.

"Why would you ask?"

"You don't seem yourself."

"This is who I am."

He didn't believe her for some reason but couldn't explain why. "Go ahead and order for me when our waiter returns. You know what I like."

She shook her head. "Actually, I don't. You're a standard Table One at Zinotti's, bolting down a large pepperoni. I have no idea what you eat other than pizza."

His jaw worked. "Give it your best shot."

"Will do, Hot Shot," she replied, using his pilot call sign.

Each squadron placed its own brand on their new fighter pilots. Once a fighter pilot received mission-ready status in his first fighter squadron, it was time to be blessed with a tactical call sign. He was good to go to war.

The naming committee comprised squadron pilots who met in a wild-ass ceremony. Semi-secret and drunken. They'd selected Hot Shot for Race. It fit him. He was assertive, confident, and short on modesty. He knew himself better than anyone else. He was exceptional at most activities and often showed off his talents. Like him or not, it was who he was. Blu didn't seem to be liking him a lot tonight.

The date was a disaster.

Race eyed Blu narrowly when she returned to the menu. She tapped her fingers on the table. All contemplative. He sensed an underlying motive on her part and swore she was out to get him. He just didn't know why. He couldn't recall anything he'd done to offend her. Not one damn thing.

"Appetizers?" Sean asked.

"H-mmm," she murmured. "I'll start with creamy broccoli bisque, and Race will have dried bean curd with celery." A short pause. "As far as the main course, mushroom ravioli for me and black bean tofu for him." She glanced at him over the menu and innocently asked, "Okay by you?"

Double the beans? He'd be a gastrological mess. No way in hell. He cut Sean a look, said, "Cancel it."

The waiter sighed heavily, appearing put-upon as he scribbled out Race's order with his pen. "What would you prefer, sir?" he questioned.

Not much appealed. Filet mignon made his mouth water. Most items on this menu sounded like cardboard. "Quinoa soup and crusty bread to start, followed by—"

"A delicious roasted red pepper and pesto wrap or cauliflower and chickpea tacos," Blu put in.

Her suggestions sucked. "What are eggplant meatballs?" he asked Sean.

"A café favorite," the waiter explained. "They're made with tender sautéed eggplant, crispy panko bread crumbs, and Italian seasonings, smothered in rich tomato sauce."

"Do they actually look like meatballs?"

"Eggplant balls, sir. The size of small plums."

"How many on a plate?"

"A child's portion comes with two, an adult's with six."

"Two balls then." The smaller the serving, the easier the swallow.

"We have a café rule," Sean stated. "You're an adult, and even with a child's portion, you'll be charged for a full-size plate."

Super. Could the dinner get any better? "Do you sell beer? Liquor?" Race could use a Coors or a shot of whiskey.

Sean shook his head. "Only fresh vegetable juices." He tapped his order pad. "Two organic carrot coming up." He left them.

There were no other customers seated in the courtyard, so Race wasn't forced to whisper. "Who are you?" he had to ask her. He wondered if she had a secret twin or unresponsive clone.

"Blu Burkhardt, why?"

"You're not the Blu I know from Zinotti's."

"What Blu is that?"

"A woman who's into me."

"Into you . . . or your tips?"

"That was mean."

"That was true."

"Are you jacking me?" he asked.

"Jacking you how?"

"Purposely making this a bad date?"

She shrugged. "Not intentionally."

Something was off. A gut feeling. He found her more calculating than she would admit. "I've wanted us to get together for years. Beyond our quick supper six years ago at Molly Malone's diner when I was home on leave." Back then flirting, sarcasm, and a sexual high had seen them through their meal. She'd seemed receptive to him. For his own reasons, he'd backed off last minute. He was only in town for a few days. Starting up with her, then taking off wouldn't have been fair to either of them. They needed time to discover each other. To feel fully comfortable and compatible. So he'd walked her to the front door then walked away without a good-night kiss.

"We're here now. Our second date."

"Can you honestly say that you're having a good time?"

"Decent enough, why?"

"I'm not." Harsh, but honest.

She blinked. "Why is that?"

"I wanted fine dining and you chose a vegetable café."

"Vegetarian café."

"Same thing."

"Would you rather eat healthy or exercise regularly?"

"I eat what I want and I'm in great physical shape." He also had a healthy appetite for sex. "I have five percent body fat." A truthful claim.

She looked him over. "Where do you store that five percent?"

"You'd have to see me naked to find it."

"I've got a good imagination."

"Imagination doesn't come close to the real thing."

"Depends on who's doing the imagining."

Their waiter returned with two twenty-ounce carrot juices. Sean placed the glasses before them. "There's a hint of pulp in each one, Blu. Prepared to your taste."

Blu nodded. She reached for a glass and sipped slowly. "Perfect, Sean," she praised, then took a second sip.

Race refused to let her get the better of him. He swallowed a mouthful of juice and choked. A hint of pulp? Bullshit. Sean had lied. It was thick and scratchy, and stuck in his throat. He nearly gagged. He followed the juice with a long drink of water.

He gazed at Blu. Was it a play of light or had a corner of her mouth twitched? Was she messing with him? He wasn't certain. Either way, he didn't like it. "The pulp belongs in a compost pile or fed to chickens," he stated.

Blu frowned. "I'm sorry you don't like it."

"You apparently do, so drink it down."

"I will."

But she did not. He leaned back in his chair and watched

her closely. She took baby sips, not full swallows. Pulp stuck to her lips, and she licked it off. His gaze held on the flick of her tongue. Blu had a very sexy mouth. A perfect upper curve. Her lower lip was full, suckable. He had wanted to feel her mouth on him from the moment he'd met her. Not so much now. Her lips had an orange tinge from the carrot juice.

She dabbed her mouth with a napkin. Then came around and attempted conversation. "Now that you're back in Barefoot William," she said, "what's your next dream, Race?"

"You." Maybe, maybe not. He said it for shock value. He wanted a reaction out of her, any reaction. She'd been his fantasy woman for a long time. Tonight's reality shifted his perspective of her.

She didn't answer him directly. Instead she looked into his future. "You've no plans to become a commercial airline pilot? To fly for private jet charters?"

Her suggestions touched on his own thoughts. He was honest. "Trace Saunders approached me before my retirement about piloting his family's private jet. A Gulfstream G650, the jet can fit up to twelve passengers and fly over seven thousand miles non-stop. The Saunders family has properties and businesses all over the world. A solid option for me."

She surprised him with, "They also attend Rogue baseball games in Richmond. In support of Shaye's brother Rylan. Ry's thirty-five now, and remains the top centerfielder in the National League East. He's consistently voted in by the fans as a starter for the All-Star Games."

"You seem to know a lot about Rylan."

"I like him, and I've followed his career."

His gut tightened, forming a big old knot. "Like him how?" He hadn't meant to sound like a jealous boyfriend, but he did. Not cool. "You do know he's married, right?"

She eyed him strangely. "He's married to Beth, a sweetheart. She's a part-time party planner. She's put together several events and celebrations in town. I've attended most. She's detailed and amazing. Her parties are always a good time. We've gotten to know each other fairly well."

"Do you know Atlas?" he asked. Ry's Great Dane was the size of a pony.

"I've dog-sat for Rylan's dogs. Not only Atlas, but his golden retriever and the two dachshunds. Atlas's favorite snack is pumpkin and oatmeal biscuits. Chicken jerky sticks are a close second."

She took another sip of her carrot juice. Her cheeks puckered and she quickly swallowed. The pulp was sticky, and she again wiped her mouth. She'd drunk less than half the glass when Sean brought their appetizers. Steam rose from both the broccoli bisque and quinoa soup. Blu picked up her spoon, scooped, and blew on a small amount. Savoring came next, followed by a low sensual moan. "Excellent," she told Sean. "So thick and creamy. Seasoned to perfection."

Race was puzzled. She was lukewarm with him, yet orgasmic over a freakin' bowl of bisque. His own yellow quinoa soup was bland. So little flavor. Warmed water with uncooked seeds. He pushed it aside. Blu delighted in her every spoonful. To the point of annoying him. He was hungry. His juice and soup didn't cut it.

He drank his iced water while watching her eat. She was happy and he was frustrated. So he winged it and played Would You Rather with her. A time killer. He said whatever came to mind. "Would you rather be here, having dinner with me, or at home eating ice cream and watching television?"

"Depends on the flavor of ice cream and what's on TV."

She'd skirted that question easily enough. "Would you rather watch a scary movie or a romantic comedy?"

"I like movies that touch me and make me think."

"Touch you where?"

"Mentally."

Sean appeared the second she finished her bisque. Her bowl was clean. Race had barely touched his soup, so he broke off a piece of crusty bread, popped it in his mouth. Chewed. Swallowed. Crumbs littered the corner of the table. The waiter picked up their bowls and refreshed their iced water with extra lemon and lime. "The main entrees will be up in ten," he told them.

Race took those ten minutes to ask her trivial questions to fill the awkward silence. "Would you rather have one wish granted right this second or three wishes granted tomorrow?"

She looked him deeply in the eyes. "I wouldn't waste a wish on having you disappear."

"Because I'm such great company?"

"We're getting through dinner."

"You've got three wishes saved for tomorrow."

"Lucky me. I will use them wisely."

She was responding to him, finally, so he kept going, "Funniest person in the room or most intelligent?"

"Everyone loves a clown."

"Run at one hundred miles an hour or fly at ten?"

"Fly."

"Invisible or too small to see."

"Invisible."

Her answers were getting shorter. She would soon shut down. Again. "A bad relationship," he eluded. "Would you rather dump someone or be the person getting dumped?"

"I don't do relationships."

Not the answer he'd hoped for. "Would you rather go forward or backward in time."

"Hindsight is twenty-twenty."

Sean delivered their dinners. Blu's mushroom ravioli smelled good and appeared edible. His eggplant meatballs were the size of grapes, not plums. Minor miscalculation by their waiter. Race wrapped up his meal in under a minute. He went on to watch Blu eat. Her full concentration was on her food. She never once looked up from the plate. She moaned and sighed with each bite. He wondered if she'd climax with dessert.

He was soon to find out. Sean collected their dishes, went on to recite the dessert menu. "Baked nectarines with slivered almonds. A chocolate, peanut butter, and avocado pudding. Or a lemon curd and yogurt parfait."

"Can you remove the avocado from the pudding?" Race asked Sean.

The waiter's eyes went wide. "No, we cannot. An avocado's neutral flavor and creamy texture makes it a wonderful substitute for dairy in desserts."

"I'll pass then," said Race.

"I'll have the nectarines," requested Blu.

The waiter beamed. "The café favorite." He left.

Race glanced around them. Outside the screened enclosure the Quaker parrots squawked loudly, their conversations far more interesting than Blu's and his own. He kept his eye on a sly green parrot with a yellow stomach as it squeezed through a small hole in the upper corner of the screen. The parrot made one overall swoop of the courtyard, then came to land on Blu's shoulder.

She didn't flinch. "Look who's here." She spoke to the bird. "Hello, Artie."

"*Ahhh, Blu,*" the parrot mimicked in a Romeo tone. He beak-kissed her on the nose. Twice.

Race sat transfixed. He wouldn't have believed it, had he not seen it. "Artie's coming onto you," he said. A gentle peck on her nose, and the bird was getting more action than Race.

"We're friends," she told him. "Best friends, actually, when he's hungry."

"*So hungry,*" the parrot moaned in a starving voice.

"He can have my remaining bread crumbs," offered Race.

She shook her head. "It's not a good idea to feed him inside the screen. Sean has patched the hole a dozen times, but Artie always finds his way back in. We don't want him leading an army of parrots. Not all customers would be so welcoming. There are bird feeders spaced around the grounds, which are filled twice a day."

Race was curious. "He's tame?"

"At times. He's the only one of the flock that seeks human contact."

"Do the other parrots talk?" he asked. Squawking was one thing, actual words quite another.

"Some will mimic. Artie has an actual vocabulary. He's gifted."

"*Feed me, baby.*" The parrot was impatient. He picked at several strands of hair over her ear, spiking them. Race rather liked the spikes.

Blu smoothed them back down. "Soon," she promised.

Sean saved the day. He hurriedly crossed the courtyard with her dessert plate in one hand and a bag of sunflower seeds and slices of fresh fruit in the other. "Artie," he scolded the parrot. "Shoo!"

"*Shit!*" Artie squawked back. But he did fly off.

Blu actually smiled. A first. "Sean is our parrot police," she told Race. "He and Artie argue daily."

"How do you know that?" She must be a regular customer.

"I've seen their interaction on occasion."

Sean apologized all over himself. "I'm so very sorry. All my fault. I forgot to fill the bird feeders at the back of the café this morning when I arrived for work. I'll do so now. Artie won't bother you anymore."

The waiter cleared the screen door with Artie flying over his head. Race was amused. The parrot had brought comic relief to a floundering date. Across the table, Blu now breathed in the scent of baked nectarines topped with melted brown sugar, almonds, and whipped cream. She was so caught up in the dessert that she completely forgot about him. His dick stiffened, and he nearly came off his chair when she finger-scooped a bit of whipped cream, then tongue-swirled it into her mouth. Bite after bite, she hummed her pleasure at the back of her throat. Lady was a sexual foodie.

"Would you rather whipped cream or ice cream?" he had to ask once she'd finished.

"Whipped cream melts faster on warm flesh."

Which he already knew. But apparently so did she.

Sean soon brought their bill. He left it with Blu. "I've got it covered," she said. "The café was my idea. There's no reason for you to buy a dinner that you didn't enjoy."

He swiped the check from her. "I asked you out. I'll pay." He did so. Sixty dollars eaten up in a vegetarian meal. He tipped Sean fairly.

He glanced at Blu as they stood simultaneously. Was that regret in her eyes? Sadness? Doubtful, but if so, she recovered quickly. He hooked his sport jacket over his shoulder, shoved in their chairs. They wound around the empty tables on the patio and entered the café through a wide, wooden door. While the courtyard had remained empty, the inside dining room was packed. Full of happy, hungry vegetarians.

The main area was filled with garden images. Wall-size color photographs depicted both residential backyards and commercial plantations. An amazing vista of produce. Tomato vines climbed latticework in the corners. Herbs grew in window gardens. Lavender, sage, and lemon balm. Heavy oak picnic tables seated four to six diners. Several tables squeezed in eight.

Most everyone knew Blu by name. She was a local. They greeted her with warmth and familiarity. She was pleasant in return, far nicer to those seated or waiting in line than she'd been to him all evening. He still didn't get it.

They reached his Lexus, and Race held the car door for her. Dusk hovered over them, ready to close out the day. He had a night ahead of him that didn't include Blu. He drove her home, breaking the silence with additional Would You Rather questions. They were less than a mile from her apartment. Sex was off the table. Nevertheless his curiosity came out to play. He wanted to know what he would miss out on.

He wrapped up their evening with, "French kiss or close mouthed?"

He wasn't sure she'd respond, but she did. "Slow, soft, moist kisses."

Prolonged foreplay. Nice. His kind of woman. "One partner or multiple partners?"

"One satisfied man at a time."

He'd once slept with twins. The anticipation had aroused him more than the actual act. "Sex with the lights on or off?"

"Darkness. Let your fingers guide you."

"Over or under your man?"

"On top. Female empowerment."

He liked to be ridden. Lastly he dared. "Would you rather have me in your bed or the vibrator from your dresser drawer?"

"Buzz."

"Batteries run down. I don't."

"You'd take longer to recharge."

He shook his head. Total gut punch. They soon arrived at her apartment complex. He parked and walked her to the door. A handshake seemed safe. Less awkward. There'd be nothing worse than seeing her eyes go wide and hear her gasp should he try to kiss her, even on the cheek. So he offered his hand, and she took it. Her hand was small and soft. His was big and callused.

She slipped away from him and headed inside. She left him staring at the closed door. So be it. He rubbed the back of his neck. What the hell had happened? He'd never been more confused in his entire life. He had truly believed she was as into him as he was into her. His mistake. After this evening he felt he'd lost something. Something special.

Blu entered her apartment and closed the door. She leaned back against the wall and exhaled, sliding down to the floor. She sat there, knees drawn to her chest, hugging them. She was exhausted from her date with Race. She'd never had any man pursue her with such intensity. He called her his fantasy lady. She'd been afraid to agree to their date, simply because she could never live up to his imagination.

Once she finally agreed to go out with him, she immediately wanted to change her mind. To decline. Sarcastic flirting with him at Zinotti's was one thing, being alone with him quite another. She'd been attracted to him for a very long time. He made her hot with a look. His smile sent her pulse racing. His touch left her panties wet.

Over the years he had asked her out during each military leave or vacation. Except for one short-lived get-together, she'd purposely held him off. Insecurity gripped her. What if she disappointed him, didn't meet his expectations? He was permanently home now. Knowing that he was in town seduced her. She needed to protect herself from the intensity of her own feelings. From jumping his bones. Race was a total turn-on. She was half in love with him.

She had seen him arrive in a shiny Lexus. He'd gotten out of the sports car and walked along the sidewalk toward her apartment. One look at him dressed up for their date stole her breath. No man wore a suit better. Clean-cut and tailored looked good on him.

Time and again she'd witnessed women flirt and fall hard for the man. He was charismatic. Irresistible. She refused to be one of many. So she protected her heart and purposely sabotaged her chances with him. She'd dressed down, made herself look ordinary. No spiked hair. No sexy black dress or stilettos. Her choice of restaurant confused him. He'd eaten little and left the restaurant hungry. She'd heard his stomach growl in the car.

She'd barely made it through dinner herself. She became aroused just looking at him beside her at the table. So much so that she'd kept her gaze lowered for much of the meal. She'd feigned lack of interest. She'd succeeded. Race had looked both frustrated and discouraged when he'd dropped her off. She'd closed him down, satisfied her objective. Then why did she feel so bad? So lonely?

A small part of her would miss his constant pursuit. He'd made her feel desirable. Truth be told, she regretted not sleeping with him. He had a sexy mouth and a big, bad body. He exuded satisfaction. Maybe she had missed out. She would never know. She'd made her decision and must live with it. She would sleep alone.

She pushed to her feet. Sighed. She'd eaten little at the café. Her meal was delicious but not terribly filling. She was a small woman with a big appetite. She decided to eat again. A thick, juicy bacon cheeseburger would hit the spot. It was still early. Beachin' Burgers was nearby. Only a five-minute drive.

She exchanged her uninspiring outfit for a red off-the-shoulder top, skinny black jeans, and ruby rhinestone leather sandals. She spiked her hair, then tipped the ends with dangerous red. The Quick Touch dye dried in seconds. She looked like herself again. Bohemian Blu.

The fast food strip was hopping. Since it was a weeknight, the townies chose burgers, tacos, and pizza over the more expensive eateries. Blu pulled her MINI Cooper into the parking lot. It was packed, so she patiently waited for a space. Ten minutes later, a family climbed into their SUV and gave up their spot.

She entered Beachin' Burgers and inhaled deeply. The scent of fried foods tempted her. She stepped up to the counter and ordered: a half-pound bacon cheeseburger, large thick-cut french fries, and a root beer float. What she couldn't finish, she would take home. The burger joint served big portions, which always provided her with a second meal.

She was a people-watcher and decided to eat there. She knew almost everyone. She felt comforted by the crowd. A small booth sat empty toward the back, near the emergency exit. She sat and spread out. She rested her elbows on the table and unwrapped her thick burger, ready to dig in.

She closed her eyes and took her first big bite. The burger was juicy, the bacon crisp, and the cheese melted over her tongue. If her taste buds could smile, they would be grinning fools.

She heard approaching footsteps and ignored them. She was too busy taking pleasure in her burger. Her second bite was even better than the first. Her third made her sigh.

"Blu Burkhardt, is that you?" The deep male voice was immediately and frighteningly recognizable. She peeked at him through narrowed eyelids. *Race Wallace.* Oh . . . hell no! He zeroed in on her food. "How's the *beef* burger, babe? Taste good?"

She was unable to speak. She could barely swallow.

He joined her, lowering himself onto the seat without her permission. He had changed clothes as well. Now wearing a scripted *I'm Your Best Option* T-shirt, gray drawstring sweatpants, and a pair of black leather double strap sandals. He brought his own bag of food and an extra-large drink, and made himself at home.

Blu died a slow death.

Race unboxed his barbecue burger. "I see you like beef," he went on to say. "Me too."

She was cornered, caught, and eating meat. There was no hiding the evidence. She couldn't have devoured it fast enough anyway.

"We're of like mind," he casually commented. He then went on to address his evening, without mentioning her by name. "I had a dinner date earlier, but it didn't go well. Total bummer. Vegetarian café and we didn't connect."

She sipped her root beer float. "There must have been a reason."

He shrugged a broad shoulder. "Not sure what it might have been. No explanation, just rejection. I've known the woman for ages. I've chased her hard. I might've come on too strong at times, but it was the only way I knew to get her attention. We've flirted. Talked sexy. All superficial turn-ons. I'd always believed we had something more. Something that went deeper." He shrugged. "Guess I was wrong."

Blu munched a french fry. Quietly attentive. Beachin' was loud. Customers talked over each other. Still she whispered, "You date a lot of women. Flirting comes easy for you, but it's no foundation for a relationship. Maybe she didn't realize you were serious about her."

"Possibly." He took a bite of his burger, tongued the barbecue sauce from the corner of his mouth. A clean sweep.

She imagined he had a very talented tongue. "Perhaps your date believed she'd fall short of who you thought her to be. Maybe she was afraid for you to find out who she actually was." Truthful . . . incredibly difficult to admit.

He swiped one of her french fries and eyed her thoughtfully. "I have enough confidence for two men, but my date had me questioning myself too. She was sexy, smart. I knew she could do better than me."

Better than him. Not possible. His admission stunned her. Her hand shook, and her burger separated. The tomato and onion broke free of the bun. Landing on the wrapper. She stared at the vegetable slices. They appeared as displaced as she now felt. Unable to wrap her mind around his comments, she returned to their date. "Sometimes we need a second chance, because we weren't ready for the first."

"A second date would include a steakhouse."

"I'm not vegetarian, Race."

He eyed her burger. "So I see. So why Lettuce Eat?"

"I own the café."

He was taken aback. "You do? Since when?"

"Since last fall," she admitted. "I had saved nearly every tip I'd ever made since starting at Zinnoti's. The previous café owner became ill, and Lettuce Eat was sold below market price. It's a solid investment. The place has satisfied returning customers, it's charming—"

"If you're a rabbit."

"The café offers healthy eating and a garden ambience. Tori designed the interior."

He nodded. "She did a good job."

"I plan to stop working at the pizza parlor in a few weeks and spend all my time at the café."

"A great strategy."

She thought so too. It felt good sharing her future plans with him. His perspective added to her own. She found him a solid sounding board.

He drew a breath, and his amber gaze darkened when he again spoke. "I want you to know, Blu, that I'm as anxious as you when it comes to us."

"I never want to disappoint you."

"You never will." He sounded so sure.

"So what should we do?"

He smiled then, suggestively. "Second chances. Compensate me for the veggies."

"How do you mean?" She had a few ideas but wanted to hear his thoughts first.

He quoted her early answers to his Would You Rather questions. "Slow, soft, moist kisses. One partner. Stroking in the dark. Riding my thighs. And . . ." He was firm. "No vibrator. I'm better than batteries. I'll make your body hum."

Sex. She was ready for him. So ready that she packed up the remainder of her meal in anticipation.

He took the final bite of his barbecue burger and collected his trash. Then slid from the booth, deposited it in the receptacle.

"What's next?" she asked.

"How about us?"

"Us is good."

They'd driven separate cars. She wasn't ready for the luxury and prestige of his penthouse address, so he agreed to her place. He followed her home. She unlocked the door and let him in. Then flipped the wall switch and there was light. Four tall metal lanterns with heavy marble pedestals illuminated each corner of the room.

"Nice lighting," noted Race. He stood in the entryway and looked around. She fidgeted, hoping he would like her place.

He went on to circle the room. Eyeing pieces and commenting. "Cool furnishings. Really different."

"It's called shabby chic modern," she told him. "Unique and quirky, and decorated by Tori."

His brow creased in thought. "Wasn't Tori's goal in high school to become an interior designer?"

"She was accepted to Pratt Institute before her parents were killed in that plane accident off the Keys."

"That was tragic. Death puts life into perspective."

"True."

"I'm grateful my parents are still alive."

"My mom and dad are gone." She still felt the deep ache of losing loved ones. "Old age. I was their late-in-life child. They were forty-five when I was born. They're buried in the Barefoot William Cemetery." More information than he needed to know, but she had a need to share with him, nonetheless.

"I'll go with you next time you put flowers on their graves." His offer sounded sincere.

Also surprising and amazingly kind. Misty eyed, she swallowed the lump in her throat. "I'd like that. I go once a month."

He continued to make his way around the living room, eventually lowering himself on the old farmhouse sofa with flared arms and a cushioned pillow-back. "This couch is comfortable." He stared at the coffee table. "Is that an ironing board?"

"Tori's creation," she said, crediting her friend. "We found an old metal ironing board at the flea market. She removed the cover and padding, lowered and soldered the legs, then had a piece of glass cut for the top." Varied height beeswax honeycomb candles added intimacy.

"Imaginative."

"Tori's a wizard with design." She joined him on the sofa.

He raised an eyebrow. "Did you drink the wine before mounting the bottles on the rustic wood squares?"

The merlot bottles were now decorative flower vases, tied with gold gauze bows and filled with artificial red poppies and yellow sunflowers. "Tori and I had a glass or two."

"Three or four," he teased her.

"I can only offer iced tea tonight, if you're thirsty."

"I'm good."

"I bet you are." Her tone was too sultry, her words too explicit. Her cheeks heated.

"We'll be good together." He took charge. "Would you rather talk or wear only a smile?"

She grinned at him, her smile broad and telling.

He looked pleased. He reached for her, drew her close. "I'm hot for you, Blu. We may not make it to your bed."

"Right here?"

"Right now." His breath pulsed in her ear.

She sank against him. She nestled her cheek at his neck. She could smell him, his skin unadorned by cologne yet appealing and male, with his own unique scent. He gently tipped up her chin. He'd recently been to the beach, and his tan intensified the color of his eyes. A glowing amber. He embraced her with a look. One of long-held desire. A deep craving. Heightened anticipation.

He went on to sketch her face. He traced the curve of her brow with his thumb, then outlined the hollows beneath her eyes. His touch was feather soft. He skimmed her nose and over her cheeks, then cupped her chin with his palm. His thumb circled her mouth until her eyelids grew heavy and her lips parted on a sigh. She experienced a crazy little tremor of warmth and arousal.

She touched him too. Stroking over his shoulder and up his neck. His Adam's apple worked. His evening stubble shadowed his jawline. The air between her palm and his face felt heated, electric. He had amazing bone structure. Strong and sexy. She could stare at him for the rest of her life.

The thought shook her. She shivered.

He clasped her by the upper arms, lifted her up and onto his lap. She straddled his thighs. He began to rub her arms. "You cold?" he asked.

His concern touched her. "I was just thinking . . ." *what?* That she could face this man at bedtime and again at breakfast, and be the happiest woman alive. She hedged, "That I like you."

He was suddenly serious. "I like you back, babe."

"Are you just saying that for sex?"

"I've never told a woman I liked her to get her into bed." He kissed her on the forehead, confessed, "You've been on my mind forever. A constant in my life. I prayed for us, Blu, but I never thought we'd be in a relationship."

Her heart stuttered. "Are we in one now?"

"In our own extraordinary way, I think we've always been in one. We just haven't admitted it."

She felt much the same way. Their connection was undefinable, yet undeniable.

"I would have dated only you, had we gotten off to a better start. But you blew me off that first night at Zinotti's, calling me Table One."

"You were a rich kid and a known heartbreaker. I was

attracted to you, but you were still in high school and I was working full-time. You were soon to leave for the Air Force Academy. I was burned in a previous relationship when the guy I was dating up and left me. I'd been emotionally invested, he, not so much. Retail sales and career advancement took him to Atlanta. I would've gone with him, but he never asked. He broke up with me by phone, at the Florida-Georgia border." She sighed. "Afterward I distanced myself from men. Sarcasm replaced serious dating. I was protecting my heart when I met you."

"It's our time now. I want you to know I'd never purposely hurt you."

She believed him. "Be nice to me tonight."

"Very, very nice."

The promise of sex filled the room. Invisible, yet tangible. Their silence became foreplay. The moments stretched out as awareness became arousal. Desire pulsed.

His gaze was hooded as he tucked her into his body. His kiss transcended the years. Close-mouthed, slow, yet passionate. Prolonged and stimulating. Expectancy played between them, a sensual tease. They kissed until she shifted on his lap and his hips rolled. They both wanted more. Their clothes needed to go.

"Leave the lights on for our first time," he said. "I want to see you."

All of her. The lanterns were bright. She momentarily hesitated. She was happy with her life. Proud of her age, her mental stability, and emotional strength. Yet standing nude in front of a full-length mirror called out her flaws. She no longer had the figure of her twenties. Her skin remained fresh and youthful, despite several crinkles at the corners of her eyes. It had become harder to maintain her weight, even though she was active. Her breasts weren't as high and perky. Her once concave abdomen had rounded somewhat. She'd kept her stress level low. Race was the only one to raise her blood pressure, in both anger and arousal.

He sensed her insecurity and put it to rest. "I've imagined you naked for a long, long time. You're as beautiful now as you were back then. You have heart, Blu Burkhardt. Don't question how I feel about you. It's real," he promised.

They began undressing each other. He slipped her top over her head, and she removed his T-shirt. He was an eyeful. This man of muscular physique and sculpted face. His shoulders were wide. His ribs were strongly defined. His sweatpants pushed low, and his hipbones thrust up. The V-cut at his groin was pronounced. The shadow of his sex visible.

His big hands spanned her belly, and he palmed upward. Her bra hooked in the front. The fastener fell to a flick of his fingers. Her breasts were exposed. His gaze heated appreciatively. He eased the straps over her shoulders. Her bra fell to her waist. His release of breath was rough, rushed. Desire flared his nostrils. He stared, and stared. His head slowly lowered, and his amber eyes were hidden by his dark brown lashes.

Light as air, he drew a fingertip from her navel to her cleavage. She sucked in her stomach nearly to her spine. Making a fan of his fingers, he palmed one breast. She arched her back, and his hot mouth fasted onto a nipple. He laved with a swirling tongue. The sensation robbed her of mind and speech. She was so turned on she could no longer sit still.

So she moved on him. She squeezed his hips with her thighs. Then rocked her hips, seeking a deeper intimacy. That closeness would only come naked. She rose on her knees and removed her jeans. She unsnapped, unzipped, and then wiggled them over her butt and down her legs.

Beneath her, Race arced his hips and tugged off his sweatpants. He was free-ballin'. They tossed their clothes aside. Their sandals came next. Skin to skin, they heated up the couch. He was hard for her. She took in his erection and inhaled her approval. He moaned over her bikini tanga wax.

He could've entered her with the slightest shift of his hips. But he did not. She flexed her thighs. He felt so good wedged against her wet heat, all solid and hard. He traced the crease of her sex with his thumbs. Then fondled her with long, lazy strokes that left her liquid. He gave new meaning to prolonged foreplay. She squirmed, and he continued to tease her. He wound her tight. She was so turned on her pubic muscles clenched. She nearly mounted his fingers.

She breathed against his mouth, bit his lower lip. "Now?" She wanted him inside her.

He slipped the tip of his tongue between her lips. "Soon."

His control nearly killed her. She stroked his erection, and squeezed from base to tip, until he threw back his head and hissed through his teeth.

Hunger glittered in his eyes.

His skin pulled taut against his cheekbones.

His lips flattened in both pain and pleasure.

She increased the pressure, and he rocked his hips. His sex thrust between her palms. He panted, groaned, and his body pumped with lust.

His breathing strained. "Are you on birth control or do I need a condom?"

"We're safe."

He cupped her bottom, lifted her easily. He eased into

her, a streamlined surge of man into woman. They seized a rhythm that fit them both. Deep thrusts and grinding hips. A fierceness overtook them. She scratched his shoulders, and he squeezed her bottom. They kissed with equal passion. He drew her outside of herself and into him. A pulsating oneness.

They were both suddenly there.

She arched against him, her body raw and reaching.

His body strained against hers.

She was about to climax. Her sanity lost to hot sex.

He let her go. A final deep thrust, and he found her on the other side of their orgasm.

Both boneless. Mindless. Replete.

Their breathing was heavy in the stillness.

Exhaustion had them moving slowly. He rolled his hips. "My ass is cramped." Not very romantic, but the truth.

Her ankle twisted at an awkward angle. "Shower?" she suggested.

In minutes, warm, inviting water cascaded from the showerhead. The spray filmed their skin. There was nothing sexier than being touched beneath the sensual spray. Slowly, their awareness built again.

A selection of sponges hung from the shower caddy. She squeezed Ocean Blue shower gel onto a natural sea sponge. A clean, fresh, beachside scent. She bathed him slowly, thoroughly. The scrape of her nails followed the scrub of the sponge, over the rounded muscles of his shoulders, the masculine cut of chest, and his flat belly. He jolted when she caressed his erection. She gently squeezed, and his eyes dilated. He groaned low in his throat.

Melting heat and thick, swelling pleasure deepened the moment when Race captured the sponge, added more shower gel. Inch by soapy inch, he massaged her neck, her breasts, the curves of her hips. Her lips parted when he eased the sponge between the V of her thighs; the teasing force had her rocking against him. Needy, her stomach in knots.

He backed her against the slick, tiled wall. Curving his hands beneath her bottom, he lifted her against him. She wrapped her arms about his neck, her legs about his hips, and received him.

He slid into her.

She took him deep.

Their joining soon quickened.

Her pulse beat in time with his racing heart.

Ultimate pleasure brought them to orgasm at the same moment. They trembled. Shuddered. Convulsed.

Sated, he supported her with one arm as he turned off the water. They toweled each other dry. He carried her to her bedroom and lowered her onto the wing bed. He followed her down. Queen-size in light oak, the head and footboard resembled wings. Both ends were the same height and upholstered in a cream linen fabric. The mattress was heavenly soft.

They faced each other, their limbs intertwined. He folded her close. She became an imprint on his skin. A sexual tattoo, invisible, yet memorable. Her cheek rested against his chest, right over his heart. They made small talk. Then grew more serious. Their lives linked. They had a lot in common. More than either had ever imagined.

She felt a calmness she'd never known. Her heart was at peace. "Where do we go from here?" she softly asked. A need-to-know on her part.

He didn't miss a beat. "We discuss moving your furniture into my penthouse."

She startled, bumped her forehead on his chin. "Live together?"

"Either before or after we get married."

She was overcome. "You don't feel it's too soon?"

"Years too late for me, babe. My mind is made up. When you're ready, I'm ready."

"Let me sleep on it."

"You won't get much rest tonight."

"So you say."

"So I know."

Morning proved him right.

Eight

"You're mighty quiet," Zane noted of Tori as they sped down the interstate in his black Impala. The muscle car growled, rumbled, and the seat vibrated. The windows were rolled down. The air whipped. Despite the early July morning, the sun had yet to heat the day. They'd been on the road for two hours, traveling from Barefoot William to Glen Glade for an on-site, three-day couples' retreat. Friday through Sunday.

He'd executed the idea with hope in his heart. There'd been no further alternatives available to him. Tired of being ignored and held at arm's length, he had nudged her. Hard. He'd caught her at a vulnerable moment that night at the pier. She'd hesitated, but finally agreed to attend. But only after forcing his promise that he would abide by the outcome. Which could be grim for him.

Still he had no choice but to go with it.

"Quiet?" Tori answered in her own sweet time. Finally she cut him a look, swift and pointed. She gathered her hair at the back of her neck, trying to tame it in spite of the wind. Strands broke free. Blew wildly against her cheek. She raised an eyebrow. "You expected conversation?"

A few words here and there would have been nice. A no or yes to his questions. A nod or shake of her head. He ran one hand through his hair. "I reach out to you, but you never respond." He felt invisible. One-sided conversations sucked.

"I've nothing to say."

Nothing to him, anyway. Emotional distance was a bitch. Her few exchanges either singed his ass or froze his balls. Still he pressed, "You've no opinion on Race and Blu?"

They had noticed Race's Lexus in the visitor's parking lot at the apartment complex. Race would never have gotten up at such an early hour to have breakfast with Blu. It was obvious he'd spent the night.

"Blu is a big girl," she slowly said. "What she does is her business."

"You were right, way back when," he admitted. "You once said they had feelings for each other. I always thought they had such a sarcastic, sniping relationship. I guess they sparred on the surface but had soft spots too."

"He better not hurt her."

"Like I hurt you?"

She clammed up.

He continued with, "Don't compare their relationship to ours. I've never seen Race so dedicated to one woman. They'll make it."

"I once thought we would too," she muttered, more to herself than to him. The breeze in the car carried her words to him.

"We can again, Tori."

"Our time has passed."

"We'll revisit our past at the retreat."

"We'll see . . ."

"We need to air it out."

"So you keep saying."

"You agreed to participate."

"Define 'participate.'"

She was going to be difficult. No big surprise. He had

expected no less. This was his idea, and he would follow through, as best he could. No backing out. "Counseling, feelings, sharing."

"Pain and bleeding?"

"Maybe it won't be as bad as you think."

"Maybe it will be worse."

She kept so much bottled up inside her. She needed to react and release. On him. To move beyond her bitterness. He would take whatever she let loose. He owed her.

"One weekend, Tori, that's all I'm asking."

She shrugged, angled a cold shoulder toward him, grafting herself to the door. Giving him her back. He'd have preferred her front. She had amazing breasts. Instead she gazed out the open window. Her silence spoke volumes. She wanted nothing to do with him.

He took in her profile with subtle glances. She'd been a pretty teenager, but as a grown woman no female was more beautiful. He admired her wild auburn hair, blue eyes, high cheekbones, and obstinate chin. Tension locked her jaw. Pinched her lips. Stiffened her neck. She had an inflexible look now that didn't suit her. Her cropped green top was hiked above the waistband on her jeans, leaving a narrow expanse of skin visible. Smooth and pale. She had a snug butt. Spectacular legs. Her body was perfect for him. He longed to touch her. But didn't dare.

"Zane! Glen Glade." Tori jerked on the seat, pointed out a rapidly approaching sign that announced their exit ramp. "You driving or daydreaming?"

He'd been stupidly distracted. By her. And nearly missed their turnoff. He flicked the blinker, downshifted the Impala. It grumbled. He took the access ramp slightly over the speed limit. He then concentrated fully on the road and the directions given him by Doctor Blackstone, relationship counselor.

Ten miles east, he located Glade Lane, a narrow, rural

gravel road. Potholes and bumps. Palms and Australian pines flanked the sides. Low-hanging cypress branches made a grab for the Impala. He swerved, not wanting to scrape the paint.

The lane tapered further, became heavily shadowed by the trees on either side, only to suddenly open into a circular patch of land. Mellow sunshine hazed the grounds. At a one-way sign, he turned right, cruising past six small cottages before pulling into a driveway marked Glade Office. "Office." He liked the discretion, the lack of formality. No Mental Health Facility. No Counseling Center. No Therapy Clinic. Casual was good. Comfortable. Private.

Nestled among the red-blossoming canopy of royal poinciana trees and wild flower gardens, buildings of a gingerbread hue and a flash of gray brick blended with the landscape. Natural, rustic. A storybook cottage. Huge stepping-stones formed a curved path to the forest green door. Stones in their organic shape, not cut or squared.

He killed the engine, removed the key, and leaned back on the seat. "We're here."

"So we are." Tori tilted her head. Narrowed her eyes. Her imagination had her suggesting, "The Brothers Grimm. Hansel and Gretel. The witch's cottage."

He'd thought the same thing at first glance. "And me without bread crumbs." He referred to Hansel's dropping crumbs in order to retrace his steps in the woods.

One corner of her mouth tipped up ever so slightly. Smile there, smile gone. Vanished happiness. They hadn't shared a smile in so long. He missed her unexpected bursts of laughter. Those moments when he'd tickle her, and she'd laugh herself silly. Those had been more favorable times. He swore to reclaim them if he had anything to say about it.

He pocketed the keys, climbed from the car. He cleared

the hood, planning to open her door. She beat him to it, stepping out before he reached her. She stood in short brown boots with a zipper in the back. She gripped the outer handle with her left hand, her knuckles white.

Their gazes locked. He was a head taller than she. He looked down as her chin lifted. "Now what?" she asked. Her words were soft, cryptic.

"We meet Doctor Blackstone. He and his wife Doctor Allison oversee patient relations."

"Therapists with relationship Band-Aids."

"Hopefully we can patch things up."

"We need more than adhesive strips." She side-eyed him. "Who recommended this place to you?"

"Al Langford." A childhood friend. They'd played sports together and had stayed in contact over the years. Al had hit a rough patch with his fiancée. The two had attended a weeklong seminar at the couples retreat. "He swore by Glen Glade."

She rolled her eyes. "Not your best testimony. Al broke off his engagement yesterday."

Zane was stunned. He hadn't heard. "How'd you know?"

"Gossip at the grocery store."

Crap. He felt bad for his buddy. He'd contact him next week. Zane remained positive, despite his friend's breakup. "Al loves Lacey. They'll work through their issues."

"They'll be doing it long distance," she informed him. "Lacey went back to Vermont, home to her parents."

"He'll earn reward air miles."

Tori's response was cut off by an older man's approach. Tall, bald, and clean-shaven, he came to them in a navy sport jacket and khaki slacks. He extended his hand to Zane, warmly said, "Hello, welcome to Glen Glade. I'm Doctor Dorsey Blackstone."

Zane shook his hand. "Zane Cates and Tori Rollins,"

he responded, including his ex. Blackstone exchanged handshakes with her as well.

The head therapist stroked his chin, commented, "You're from Barefoot William, and the first to arrive. Two more couples will be joining us. You will meet the others at a buffet dinner at the main cottage tonight, but no one will socialize beyond the meal. No group sessions; it's all individualized. I will go over and explain the program this evening."

Zane exhaled, relieved. It would be difficult enough for Tori to open up to him. She'd totally shut down in unknown company. He nodded. "Fine by me."

"Good for you too, Tori?" Blackstone asked, including her.

"As good as it's going to get."

"It will only get better," he assured her.

She didn't look convinced. Contemplative lines appeared at the corners of her eyes, her mouth. She didn't agree with the man, but she wasn't disrespectful. She bit her tongue.

Blackstone shared his philosophy with them. Starting with, "Glen Glade is quiet and peaceful. A place to recharge your soul and reevaluate your life." He swept his arm wide, encompassing the grounds. "The cottages are old-fashioned, quaint. Secluded. Each is situated on an acre. You've space to breathe. The land grows wild, as nature intended. As the first couple to arrive, you have your choice of lodging. Feel free to check out all six. Once you've chosen, park your car in the driveway. Your vehicle marks your territory. The doors are unlocked. House keys are on the entrance table. Lock up when you come to the main house for supper at six and for our daily sessions."

Zane gave him a thumbs-up. "Got it."

Dr. Blackstone waved them off with, "Should you need to make any last-minute phone calls, do so before dinner. I'll confiscate iPhones and Tablets at that time." He walked away.

Tori paled. "No outside communication?"

"We're here for introspection."

"But what about Nana Aubrey?" she worried. "Your cousin Karen is a registered nurse and will take good care of her while I'm away. But I can't go three days without hearing her voice. Don't ask me to."

Zane understood and had planned ahead. He lowered his voice, assured her, "I've got you covered. I hid a burner phone in the glove compartment."

"Thank you." There was raspy relief in her voice. She looked at the ground, then up to the sky, anywhere but at him. Clouds gathered. Thick, fluffy cumulus in odd formations.

He rested a hip against the Impala. Scanned the sky too. "We were cloud-watchers in high school," he recalled. "We'd look for shapes in the formations. You always saw castles and I'd find cartoon characters. Whatcha see now?" he asked.

She squinted against the sun. "A half a heart."

He saw it too. He pointed east. "There's the other half. It should arrive if the breeze holds steady."

"The heart will remain broken if the breeze dies."

They stood and stared. Anticipating the outcome.

The symbolism wasn't lost on either one.

Here were two halves seeking a whole.

Tori was skeptical.

Zane rooted for the light wind.

The two halves were almost aligned when the gusts stilled. Zane held his breath. So close, yet so far away. A second cloud bank drifted by and nudged the halves together.

He pumped his arm, victorious. A positive sign.

She shook her head, scuffed her boot on the gravel,

and put everything in perspective. "The clouds aren't us, Zane. Don't read more into them than is actually there."

He refused to be dissuaded. The heavens had sent him a message. He held on to that hope. He motioned her back into the car. "Hop in. Cottage time."

They had six to view, and went from door to door. They were all basic, quite similar, with wrap-around porches and sparsely furnished interiors. He held back at each entry in order to catch her expression as she took in the contents. Like or dislike. He would settle wherever she'd be comfortable. It was her call.

The initial five cottages held no appeal for her. Together, they slowly climbed the wooden steps to the porch on the sixth. Entering, they were greeted by a crescent moon hardwood entrance hall that flowed into an open-raftered, high-ceilinged living room. The layout of the cottage was similar to their first home as a married couple. A stark reminder of their past.

Tori had placed her own designer stamp on their place. The Glen Glade cottage paled in comparison to her unique and quirky style. The furnishings were simple and functional. The basic blue fabric couch, matching ottoman, and mosaic coffee table had little flare. There were no chairs. The two of them would be forced to sit together on the sofa. He smiled to himself. Tori visibly frowned.

Three books were stacked on the coffee table. He checked them out. *Love and Respect. Please Understand Me. Men Are Like Waffles—Women Are Like Spaghetti.* The title of the third made him smile. He read the book jacket. The authors explained that men and women were wired differently. A man was like a waffle—each element of his life was in a separate box. And a woman was like spaghetti— everything in her life touched everything else. It made sense to him.

Two life-size wall posters drew their attention. The first

was a soft-focus black-and-white art shot of two nudes. The man rested his forehead against the woman's. Their eyes were closed. Their bodies engaged. *My Soul Mate. My Best Friend. My Love,* was scripted across the bottom in wavy blue type.

The second photo depicted two pairs of clasped hands. A callused man's fingers laced with a woman's smoother ones. Both wore wedding bands. Their wrists were bound by a golden ribbon, flowing with the words: *I Want to Be the Only Hand You Ever Hold.* He thought it charming. Poignant.

No television. No radio. They were meant to converse.

It could be a quiet weekend.

A pocket door parted to reveal the single bedroom. They peeked inside. Tori bit her bottom lip. "I'd hoped for two bedrooms."

Instead they faced twin beds.

The previous cottages all had one bedroom as well. But each had featured queen-size beds. Here, twins. No sharing a mattress. But they would share four drawers in the dresser. One closet. A tiny bathroom. Walk-in shower. After a second glance at the beds, Tori headed for the kitchen. He followed her out.

The kitchen unfolded at the back of the cottage. It was small, with basic appliances. He opened the refrigerator door and found it fully stocked. There were lots of food choices.

Tori stepped around Zane and rummaged through the cupboards. An assortment of paper products and bags of snacks were to be found inside. Cheese Doodles caught her eye. Her heart squeezed. A snack once enjoyed by Zane and her in high school. They'd laughed when their lips and fingers turned orange. Their kisses tasted cheesy. The memory slammed into her, sharp and suffocating. A sweeping sadness unsettled her soul. It was more than she could handle at the moment.

Unmindful, she backed up and into him. The unintentional contact was startling. Their bodies brushed. Her back against his front. His heat jumped her with a smoldering intensity. Her cheeks flushed. Her stomach constricted. Her knees bumped each other, then buckled. She was thrown off balance. His arms went around her waist, and she clutched his forearms for support.

He held her easily. Loosely. His hands flexed, but he didn't tighten his hold. She heard the tick of the coffee cup–shaped clock on the wall above the sink, along with his breathing near her ear. Deep, steady. Warm.

His grip shifted to her shoulders as he turned her toward him. Then he let her go. "Sorry," he quietly apologized. "I didn't mean to touch you, but I was afraid you'd fall."

She would have fallen and was glad he'd been there to catch her. "Thanks, I'm fine."

He glanced at his watch, said, "Three thirty. Time to unload the car and settle in. I'll get our bags."

Tori refused his help, however considerate. She took off ahead of him. "I can get my own."

"I figured you might."

She beat him to the Impala. He arrived close behind her. He popped the trunk. It was only a three-day stay, and they had minimal luggage. There would be no dining and dancing. They faced hours of conversation and communication. If that were even possible. She wasn't sure. She had promised him she would try, and she would. Despite fighting him every step of the way before their arrival.

He hefted his black Nike duffel bag onto his shoulder. A wide shoulder that could carry the weight of the world if he had to. His inner strength and indomitable will defined his character. In many ways he was a good guy. But was he the best man for her, after all this time? Tori couldn't be certain. He'd lost her trust. And trust was the glue in any relationship.

She'd traveled with a small mauve carryall. She raised the handle and tugged it along. The wheels fought against the gravel drive, twisting and making her progress difficult. She carried it up the steps and onto the porch. Then inside. Zane followed her.

Her steps dragged as she crossed the living room. He entered the bedroom ahead of her. She leaned against the pocket door. Such a small space, suggestive of awareness and intimacy. She wasn't certain she could sleep in the same room with her ex-husband.

He dropped his duffel on the bed nearest the dresser, asked, "Top or bottom drawers?"

She hadn't planned to unpack. She could live out of her suitcase. She wasn't bothered by a few wrinkles. However Zane was thoughtful and had given her a choice. She went with, "Top."

She dropped her carryall on the second twin. The burgundy-colored comforter rippled. She unzipped it, removing jeans, tops, panties, socks, and a pair of tennis shoes. A casual weekend, Zane had told her when she'd asked what clothes to bring. She would climb into bed in a pair of black cotton pajamas. Baggy and mannish. She neatly folded the items, stuck them in the drawer. Then shoved her sneakers beneath the dresser. The round canvas toes peeked out.

No chairs in the bedroom either, so she settled on the foot of her twin. Carefully, cautiously, attempting not to leave a butt imprint. She didn't want to leave any impression on this place, didn't want to be there to begin with . . . there with him. Regrettably, the mattress was soft, and her ass sank deeply. She saw Zane grin from the corner of her eye. She glared at him. He swallowed his smile.

She bent her head and absently traced an imaginary design on the comforter. Circles, triangles, stars. She discreetly watched him unpack from beneath her lashes, pretending not to care about his clothes, yet she was still curious. Out came worn jeans and pressed khakis. Sweatpants. T-shirts. A white button-down that he hung in the closet. A pair of brown leather loafers. Underwear? She looked more closely. None. She sucked air and pushed off the bed. Moved into the living room.

"I'm going to grab a shower before supper," Zane called after her. A warning he'd soon occupy the bathroom.

She hadn't planned to clean up, not much anyway. A brush to her hair, a bit of lip-gloss. There was no reason to impress her ex. Or the relationship specialists. She could care less about the other two couples. She had her own issues, and they had theirs. They'd meet, eat, and go their separate ways.

Or so she'd thought. But the evening seemed to drag on and on. The main house opened its doors to a welcome buffet and comfortable seating around the living room. But the participants were an ill-assorted group, several seeming to repress animosity while others demonstrated forced pleasantry. Tori barely survived the first hour of stilted conversation.

The initial comments centered on the doctor's home and furnishings. It was tastefully decorated for a Hansel and Gretel cottage with oil paintings, oriental carpeting, and antiques. Dim lighting was easy on their eyes. But couldn't hide the glares and daggers thrown between the couples.

Tori worked her way through the buffet, then took a seat beside Zane on a short brocade couch. She'd known him as a teenage boy, not as an adult male. He'd filled out, a large man on a delicate sofa. They had barely an inch between them, if that.

She was balancing a plate of food on her lap. Pasta salad and fresh fruit. She ate slowly. In contrast, Zane was on his second helping of baked ham and potato salad. Their bodies shifted with each bite, vying for space. They were significantly aware of each other. Hips and thighs brushed. There was a physical charge between. They might not get along now, or ever again, but past familiarity made her feel safe. A strange sensation. Unexpected, yet undeniable.

She ate, listened with half an ear. The couple seated on the shellback love seat in deep plum velvet spoke in sharp undertones. Michael and Cynthia Foster. Mick and Cyn, as they preferred to be called. They'd dressed formally for an informal meal. He in a suit, she in a little black dress. He was of average height. She stood six feet in staggering high heels. She was a woman with fluffy blond hair and flashy jewelry. Their whispers traveled. It didn't take long for Tori to assess their situation. Money issues. He worked, she spent . . . and spent. Mick wasn't happy with her new Mercedes-Benz. Shiny, black, and parked beneath a carport at one of the cottages. Cyn had complained there wasn't a garage.

Tori inwardly cringed. The Fosters made her uncomfortable. But then so did the third couple, Trig and Missy Madison. Missy had clenched her jaw and chastised Trig in the buffet line for eyeing Cynthia Foster's cleavage. Her very deep cleavage. He irritated her further by openly staring at Cyn's butt as she swayed across the living room to join her husband on the love seat. Her hips were a human pendulum. When Cyn attempted to engage Zane in conversation, he paid her little attention, giving only monosyllable responses. That pleased Tori, for some reason.

For dessert, a maid served a delicious assortment of petits fours on a silver platter. They were bite size, the mini butter cakes covered with dainty icing. Tori chose a lavender-frosted cake with a tiny pink rose. Zane selected one with vanilla frosting decorated with a blue bow. Tiny cake. Big-man hands. The petit four got lost between his fingers. He managed his bite, then whispered from the corner of his mouth, "Too sweet."

A memory surfaced. "You'd rather have apple pie?" escaped her without thinking. She remembered them sitting at Molly Malone's Diner on the boardwalk. He'd eaten three slices à la mode after football practice.

He nodded slowly. "You once tried to bake me an apple pie."

Her face heated. "Not my best effort." She'd forgotten the cornstarch. It had turned out soupy.

"Not all that bad. I ate it."

He had. Scooping the pie into a bowl, and complimenting her baked apples. The dessert hadn't tasted bad; it just wasn't the pie she'd intended. He had encouraged her to try again. And again. Without great success. He liked her microwave brownies from a box mix. Her chocolate chip cookies. The Pillsbury rolled dough became her staple, an easy slice and bake.

They looked at each other then. A long, telling stare. A visual touch. His brown gaze was a window to their past. The intensity of his scrutiny made her heart skip and softened her stomach. She was first to look away.

Seconds later, Dr. Blackstone stood and addressed the group. "I have greeted you individually upon arrival, and now I welcome you all together. My colleague Dr. Mavis Allison and I sincerely hope you enjoy your stay and that you make the most of your weekend with us. Our approach is unconventional, but we find our relationship guidance to be as beneficial as structured therapy sessions.

"Tonight will be your first exercise. Once you are back at your cottages, I want each couple to recall the setting where they initially met. A coffee shop, a book store, contemplating produce at a grocery store, whatever it may have been."

"A bar?" came from Trig Madison. "That's where I first picked up Missy."

Missy huffed. "You flirted with every woman at Hazy-eyed Crazy."

"You got to me. Drinking Manhattans and tying cherry stems with your tongue." Pause, a sneer. "She was a one-trick pony."

Missy winced, embarrassed.

Dr. Blackstone cleared his throat. "A bar is fine. Start from the very beginning. Try and remember that first spark of attraction. Approach the person with newfound interest. You may not fully recall your early dialogue, so develop whatever introduction gets you talking."

"Tampa Federal Bank," Cyn muttered. "I was there for a loan. Who knew my future banker husband would be tight as a vault."

Mick squared his shoulders. "Money's meant to be spent, just not my last dime," he defended.

A mean expression and unladylike snort was Cynthia's only response.

Blackstone held up his hands, palms out, and kept the peace. "Breathe deeply, inhale and exhale," he encouraged. "Erase, disregard where you're at now and what you're presently feeling. Go back to where it all began. A pleasanter time. No discussion beyond that first meeting. We'll progress further on Saturday. Slowly move forward."

Tori sat quietly. Zane fingered the cuff on his white, long sleeve, button-down shirt. Neither commented. The Cates family was a grapevine of news and gossip. The relatives were aware of Zane and her past. Their high school years and beyond. Their fights and arguments. Here at

Glen Glade, she had no desire to air their differences with strangers. They'd take their disagreement to their cottage. Keep their conversation private.

Doctor Allison joined Blackstone. They stood close to the same height. Platinum haired, wearing cat's eye glasses and a genuine smile, she appeared distinguished, yet feminine, in a dove-gray skirt suit. "Enjoy a second cup of coffee, another petit four," she offered. "Talk among yourselves if you like. This will be your first and last social hour. Once you leave and return to your cottages, be honest with your partner. No hedging, no placating. No purposeful wounding. No stressful surrendering. You are equals. Let your communication be organic. Be yourselves. Open your hearts. Open your minds. Be kind. Macho and bitchy won't see you through the weekend."

"There's a red call button by the front door should you become overwhelmed," added Dr. Blackstone. "Push it, and either Dr. Allison or I will make an appearance."

"A referee?" joked Trig Madison.

"A mediator," Dr. Allison counseled. "You must work through your own issues. That way, your reconciliation will be a personal triumph. We can offer logical suggestions but will not advise. Oftentimes a third party brings stability to a shaky situation. Without taking sides."

"Do you have beer or wine?" asked Trig.

Blackstone shook his head. "No alcoholic beverages on the premises."

Missy sighed, openly relieved. "Good. Trig can be a mean drunk."

"Sober solves problems. Drinking blurs lines," noted Blackstone. "Promises made under the influence seldom stick in the morning."

"Whatever." Trig stood. "I'm gone."

"I'll join you shortly." Yet Missy lingered.

"See you at the cottage, barfly." Trig left.

Tori had had enough. She glanced at Zane, noted his contemplative expression. His shoulders were tense, his hands tightly clasped. He was a man who respected women. Trig Madison was rude. Discourteous. His and Missy's exchange was disturbing. It would be a long weekend for the Madisons. She shifted on the sofa. "Coffee or the cottage?" She left it up to him.

"I'm ready to go if you are."

The cottage meant intimacy. Conversation. She felt the color drain from her face. An apprehensive shiver skimmed her spine. Time to face the music. She had agreed to the weekend, to prove to Zane their relationship was over. In spite of the heart-shaped cloud and his belief they could fix what he'd broken.

He'd shattered her spirit when he'd left all those years ago. The wound was still jagged. She pulsed with every emotion she'd ever felt toward him. A flitting happiness textured with anger.

"Let's do this," she agreed. *Let's get it over with,* was left unsaid.

They rose, crossed the living room together to their hosts, and spoke to them briefly.

"Thank you for supper." Tori was appreciative.

"Tasted good," from Zane.

"We always enjoy the initial meet and greet," said Doctor Blackstone. "We try to keep conversation light and the atmosphere relaxed. Unfortunately, on occasion, couples bring their baggage to dinner, as we witnessed tonight."

Dr. Allison walked them to the door. "Please leave your iPhones or Tablets in the wicker basket on the entrance table. It's just the two of you this weekend. No outside world. Have a productive evening."

"Productive." Tori mentally repeated the word when

she next sat across from Zane at the café-style kitchen table. He'd changed from his white button-down to a plain gray T-shirt. Sweatpants replaced his khakis. He'd kicked off his loafers. Now barefoot.

She still wore the same clothes from earlier in the day. Her cropped green sweater, jeans, and short boots had survived the car ride, supper, and would get her through their dialogue. She would've liked to remove her boots but didn't want to get too comfortable. Her body was on hyper drive. Erratic heartbeat and shortened breaths. She felt jumpy. She sat on the edge of her chair and gripped the table's edge.

Zane rested his elbows on the tabletop, steepled his fingers. His gaze was steady, yet guarded. A corner of his mouth slowly tipped up. "I half-expected you to sit for sixty seconds, then disappear."

She noted the second hand on the coffee cup–shaped clock. "I've lasted two minutes."

"How are you doing?"

"Ask me in an hour."

"Are you able to discuss us?"

"High school. First love. Not much to talk over. We were short-lived, Zane."

His jaw worked. "Be eighteen again with me tonight."

A long time ago, yet still fresh in her mind. They shared such a memorable past. Difficult to ignore. Harder even to forget. Eighteen was a good year for the two of them. So good. But beyond that, their lives had diverged. Dr. Blackstone had requested that the couples go no further than their initial meeting. Those moments when interest and attraction hinted at dating and kissing under the boardwalk. She would push through it. For closure.

"You start." His voice was deep, gentle. Hypnotic. "Take us back."

She shrugged, fudged, "I don't remember much."

"Hard to believe," he stated. "Come clean, Tori. You remember as much as I do. That would be everything."

Everything was overpowering. Emotion choked her. Cut off her breath. She stared at him, summoned up their past. Memories ran toward her. The past claimed the present. Their first meeting came to her, fleshed out and fully blown. "I was sunbathing on Barefoot William Beach," she recalled. "It was October and the winter people hadn't yet arrived. A secluded spot. Your voice echoed across the beach." It was as clear now as it had been then. Stern-toned, concerned, and his command directed toward his rambunctious pup. She quoted, "*Oswald! That bikini top better have come from the lost and found at the lifeguard station.*"

"No lost and found." Zane chuckled. Amused. "It was yours. You lay facedown on a beach towel. You'd untied your top, not wanting tan lines. Fallen asleep even."

She'd been so tired. She remembered how hard she'd worked that year, attending high school, then taking the night shift at Zinotti's Pizza, all so she could save money, make the grades necessary for college. It had exhausted her. That Saturday afternoon, the warmth of the sun soothed her so that it was easy for Ozzie to take advantage.

"My pup tugged and stole your polka-dot top out from under you," he stated.

Her lips parted in surprise. "You remembered the polka dots."

"Unforgettable. White on black. You looked hot."

His compliment touched her. She shook it off.

The puppy's image was vivid in her mind. "Sneaky Oz." She'd loved the dalmatian. Still did. A soft frisson of emotion stirred in her hardened heart.

Zane pushed back on his café chair, tipped it onto two legs. A risky balancing act. He crossed his arms over his chest. Thoughtful. "You scrambled to cover yourself."

"With my ragged cutoff shorts."

A smile played at the corners of his mouth. "You concealed most of your chest, all but one nipple."

She pulled a face. "Don't remind me."

"A memory I'll hold forever."

She wished to wipe it from her mind.

He cocked his head, curious. "What was your impression of me?"

"Looking for an ego boost?" she sarcastically asked.

"Maybe. It's been a long time since you've been nice to me." He eyed her with an intensity that made her stomach quiver. "Be pleasant now. I'm only asking for an hour."

The longest hour of her life. She went back to high school. "I was the new kid. I'd only seen you in passing. We hadn't spoken. You were popular. Everyone's friend. A presence unto yourself."

"Presence, huh?" he asked with a cocky grin.

"Get over yourself."

"This is my moment. I want details."

She gritted her teeth. "You'll get details only once. They'll never be repeated."

"Once is good. Was it love at first sight?"

Darn close to it. She kept that to herself. Gave him, "You were tall."

"Six feet by sixteen."

"Good-looking, I guess."

"One to ten, how handsome?"

Solid ten. "Seven, maybe."

He pressed his hand over his heart. Grimaced. "Eight, at least."

She went on to say, "You were clean-cut."

"Smart, athletic, outgoing, confident."

"You're putting words in my mouth." Words she could not deny. They were all true. He was a Cates, and he carried their genes.

"I did impress you though, right?"

"A little, maybe."

"Enough to start a dialogue."

"You had my bikini top," she reminded him.

"Which I returned."

"In your own good time."

"I was playing with you."

"I never liked being played."

He knuckle-scrubbed his chin. "For what it's worth, I thought you were the prettiest girl around. I was nervous as hell to talk to you. That night, I stuffed myself with pizza to get your attention."

Quite the confession from the boy who could have dated any girl in the senior class. Females had sought him out, surrounding him between classes, during lunch, and after school. She'd never have imagined he would find room for her in his life. He had. They'd shared such magical times.

"I never thought you'd go out with me."

She had gone out with him and later lived to regret it.

"I was half in love with you that night on the Ferris wheel," he confessed. "How'd you feel about me?"

"I . . ." She let out a broken sigh.

"Don't quit on me, Tori," he was quick to say. "We've just gotten started."

Start. Stop. Rehashing the past shouldn't be so difficult. Hurt snuck in and stole what little healing she had achieved. She swallowed hard. Rubbed her throat. Couldn't express her feelings.

He rose then and cut her some slack. "Break time. Something to drink?" he asked, heading for the mini-fridge.

"A bottle of raspberry iced tea."

He chose a root beer. He filled two glasses with ice and

returned to the table. He scooted one glass and the bottle of tea toward her. "You once liked ice with your beverages."

She was touched that he remembered. "I still do."

They sipped silently. She tightly clutched her glass. The condensation moistened her palms. He didn't hurry her. The tea was refreshing, calming. The intensity between them eased.

"The Ferris wheel, Tori." He soon took up where they'd left off. "How'd you feel about that night?"

She mentally fought against returning to the ride. Dr. Blackstone had stressed honesty. Yet it hurt to speak the truth. So damn much. Still she tried. "You'd bought me sunglasses I didn't want, and we argued over the gift." Never would she tell him that she still had the two quirky pairs. She couldn't bear to part with them. "We made up on the Ferris wheel." She met his gaze across the table, sensed his vulnerability. She exposed her feelings too. "Yes, I liked you. My parents were dysfunctional. You"—she drew a deep breath—"made me feel safe and protected."

"How about loved?"

"At one time." She'd once believed that they were meant to be. False hope.

He lowered the chair legs back onto the floor. His gaze was dark and direct. "What about now?"

She stopped him. "Don't get ahead of ourselves. We discussed our initial meeting and first date. The past ends here. No more tonight."

He backed off. "We remembered a lot."

Too much in some places, she feared.

"Our memories are strong because they're still important to us."

"*Were* important, at one time."

"Still important, Tori," he persisted. "Our past affects our present, our future. We're stuck in what might have been."

"Yet what never will be again." She left it at that.

They had two days left at Glen Glade. Somehow, she would survive and endure. Mental exhaustion now claimed her. "I'm tired," she told him. "I'm going to grab the burner phone from your car. I want to wish Nana Aubrey good night."

He nodded. "The glove compartment's unlocked."

"Gram, shower, bed," she tossed over her shoulder as she left the kitchen.

"Happy chat. Dream sweet."

Nine

Tori tossed and turned all night. She woke with bed head and a pillow crease on her cheek. Dry mouth and morning breath. She'd kicked off the sheet and comforter. Her pajama top had ridden up, exposing her left breast. She covered herself. Then plumped two pillows behind her head and sat up. She felt oddly disoriented. Until she recalled her surroundings. Glen Glade, couples counseling, she'd spent the night in a cottage with Zane.

A rustle of bedding, and she found him seated on the edge of his twin bed. He was bare chested, with a beige cotton sheet wrapped about his hips and a tented erection. He stretched his arms wide, rolled his neck and shoulders. His muscles rippled. He looked good in bare skin. Healthy and strong. Military fit.

They might not be together now, but the attraction between them still sizzled. He appealed to her still. There was something sexy about a man waking up. Something warm and inviting. All sleepy eyed and scruff chinned. His yawn. Scratching his belly. She stared overly long, embarrassing herself.

Zane didn't seem to mind her eyes on him. He gave her his own sunrise once-over. A thorough scrutiny. Her nipples puckered and her inner thighs warmed. Her skin itched.

They'd raised the slatted shades and left a screened window cracked between their beds for fresh air. Sunshine tapped them on their shoulders, went on to streak the hardwood floor.

"How's your grandmother?" he asked.

She hadn't spoken to him since they'd parted ways last evening. "Nana Aubrey's doing fine, thanks. I also talked to Karen. She understands Gram just fine. They were getting ready to order a pizza when I called."

"Good to know. You were able to exhale."

"I get keyed up when I'm away from her for long."

"One day down."

"Two to go." Sounded like forever to her.

"Dr. Blackstone stopped by last night when you were in the shower. He left today's agenda. We start with individual sessions. You with Dr. Allison and me with Blackstone. It's all about getting reacquainted with ourselves so we can be more accepting of others. Afterward we return to the cottage and work on listing five moments of importance in our relationship. The three best and the two worst."

"Just two, huh?"

"It wasn't all bad, Tori. Surely you see something good in our relationship."

She squinted at him.

He rolled his eyes, went on to say, "We have time for breakfast. We're not due at the main office until ten."

"I could go for a cup of coffee."

"I'm thinking bacon and eggs."

In such close quarters, she found their conversation came easy. That bothered her. She didn't want to fall into familiar patterns. "We could eat in shifts," she suggested.

"We eat together, Tori." He stood firm. "You're not avoiding me at meals, especially if I do the cooking."

"I never asked you to fix my meals."

"Cooking for two is as easy as one."

"Pour cereal in a bowl for me then."

He pushed off the bed, and the sheet dipped sharply over his left hip. He turned in profile and flashed her half a butt cheek. "I'm not going into the bathroom to dress. My clothes are out here. Close your eyes or look, your choice."

She'd been warned.

He dropped the sheet.

She jumped.

He started to dress.

He no longer looked at her, but she still eyed him. She couldn't tear her eyes away. Bulked-up shoulders. Sinewy roped arms. Solid back. Firm ass. Athletic legs. He was efficient in dressing. Each movement was precise. His stomach flexed as he drew on his jeans. He tucked his sex, avoided the teeth on the zipper. He chose a black T-shirt. Then slipped on his loafers, without socks. He was ready to go in minutes.

He ran one hand over his short hair. The military cut didn't need combing. "Your turn," he said, as he dropped back on the bed to watch.

She rolled her eyes. "I don't think so."

"You forget I've seen you naked."

"How long ago?" Years, not yesterday.

"Too long, Tori."

He would wait a lot longer, she decided, maybe forever. They weren't even friends at the moment. While she appreciated seeing him in nothing but skin, she wasn't about to grant him the same privilege. She was aware of her weakness with this man. Nakedness would lead to lovemaking. Lovemaking would take her back to a beginning that she was trying to end.

She slid off the bed in her black, mannish pajamas. "No show," she told him as she crossed to the dresser and selected her own clothes. She went with her favorite flag print shirt. An abstract amethyst medley of stars and stripes worn over dark-wash cuffed jeans. She claimed a pair of multicolored socks and her boots, then walked into the bathroom. Closed the door on him.

She debated a second shower, even though she'd taken one the previous evening. Just to kill time. They faced a two-hour stretch before meeting with their counselors. That time would include breakfast. She'd have to eat a lot of cereal to fill the interval. Maybe if she chewed long enough, she wouldn't have to talk.

The scent of coffee reached her shortly. A tempting siren call. She put on her clothes and faced her day. She focused on the fact that there were only two more days at Glen Glade before she would head back home. The idea of returning to her grandmother and Oswald lifted her spirits. However the thought of resuming her job at Zinotti's depressed her. She'd worked for Eddie for eighteen years. Time had slipped by and gotten away from her. She wanted more than she now had. She would have to initiate a career change for herself. She just wasn't sure when or how.

She brushed her hair, left it wild. A final look in the mirror, and she found herself pale. She pinched her cheeks for color. Then headed to the kitchen. She found Zane in front of the stove, confident in his cooking skills. Scrambling eggs and turning bacon in a small skillet. He saw her enter and popped rye bread in the toaster. The food smelled good. Her hunger spiked.

"There's orange and apple juice in the fridge," he shared. "Raisin Bran and Fiber One in the cupboard."

She pursed her lips. Sighed. Now she'd have to admit that she'd changed her mind, preferring his choices for breakfast over her own.

He cut her a look, shrugged one broad shoulder innocently. "I made extra, enough for two. Cereal sounded boring when you could have pepper-smoked bacon and scrambled eggs with chopped vegetables."

The toast popped, and he lightly buttered the slices. He split the food on two plates and nodded toward a chair. "Have a seat, if you like."

She liked. A lot. She tried not to show how much. The aroma drew her to the table like a crooked finger. She sat and ate. Conversation lagged as they dug in and cleared their plates.

Zane passed her the pot of coffee, and she poured a second cup. She felt full, satisfied, and expressed her gratitude. "Thank you," she managed. "You always knew your way around the kitchen, far better than me."

"I can fix the basics. You made the best pizza."

"I took home what I learned at Zinotti's." She could also make spaghetti sauce and a mean meatball sub.

"Your grandmother was never particular. Neither was I," he said. "It never mattered what we ate, as long as we ate together."

Together. Seemed a lifetime ago.

She shifted on her chair, feeling twitchy. "I'm restless, Zane. I'm used to being active. Working and running errands. It's hard to–to . . ."

"Sit and make conversation with me."

He stood, collected their dirty dishes, and set them in the sink. "We have an hour. Let's take a walk."

"We're not supposed to leave the cottage except for therapy sessions."

"Says Dr. Blackstone." He grinned at her, then conspired, "I say we go out and get some fresh air. There's a path behind the cottage that leads into the woods. No one will see us." He held out his hand. "Ready, set, go?"

She jumped up, took his hand, and escaped with him. It seemed natural. He drew her out the back door and down a ramp to the yard. Tori turned her face to the sun, and contentment warmed her. A mellow-yellow day. Zane gave her hand a tug, and she followed him. The path was narrow and weedy. Her troubles scattered on the gentle breeze. Her mind cleared.

They came upon a clearing and looked around. They took in the trees, flowers, birds, and then each other. They couldn't avoid the obvious. They stood close together and still held hands. Human contact. The touch of their fingers was powerful. Intimate and instinctual. It felt right, yet wrong. She hadn't held another man's hand since Zane's own. Uncertain, she let things play out as they would. Their fingers remained laced.

After some time, he glanced at his watch, calculated, "We've walked for thirty minutes. Communicated with Mother Nature for ten. We're due at the main house in twenty."

"Power walk or jog?" she asked.

He glanced down at their feet. "You're in boots and I'm wearing loafers."

"Your point being?"

He squeezed her hand, then freed his own. "Last one to the main house explains why we're late."

"It was your idea to take a walk."

"I thought it was yours."

She gaped, and he took off. He'd always been athletic and hadn't lost his speed or endurance. She barely kept him in her sights as they covered the path in record time. He ran up the ramp to the back door, paused to check on her. Tori sprinted past him. She made it through the cottage, out the front door, and halfway across the circular driveway before he caught up to her. He reached the wide yard of the main house mere inches ahead of her.

They were adults acting like children. Neither cared. The win took on a life of its own. No rules, rather a free-for-all. It suddenly meant everything to her. She refused to lose. Even if it meant cheating. She reached out, grabbed the back of his shirt, and held on tightly. The cotton stretched and ripped at the side seam. He dragged her for several yards, then lost his footing. They both went down. He twisted, protected her, and took the brunt of their fall. He landed on his back and the air left his lungs in a rush. He closed his eyes and caught his breath.

Tori sprawled across him, panting. Her knee was wedged at his groin. She pushed up on her elbows, spied the stepping-stone pathway. Twenty feet to go. So very near. Adrenaline fired, and she rolled off Zane. Her legs had weakened and wouldn't support her. So she began to crawl the remaining distance.

Her life had been so serious for so long. Yet there was something both funny and absurd about their situation. Laughter rose, spilled out. Sounding rusty. It slowed her down. She couldn't remember the last time she had laughed. It was almost painful.

A tug on her ankle, and she realized Zane was on all fours, coming up behind her. She was afraid to kick out, afraid that she would hurt him. She lunged the last foot and slapped her palm on the winning outdoor stepping-stone. The sound reverberated. In her mind. In her heart. Down to her toes.

She heard the click of high heels and raised her head. Dr. Mavis Allison stood over them. Tori lay flat on her stomach, and Zane had collapsed beside her. His left leg pinned down her right.

"Interesting way to arrive at your sessions," Dr. Allison commented, mild amusement in her tone. "You're seven minutes late."

"I hope we don't get detention," Zane said under his breath. Tori dipped her head, grinned. He pushed to his feet, then offered Tori his hand and drew her up too. "We needed the exercise and raced," he said, hedging his explanation. Keeping their walk a secret. He drew his T-shirt away from his chest, displayed the tear. "We would've arrived on time had Tori not pulled a fast one."

"I needed the advantage."

Dr. Allison observed them both. "Win or lose, did you enjoy yourselves?"

Tori looked at Zane. He nodded. She managed one too.

"This way." Dr. Allison motioned them forward. "My office is situated off the living room. Dr. Blackstone is located on the second floor. Take the stairs," she instructed Zane. "Third door on the right."

They entered the main house, parted ways. "Catch you after," he said as he left her.

They would only be separated for an hour, yet a small part of her looked forward to seeing him again. She watched him walk away. A man's stride. Purposeful and athletic. He reached the staircase and took the steps two at a time.

"Eyes dilated. Expression dreamy. Heart on her sleeve," noted Dr. Allison.

Tori started. "Who?"

"You."

"Impossible."

"All things are possible. Go after what you want."

Tori shook her head, denied, "I don't want Zane."

"Perhaps he wants you bad enough for both of you."

Dr. Allison's statement became the topic of their session. Could one person's love overcome another person's pain? Tori was not sure. She was aware that Zane wanted her, but their past held her back. He'd left her when she'd needed him most. She was afraid to love again.

This morning during her meeting, she vowed to be strong. Confident. To be her own person. To take back her mental and emotional freedom and not to rely on another person for her happiness. The future was hers; she only had to make that all-important decision. Would she now move forward with Zane or without him? It was her choice. She would make a fresh start either way. Still, the outcome weighed heavily.

Their afternoon assignment was to separately list five moments of importance in their relationship. Those poignant and significant. The three best and the two worst. How did the two worst become so bad? Could they have been prevented? Tori and Zane would later come together and discuss each point. Conversation was to remain amicable, peaceful, balanced. Honest.

Good luck with that, Tori thought.

Dr. Allison released her on the hour. The counselor's schedule was rigid. There was no making up the seven minutes lost with their late arrival. Tori slipped out of the office, quietly closing the door. She crossed the living room as Zane came down the stairs. She sensed his presence before she heard his steps. She glanced his way.

"Wait up," he called to her.

Without any hesitation on her part, she hung back until he reached her. He grinned down at her. "I see you lived through the session."

"I've lots to think about." She didn't give further details.

"Yeah, me too."

He tentatively curved his hand about the back of her neck, gently massaged. "It's going to be fine, Tori. I don't doubt it for a minute. Whatever's meant to happen will happen. I have faith in us."

She swallowed her apprehension. So much rested on her shoulders, which now included his hand. He rubbed her neck, relaxed her, and then walked his fingers along her left shoulder. He massaged away her tension. He had great hands. Strong and soothing. He'd given her many backrubs early in their relationship. Maybe she should list his hands as a positive on her list.

The cottage welcomed them home. A temporary retreat that might just change lives, hopefully for the better. But that outcome was yet to be seen. Zane held the door for her. She scooted in ahead of him.

He pressed in behind her. She glanced over her shoulder, caught his determined expression. "Paper and pen?" he muttered aloud.

She blinked. "You plan to start your list now?" He was way ahead of her. She was tempted to procrastinate when it came to making her own.

"Way back when, you always wanted to do your homework right after school, before we went out and had fun."

"You consider our lists homework?"

"Yeah, although there's no teacher. We grade each other."

He was raring to go, but she was far less enthusiastic.

He checked the entrance table for supplies and found what they needed. "Pen or pencil?" he asked her.

"Pencil." Ink was too permanent. "I'd rather erase than scratch out."

He handed her a sharpened basic number two pencil and a small, yellow-lined writing pad. He hooked an ink pen to his own pad. "Sit together or apart?"

She shook her head. "Doesn't matter to me."

"Apart, then. I don't want you cheating off me."

Oh brother. Like she would.

"I'll be in the bedroom," he told her. "I need to change my shirt. *Someone* ripped it and owes me a new one."

"Tell *someone* who cares."

He threw back his head and laughed. "Damn, I've missed the old Tori."

She'd often been flip or sarcastic with him, but in a loving way. She momentarily slipped into her old self. She shivered, then warmed. Surprisingly the warmth stayed with her.

She glanced toward the bedroom, just as he tugged his black T-shirt over his head. She'd always admired his chest. Thick and rock solid with an arrowed treasure trail to his groin. He selected another shirt from his dresser drawer, one worn and faded from the Air Force Academy. She now faced their past on his chest.

"I'm going to work from the bed," he called to her. He stacked pillows against the headboard and dropped down. Sprawled out. He looked comfortable. And incredibly sexy.

"No time limit," she added.

"As long as we discuss our points before our next session."

That would be tomorrow. "I'm going to give Nana Aubrey a quick call before I get started."

"Tell her 'hi' for me."

Very thoughtful. His greeting would mean a lot to the older woman.

She sat on the front seat in the Impala, popped the glove box, and made her call on the burner cell phone. Karen answered on the second ring, her voice cheerful. The nurse revealed that Tori's grandmother was fairly alert and feeling strong. She'd used her walker to stroll outside, taken a short turn on the circular sidewalk. Oswald by her side. Karen then handed the phone to Nana Aubrey. Tori did most of the talking, finishing with an "I love you."

Her gram soon hung up, and Tori closed the cell. She held the phone on her palm. Zane had made the purchase, allowing her to stay in touch with her gram. He was thoughtful. She was grateful.

She gazed through the windshield, lifted her eyes to

the sky, and found a pileup of cumulus clouds. All puffy, fluffy, whimsical, and thick as cotton. Undercurrents pulled them apart, then stuffed them back together. The new image resembled the cartoon character Scooby-Doo. Zane would love the formation. She realized her loneliness diminished when she shared with him. Still, she struggled with her future and the question of whether she should face it alone.

She closed her eyes and contemplated her list.

She thought so long and hard that she jolted awake when Zane tapped on the passenger window, which was rolled down halfway. "You okay?" he asked, looking concerned. "You were gone ninety minutes. Long chat with your grandma?"

Tori shook her head. "Short-short with Gram. Karen has been a lifesaver . . . everything's fine. I was reflecting on my list and must've fallen asleep."

"Thoughts of me put you to sleep?"

"To be honest, I was tired to begin with. I didn't sleep well last night. Only an hour or two."

Zane understood. He'd lain awake himself. Flat on his back and staring at the ceiling. He'd been horny as hell, knowing Tori was just feet away from him, yet they couldn't share a bed. She was a turn-on in spite of her mannish pajamas.

"Are you hungry?" he asked her.

"Too on edge to eat," she disclosed. "My stomach hurts."

He opened the car door, hoped she would get out. She did. "Forget the lists," he decided. "Let's go in the living room and wing it."

"Fine by me," she hesitantly agreed. They continued to break the rules. They'd taken a walk and now disregarded the lists. There was freedom in doing things their way.

He went on to gather beverages and light snacks.

Whatever it took to relax her. That meant most to him. He poured a root beer for himself and a raspberry iced tea for her. They needed something to munch on. Something to take up the lull in conversation. He filled three glass bowls with potato chips, mixed nuts, and Cheese Doodles.

He returned to the living room and found Tori huddled at one end of the short sofa. Her brow was deeply creased, and apprehension darkened her eyes. She drew up her legs and hugged her knees, a protective shield against him. She looked more little girl than adult woman. He hated that she feared their talk. It had been a long time coming.

He set the drinks and snacks in the center of the coffee table, then took the middle couch cushion. They were close enough to touch but distanced by emotion.

He ran his palms down his thighs, said, "Well, here we are."

"Here . . ." Obviously, she wished to be anywhere else.

"We need to hash things out, however painful."

"Painful for who?" she asked.

"For both of us."

"You too? Could've fooled me." Sarcasm was her weapon, always had been.

How could she not know how much he cared? How gutted he felt whenever she pushed him away? "I miss *us,* more than you'll ever know."

"You miss us?" she repeated, her words stilted, snide, disbelievingly.

"Truth, Tori." He ran one hand down his face. So much for gentle dialogue. There'd be no easing into this conversation. It wasn't who they were. They had baggage to unload. He pushed everything out in the open. "I can't shake the past. It haunts me. Relentlessly. I've made mistakes and felt guilty as well. I'm seeking your forgiveness."

No comment from her, but at least she was listening.

He continued. "Memories return me daily to when I was eighteen and crazy in love with you. I've never been closer to anyone in my life, not even my family. You believed and supported my dreams. The Air Force Academy was always my goal, just as Pratt Institute was yours. Life got screwed up somehow. Bad. Our plans fell by the wayside. A lot happened between high school graduation and my late acceptance. You lost your parents—"

"And then I lost you."

That shook him. "I didn't die."

"But you could have." Her sad expression tore him up inside. "After my parents' accident, I prayed you wouldn't be admitted to the academy. That was selfish, maybe, but a fear of flying paralyzed me. I would picture you leaving and never coming back. I couldn't breathe. My insides went numb."

He was stunned. "I had no idea."

She straightened her legs, squared her shoulders. "I had planned to tell you after we were married. Following the deadline for late acceptance. But then your letter arrived last minute, and you were so happy. Your family and friends celebrated." She reached for her glass of tea, sipped slowly. She poked an ice cube with her finger and watched it bob. Then focused on him once again. "You faced a decision. You couldn't have both the academy and me."

"We talked it over, Tori. You encouraged me to go."

"You'd lived and breathed the academy all your life. I only came along your senior year. I felt I couldn't compete with your dream."

"You were my wife. I looked to you for answers, and you pushed me out the door. Had you asked me to stay—"

"I did—you just didn't hear me." She placed her palm to the center of her chest. Her expression was miserable.

"You listened to my words but not to my heart. I never wanted you to go." A telling pause. "For a foolish second I thought you'd pick me and stay."

"Instead I chose the academy." He hung his head. "Our divorce was only meant to be temporary. I'd planned to marry you the moment I graduated from the academy."

"Convenient for you but not for me. I fell apart."

"I wasn't there to hold and help you."

"You were there for me when my parents died, so I didn't have to go it alone. I relied on you when I should've depended on me. Only me. Not once did I feel sorry for myself, but the pain followed me everywhere. To work. To bed. I never regained my strength after their deaths. Instead I took the easy way out and walked into your cottage and married you. I leaned on you and lost myself."

"You are the strongest woman I know."

"I grew into my strength. I had to. I was married and divorced in a week. Alone and misplaced. I had my grandmother to support. I had to recover from my head-on collision with grief."

He felt like shit. Tori had held on to her hurt as tightly as her memories. She'd kept everything so bottled up inside she couldn't breathe. She was having trouble breathing now.

A white-hot pain jammed his own chest. Remorse choked him. He had little defense. "No one ever told me how bad you felt after I left."

"I walked around like a zombie for months."

"My family kept that from me."

"I can understand their reasoning," she tried to be fair. "You were at the prestigious Air Force Academy. All your energy had to be directed at studying and holding your own. You couldn't be distracted. They didn't want you worrying about me."

Zane's jaw locked. His parents had thought they were

doing him a favor by not sharing Tori's pain. She'd suffered alone. Had he known, he would've found a way to make things better for her. Somehow. Instead his family's silence had only deepened their falling out, adding misunderstanding and false impressions to their miscommunication. "You moved out of the cottage," he said.

"*Our* cottage. But there was only me left."

"I wanted you to stay there."

"What you wanted no longer mattered. You were gone."

"Damn, Tori, I'm so sorry."

The years stacked up, and her pain became too much for her. Emotion misted her eyes. She'd never really cried, hard and cleansing, yet a single tear escaped now. "You risked your life almost every day," she choked out. "You were deployed to Iraq, flew F-16s. Air strikes and flyovers." Her words were sharp and angry, as rapid as her breathing. "Ten years later, instead of retiring, you transferred to the Air Force Reserve, to the 53rd Weather Reconnaissance Squadron, and became a hurricane hunter. For four years you flew directly into tropical depressions and the eyes of hurricanes—Joaquin, Hermine, Irma—facing winds of one hundred fifty miles per hour. *You could've died.*"

She had followed his career. He hadn't known. She'd never responded to his letters or emails. Nonetheless she'd held her breath with each mission, afraid that he would miscalculate or jeopardize his life and die. Beneath her anger, she still cared for him. That knowledge restored his soul.

He calmly reminded her, "You were aware of the danger involved in flying for the Air Force and as a hurricane hunter when we dated. You never seemed opposed to my plans."

"That was before my parents died."

"I was well trained in the service. I did a damn good job and didn't take unnecessary risks." He added sympathetically, "I'm not your parents, Tori. We each have our own paths to follow. Some lives end earlier than we would like, while others allow us to live to be one hundred. If it's within my power, I've no plan to leave you again."

"I–I missed you." At no time had she spoken those words out loud, but they slipped out today on an anguished sigh. She looked vulnerable and very tired.

"I missed you too." In the past their opportunity to reconcile had never materialized. Could they recover now? He damn sure hoped so. "Help me to help you. I don't know how to make it better for us."

"I've survived the years. I don't expect you to fix me."

He reached out to her. "Not fix you. I just want to love you. You don't have to love me back, if you're not ready or simply can't. Maybe someday."

"Someday . . ." She broke down in front of him then. A fractured shaking, followed by a stream of tears. For years she'd held him at arm's length. Today she reached for him, her arms outstretched. "Hold me, I hurt."

Zane hurt too. He crushed her to him. He kissed her forehead and let her cry. She cried her eyes out. Her body trembled, and he absorbed her fears and heartbreak. Her disappointments and despair. He lent his strength.

She wept so hard she crumpled. He handed her a Kleenex from the box on the coffee table. Then smoothed back her hair and rubbed her back when she hiccupped and couldn't catch her breath. He gently patted her shoulder.

She sniffed, sighed, and sobbed some more. He handed her tissue after tissue until she'd gone through the entire box. He passed her the iced tea to soothe her throat.

Long after her tears had dried, he offered soft words and comfort. She nodded against his chest, accepted his reassurance and support. He recognized her vulnerability and all she had endured. He silently vowed to make it up to her. Somehow. In his own way.

She eased back just a bit. Her hair was tousled and her eyes were red. "Feeling better?" he asked.

She dipped her head, let out her breath. "Getting there." She eyed the front of his T-shirt. Her tears had soaked his Air Force logo.

It seemed appropriate that she had released her pain on his past. He was no longer in the service, though it would always be a part of him. He prayed Tori would be part of his future.

"You expressed your sadness and I felt your sorrow."

"Over time, I went from being sad to being mad."

"You've channeled your anger quite well, if I can say so."

"I have, haven't I?" Her tone lightened, but she didn't smile. "Today the pain rose and came out."

"What about your anger?"

"Still at large."

He glanced over his shoulder. "Should I watch my back?"

"No ambush, Zane. Promise. I feel—" She clasped her hands in her lap, wavered.

"How, Tori?"

"At peace."

She shifted and lifted her chin—just as he turned his head.

Their mouths were separated by nothing but breath.

She inhaled.

He exhaled.

Awareness warmed the air and stirred with an undeniable need. Their bodies heated from closeness and familiarity. The slightest move, and sex would take them to the bedroom.

They stared at each other, the stare of two people who connected and communicated even in silence. Their healing had just begun. He wanted her to make the first move. When she was ready. Today, tomorrow, next month, he would wait for her.

He lightened the mood with, "Cheese Doodle?" He reached for the bowl, set it between them.

She picked up several, set them on her palm. "I could eat a bag of these all by myself in high school."

"That's why we always bought two . . . one for me and one for you."

The memory of the snack settled between them, but neither frowned nor cringed. They'd missed lunch and now devoured the melt-in-your-mouth puffs within minutes. They finally looked up. Tori's gaze fixed on his mouth. Her eyes went wide and her lips twitched. "Orange doodle dust, Bozo."

She'd called him a clown. He touched his face and found cheese dust beneath his nose and over his chin. "Your hands look like you're wearing orange gloves."

She didn't take offense. Instead she surprised him by licking the fingers of her right hand. The swirl of her tongue started out playful, only to mesmerize and arouse when she reached her thumb. She sucked it into her mouth and it came out clean. She ran her tongue over her palm, and Zane growled low in his throat. He stood while he still could. Before his sex spiked and he couldn't leave the sofa. There was nothing so uncomfortable as walking with an erection.

"I need to wash my face." He took off toward the bathroom.

"My hands too." She headed to the kitchen sink.

It took a while to settle his body down. Afterward he returned to the living room. Tori had cleared the coffee table of their drinks and snacks. She now stood at the back door, looking out.

He came up behind her. "What do you see?"

"Sunshine, a clear blue sky, and"—she stretched her arms—"a new start."

He nodded. "I see it too."

"We've lost a lot of time."

"But found each other again."

"I can't rush into a relationship."

"There's no hurry. No more Cheese Doodles for you though, if sex is off the table."

"No climbing out of bed nude," she requested. "You got to me this morning."

Good. Their sexual attraction remained strong.

Their emotions were on the mend.

Life had improved already.

"Plans for this afternoon?" he asked her.

"Other than conversation?"

"We talked it out earlier. No lists. No rehashing. We did it our way and it worked."

She grew thoughtful. "I'd like to sit with you on the sofa. Your arm around me, and me holding your hand."

Seated the same way they'd so often sat in high school. He liked her idea. "That can be easily arranged."

He made it happen. He took her by the hand and led her to the couch. He lowered himself at one end, beside the armrest, and drew her down beside him. He curved his arm about her shoulders. She tightened her hold on his hand, as if she'd never let him go. Then snuggled as close as skin to skin. It was an intimate, yet innocent moment. Time was their friend. They had nowhere to be. There would be no disruptions.

Contentment relaxed them. Her body grew lax, her eyelids heavy, and her jaw slack. She slept against him. Her breathing was soft. She hung on to his hand, even in sleep.

He closed his eyes too, not intending to nap. But once

he stretched out his legs, put his feet up on the coffee table, sank deeper on the cushion, and laid back his head, he was out like a light.

He eventually stirred and found dusk spying on them through the open window shutters. He glanced at his watch. He and Tori had slept for six hours. She was still zonked out.

He wasn't about to wake her. She'd released years of emotion earlier and now needed to recharge. He managed to squeeze out around her, and she slumped sideways when he stood. He bent and scooped her up, carried her high against his chest into the bedroom. He gently laid her on her twin bed, stepped back, and debated. He wanted to sleep with her tonight, even if they both remained fully clothed.

He slipped off her boots, then kicked off his loafers. She lay on her side on the mattress. He slipped in, spooned her, and soon slept as deeply as she.

Morning dawned with shafts of sunshine squinting through the slatted shades. Zane sensed Tori had wakened ahead of him, but she hadn't moved. His hand rested low on her stomach. "Feel me," he whispered as her back molded to his front.

Her shoulder blades pressed into his shoulders as tightly as her bottom snugged his groin. His strength surrounded her, bold and seductive. His erection strained against the small of her back.

Ever so gently, he brushed her auburn curls off her neck. Then placed an openmouthed kiss behind her right ear, and lightly blew on the spot. Her hot shudder echoed down his body. He skimmed his fingers over her belly and up her chest, then flattened his palm over her heart. "I'm listening," he said.

No words were spoken. She rolled toward him, and

they communicated through deep kisses and exploring hands. No part of her body escaped his touch. They were eighteen again in their urgency. Adults in their need to satisfy.

"Skin." His voice was deep and dark with sexual intent.

He glided his hands down her sides to the hem of her top, then eased it up and over her head. All along the way, he teased her belly, her ribs, her breasts through the black satin cups of her bra. He tossed her shirt aside. Unhooked her bra with finesse. He ran his fingers beneath the straps, inching the satin off her shoulders and down her arms. Her freed breasts now rose with a woman's fullness, round and firm, and catching the morning light on their upper curves. Cupping the underside of one breast, he flicked his thumb over the nipple, until it swelled and pebbled. He traced down her ribs to the smooth, taut hollow of her stomach. Slow hands. Slower burn. He wanted her hot for him.

Tori refused to go it alone. She wanted him with her. The sexual climb was better together. She tugged off his T-shirt with minimal struggle. Breasts against chest, they went to work on their jeans. The sound of their breathing sharpened as they unsnapped, then scraped down zippers. He searched a side pocket for a condom, located a Trojan Bareskin. He kept the packet close by. He then rolled his hips, and she wiggled her butt, and the denim was worked down their legs and over their ankles. He was completely nude. She wore a black lacy thong. She'd worn cotton bikinis in her teens. He preferred her sheer lady lace.

Her skin was flushed, her lips moist and parted when he glossed his hand over the curve of her hip, then slid his hand beneath the elastic on her thong. He stretched his fingers toward her sex. He stroked beneath the satin. Goose bumps scattered across her belly. He penetrated her with one finger. She grew damp and slick, and radiated heat. She rocked against his hand, arched her back, and tossed her head. He lowered her panties. The callused pads of his thumbs sketched the soft flesh of her inner thighs, the sensitive backs of her knees, then trailed down her calves. The thong fell off her ankles.

His hands were steady as he opened the foiled packet and fitted the Bareskin. He'd bought a box before leaving town, on the slim chance they would have sex. They were now, and he was insanely turned on. Out of his head crazy for this woman.

He worked his way back up her body. Remembering her softness while imprinting new memories. She met him halfway. She clutched his shoulders, scored him with her nails. Left crescent moons of her arousal. She brought him higher and closer to her. He was fully erect. She wrapped her arms about his neck, and her thighs about his hips. She was positioned where he could slide into her any second.

He played out that second, turned it into a minute. Kissing her deeply, continuing their foreplay with ongoing caresses. Until he moaned and she whimpered. He cupped her buttocks, his legs straining as he sank into her.

Concern slowed him. "You're so tight."

"I haven't been with anyone but you since high school."

"My hand can attest to satisfying myself."

Her smile warmed his mouth. "Let's take care of each other."

Their hearts and bodies pulsed as one. Need and want collided. Lust and lack of control intensified. He moved inside with deep circular motions that changed the angle of each thrust. The tension in his body strained every muscle. Her body was as taut as his. They were relentless in their pursuit of pleasure.

Gratification pushed them to the edge.

Raw release sent them over.

She shattered in his arms, slick and explosive.

He spun out with such force, he swore he'd lost his sanity.

Muscles slack, they lay boneless, motionless, for long minutes, lacking the energy to roll apart, yet sustained by the warm tangle of arms and legs and remnants of passion. They were amazing together. The sex was phenomenal. His love for Tori unparalleled.

He rose and disposed of the condom. While up, he heard a knock on the front door. He grabbed a pair of sweatpants from the dresser drawer and walked into the living room bare chested. A note was slipped under the door, indicating their final Sunday counseling sessions were scheduled on the hour. They had forty minutes to shower, dress, and arrive at the main house.

Zane hated short notices. His woman was naked in bed and he was in sexual recovery. He wanted her again, but that was no longer possible if they were going to make their meetings. He scratched his belly and silently swore his disappointment. Then wandered back to the bedroom to inform Tori of their day ahead.

The counselors held both of them longer than the designated hours. In their separate meetings they got serious. Where were they now? Had the weekend improved their relationship? Where would they go from here? Their assignment before they left Glen Glade was to make one last list. They were each to write down three short-term goals and one long-term.

Back at the cabin, the couch became their focal point for conversation and comfort once again. They sat at opposite ends, pen and paper in hand, and jotted down their plans. It took them an hour. It would have been quicker had they concentrated fully on their task and not leaned toward each other every other minute for a kiss.

Tori had never looked more beautiful, Zane thought. Makeup free, she'd clipped her hair in a loose ponytail. Wispy strands arced over her cheeks. Her eyes shone with happiness. She smiled often. She'd always loved baggy, comfy clothes, and had often borrowed his workout gear. Today she'd snagged one of his Air Force T-shirts and a pair of his drawstring gym shorts. The shorts were tied loosely, and he anxiously waited for them to slide off her hips. A sex break.

"I'm ready if you are," she finally managed.

He set his ink pen on the coffee table. "Good to go."

"I'll go first."

Fine by him.

"I've been thinking that it's time for me to commit to a new life and move forward."

He liked how that sounded. He silently hoped he was part of whatever she now planned.

"Short-term, I want to move out of the White Heron. It was my first apartment in town, but I don't want it to be my last. I need something nicer for Gram, Ozzie, and me."

He liked her idea. He tapped his paper with his finger. "One of my short-term goals was to offer you a place to live. Help you relocate. There are several Cates properties available. Low rent. Our old cottage is still empty. Charmingly decorated, as you know. I'm acquainted with the decorator personally," he added, tongue in cheek.

She smiled, tentative, yet positive.

"Aidan's construction company just finished a condo village near the hospital. My brother's indicated that there are several units still available. Pets are welcome."

He paused, debated, and went out on a limb. "Or you could always move into Grandpa Frank's stilt house with me. It's plenty big. Surrounded by fruit orchards. Wide porch for your grandmother's rocking chair."

She took it all in. "Places to consider."

"Second short-term goal?" he next asked her.

"To quit Zinotti's. The pizza parlor is a dead-end job. It has been for a long time. I'm going to insist that Eddie give me the money I've invested over the years."

He couldn't agree more but didn't say so. It would be too in-your-face. He didn't want to hurt her—ever again.

She shifted on the couch cushion, tucked one leg beneath her. "Were you aware Blu has invested in Lettuce Eat, the vegetarian café?" she questioned. "A new direction, and I'm thrilled for her."

"My mother mentioned the purchase recently. She heard through a Realtor at church Bingo. Good for Blu."

Tori pulled a face. "Nothing gets by the Cateses."

"It's our town, and we keep our fingers on the pulse of all that goes on."

"I'd like to follow Blu out the door of Zinotti's when she gives her notice."

He raised an eyebrow. "Your timetable?"

"We agreed on two weeks."

"That's right in line with my second short-term goal, to suggest new jobs for you."

"Oh really?" she sounded skeptical.

"Swear."

"These goals aren't all about me. What about you?"

"My life is in order." More or less. They'd yet to discuss their future. Coming up shortly. "I'm retired, back in Barefoot William, and I'm half owner of Gray's Garage. I'm pretty well settled."

"I wish I were."

"Give yourself time, Tori. All will fall into place."

"You're sure?"

"I have faith in you."

Her eyes misted, and she bit down on her bottom lip. "I finally believe in me too." She drew a deep breath, said,

"My third short-term goal also includes a transformation. I may or may not succeed, but I still have to try."

"I'll always support you." He listened closely.

"I want to submit a design for the lifeguard tower renovation," she slowly shared. "I'm not qualified. I have no real experience, no portfolio. Although I did decorate Lettuce Eat. There've been lots of customer compliments. Interior decorating was always my dream. The idea has been nagging me. I can't let this opportunity pass me by. This is Shaye's beach project. You're her brother. *Promise me*," she stressed, "that you won't influence her on my behalf. I want to succeed or fail on my own merit."

"I promise." He would keep his word. Tori had no idea how talented she truly was, and she would nail the job without his help. "Shaye will be fair. She's decided that there won't be any names attached to the submissions. She wants to review each one openly and honestly. Without knowing who proposed what. She's looking for both formal designs and unique plans. She doesn't want to favor a big-name firm over a promising up-and-comer."

Should Tori be chosen to remodel one of the towers, a new career could open for her. She'd be noticed, acknowledged, and sought after. This was her chance to live her own dream. "Go for it," he encouraged.

Her eyes brightened. "The concept for a tower came to me this morning, during my session with Dr. Allison. I started doodling on the piece of paper she'd given me to take notes. She thought I was paying attention, but all the while I was at the lifeguard stand."

"Share your vision."

She did so. Her excitement was contagious. "Picture this . . . rising from the beach to the tower are wide transparent steps, embedded with pure white sugar sand. The door opens on a turquoise Gulf Stream wave, painted on a blond hardwood floor. A wave that appears to flow into the entrance hall. Construct two floor-to-ceiling windows on the east and west walls to receive the sunrise and sunset. On the south wall, mirrored sunshine. Gold Coast amber glass will be cut and fitted to form an actual sun, enhancing the room and visually expanding the space."

She paused, having run out of breath. "What do you think so far?" She valued his opinion.

"Very distinctive," he approved. "Run with it."

She continued with, "Thick, woven, sage-green sea grass rugs scattered across the floor. I want contrast. Tropical wicker furniture in deep sea coral and parrot green with red hibiscus print cushions, along with vintage black-and-white photographs of early Barefoot William, framed and positioned throughout." She grinned at him. "That's just the living room. Don't get me started on the kitchen, bathroom, and second story."

"You are amazing, Tori Rollins," he praised. "Your interior designs would enhance any tourist's stay."

"I can only hope."

He then broached their final topic. "Last but not least, our long-term goals. What happens to us?" He hated to ask, but needed to know. His question stretched between them. Hanging heavy in the silence.

She inched toward him on the sofa, until they were nearly touching. "We've become friends again—that's big."

Not big enough. Friends were good, but it didn't carry the same connotation as lover or wife. "The goal I wrote down was to win your heart and love you forever."

"Mine was for you to kiss me, at the beach, behind the NO KISSING UNDER THE BOARDWALK sign."

That was the first place they'd ever kissed. Private, secret, and high school hot. Incredibly special.

"So you want to be with me then?" He needed reassurance.

"We are a given."

"No doubts?"

She reached for his hand, pressed his palm to her heart. "Listen to me," she softly said.

Her heartbeat spoke to him. Steady and true. He understood. "I hear you, and I love you too."

"So what now?" she asked.

"Cheese Doodles, sex, home."

"I'm looking forward to all three."

One year to the day

Tori and Zane were remarried on the beach in a close-knit, supportive family ceremony. She wore a flirty, gauzy pink dress that fluttered on the Gulf breeze. He wore a white button-down and black slacks. They stood barefoot at the water's edge. Nana Aubrey stood up for Tori. She leaned on her walker, wearing a white pillbox hat and a pale blue suit. Zane chose dalmatian Oswald as his best man. Race and Blue were in attendance too . . . this time as man and wife. Twilight captured their vows, as Tori again became a Cates. Forever. Hugs sealed the two families. Nurse Karen escorted her Gram and Oz back to the cottage. She would spend the night so the newlyweds could have their honeymoon.

They would honeymoon at the Sun Spirit Suite, Tori's newly renovated lifeguard tower. It had been a spectacular hit with the community. Her interior design, everyone agreed, was phenomenal. She'd won the contract fair and square, without his influence. Clients were already lining up for her unique flair. For her kaleidoscope of colors. She would soon be a very busy designer.

As darkness laid the day to rest, Zane's heart swelled

with love for his wife. He knew she loved him too; her own heart told him so.

They'd found their way back together. They'd been given a second chance at falling in love for the first time. This new first would be his last. All his lasts would be with her. Always.

Connect with

Us

Visit us online at
KensingtonBooks.com
to read more from your favorite authors, see books
by series, view reading group guides, and more.

Join us on social media

for sneak peeks, chances to win books and prize packs,
and to share your thoughts with other readers.

facebook.com/kensingtonpublishing
twitter.com/kensingtonbooks

Tell us what you think!

To share your thoughts, submit a review,
or sign up for our eNewsletters, please visit:
KensingtonBooks.com/TellUs.